<u>Special Thanks:</u>

To Alex and Leo and Max—You boys are my world! я тебя люблю!

To my family—I love you!

To Stacia—Not only my editor but a best friend as well.

To Kristie and Michael—For your very heartfelt, very imaginative, and very LARGE surprise!

TIME IS MONEY

First edition. October 26, 2021.

Written by Gina LaManna.

To my Lacey Luzzi & Kate Rosetti readers!

Synopsis

When Kate Rosetti returns from a rare week of vacation in Hawaii, she finds herself immediately immersed in a case more complicated than any she's faced before. A man's body has been stuffed into the back of an ice cream truck, and it seems like everyone—including his three girlfriends—had a reason to kill him.

But when the case blows up into a bigger sensation than Kate could ever have anticipated, she finds herself forced to work side by side with her ex-boyfriend, FBI Agent Jack Russo, and his very new, very attractive female partner. As they start to close in on the murderer, Kate becomes acutely aware that if she doesn't catch this killer soon, someone she loves might be dead next.

Chapter 1

"There she is."

"Kate Rosetti!"

"Long time no see."

Walking into the precinct on an otherwise average Monday morning, I was completely unprepared for the welcome I'd get after a week away. In my coworkers' defense, my taking a long weekend was practically unheard of, let alone a full week away from the job. It felt like I'd spent lifetimes away from the office.

"You tan so well." Asha sauntered up to my desk. "I'm jealous. You look like you did nothing but lay on the beach all week."

"I mean—"

"Did you meet any cute guys?" Asha asked. "Remember what I said about letting loose and finding yourself a little Hawaiian fling? I hope you considered my advice."

I wrinkled my nose. "Being there with my parents sort of cramped my flinging style. Not that I know how to *fling*."

"Oh, come on." Asha rolled her eyes. "Your parents are totally obsessed with each other. Plus, this was like a honeymoon for them. You were probably cramping *their* style."

"I wasn't cramping anyone's style. They had plenty of alone time."

"How was it?" Jimmy asked. "The first vacation of your entire career. What do you think, Rosetti? Do you feel refreshed?"

"It was weird." I sat behind my desk, feeling the eyes of every detective in the room on me. "I feel like I missed everything. What's going on? Who died? I don't know what's happening in my own city."

"Believe it or not, we functioned just fine without you," Jimmy said. "Not that we didn't miss you, but we had Chloe in town for the week to help. We didn't even catch a case. The only dead body that came in went to Dunkirk."

I glanced over at Frankie Dunkirk, the guy who sat a few desks away from me.

"Don't look at me," Dunkirk said. "I just follow orders."

"Anything interesting?" I asked. "Did you get a big case?"

"Not anything particularly thrilling. The victim was an older woman who got bumped on the head. We're still working out the details," Frankie said. "Dr. Brooks is still trying to piece together the murder weapon for us, which might give us a lead."

I turned back to Jimmy. "I really didn't miss anything important?"

"Nope," Jimmy said.

"You missed a few of Jimmy's three-hour lunches," Asha said, "but I'm not supposed to tell you about those."

I grinned and switched on my computer. "I have to admit, I'm disappointed to realize y'all can survive without me."

"The killers were just going easy on Jones," Asha said, giving him a playful smile. "If Jimmy had caught a case, he would've been on the phone with you every five minutes asking your advice."

"Probably true," Jimmy admitted without hesitation. "I have no shame in slacking to the best of my abilities."

The chatter around me died down. It was amazing how time away from my caseload seemed to work. On one hand, it felt like I'd been gone forever. On the other hand, having sat in my chair for a total of two minutes, I also felt as if I'd never left.

As I mindlessly scrolled through some emails and sipped the familiar black coffee I'd nabbed from the shared pot, I had to admit it felt good to be back. In a way, this was the place I felt the most comfortable. I wasn't sure exactly what that said about me, seeing as it was a place surrounded by death and murder and killers, but it was true.

As much as it'd been nice to escape to Hawaii to celebrate my parents' renewal of vows, relaxing on the beach wasn't my forte. Sitting still made me anxious. Bathing suits weren't really my style. Neither were vacation flings. In fact, I was on a diet from men and dating after my recent breakup with Jack Russo. Getting involved with someone at this point seemed like it would bring more pain than it was worth. I preferred to throw myself back into work where I could make a real difference.

I slipped on a pair of headphones and set to reading through a few reports that'd made their way across my desk while I'd been out. I updated my stupid timecard so the chief wouldn't get on my case about it again. By the time I'd switched back to my inbox, Jimmy was standing before me gesturing for me to take my headphones off.

"Seems like the murderers are back from vacation too," Jimmy said, peeling back a string from his never-ending stack of Twizzlers and popping it into his mouth. "We've got a live one. Let's go."

"You mean a dead one?" I rose from my seat and grabbed my keys.

"Ah, I missed that dark sense of humor. You've got dad jokes, Rosetti."

"That's why you can never retire," I said. "You'd miss me and my dad jokes too much."

"Uh-huh. Sure."

"That, and I can't seem to get an assistant to stick around," I said. "Chloe was stolen first by a hot FBI agent and then by Asha."

"You've only tried one trainee. You could give it another go."

"I wouldn't have to try anymore if you'd just man up and do your job instead of retiring."

Jimmy snorted a laugh. "You're right. I did miss you."

We made our way out to the car in amiable silence. We had our routine down pat, and we could make decisions together at times without saying a word. We headed to my car and hopped in, and it was several minutes later before either of us spoke.

"How is Chloe doing?" I asked. "Does she like life in DC?"

"If I didn't know better, I'd think you sound hopeful that she hates her life and wants to move back. That's almost sweet of you, Rosetti."

"I don't want her to hate it," I said. "But if she did break up with Agent Brody, I guess I'd consider having her back."

"You miss her. It's cute. Unfortunately for you, she's doing great out there."

"I'm happy to hear it. Really."

"Me too. She seems to be really enjoying her life. Not to mention, Asha raves about having her on her team. You know how impossible it is to find someone who can keep up with Asha."

"Yeah. Almost as impossible as it is to find someone who doesn't mind working with me."

"I work with you."

I glanced over at Jimmy. "You don't count. I'm driving you away from the job."

"I'm pretty sure that's my advanced age and high blood pressure. Not to mention my wife. But that could be related to the high blood pressure situation the doc keeps droning on about."

Still smiling, I reveled in how comforting it was to be back in a place I belonged. In a place where people understood me. There weren't many people who would prefer to be in the frigid January winters of Minnesota, peeking around dead bodies for clues as to who killed them, instead of lounging on a chair in Hawaii, but I was one of them. Hawaii was nice in theory, but it wasn't for me more than once a decade.

"How'd it all go on your trip?" Jimmy asked. "I mean the real deal, not the nice stuff you tell everyone else."

"It was great," I admitted. "It really was. I had a nice time, but more importantly, my parents loved it. They loved having our family together for a whole week."

"I'll bet."

"There were lots of family dinners, family lunches, you name it. Volleyball games on the beach, after-supper walks, late nights around the tiki bar."

"Sounds like a slice of paradise."

"It was a great time. Though I couldn't help but feel like they were doing some of it for me."

"What do you mean?"

I shrugged. "My parents were there getting married. Well, married again. My sister and Wes are newly engaged. Don't you think they should've wanted a little more alone time?"

"Take it from me," Jimmy said. "I've been married a long time. I love my wife, and I love getting away with her. But there are different sorts of vacations. How often is your family going to be doing this? Soon enough your sister will get married. Maybe they'll have kids. You've got a career that keeps you crazy busy. Your parents are getting a little older. I understand why they'd want to savor the time together as much as they could. They've got a lifetime to stare at one another over the breakfast table all alone."

"I can't figure out if what you said is incredibly romantic or sort of morbid."

"A little bit of both?"

"I guess that's life."

"Speaking of life," Jimmy said in a clumsy segue, "have you heard from Russo?"

"No."

"Have you been thinking about him?"

"What sort of question is that?"

"Not a stupid one," Jimmy said. "You're making it sound like a stupid question."

"It is a stupid question."

"No, it's just one you don't want to answer. I'll take that as a yes."

"I just broke up with the guy. I just spent a week surrounded by a love fest. Sure, I thought about him a few times."

"Not enough to call him?"

I hesitated. I'd thought about it. One night I'd even hit dial on my phone, but I was blaming that on the number of mai tais I'd had over our family game of Clue and not my actual feelings for my ex. I'd hung up before the phone call had connected, and I hadn't gotten any sort of response from Jack in return.

"You called him," Jimmy said knowingly. "Let me guess, he didn't answer?"

"I don't know if the call actually went through and registered on his phone," I said defensively. "It was a moment of weakness where my thumb hit dial without my brain being attached."

"A few adult beverages might've been responsible?"

"That and Colonel Mustard in the library with the candlestick."

"Am I supposed to understand that somewhat creepy reference?"

I shook my head. "Anytime I think about talking to Jack, I wonder what it would actually change. The answer has always been nothing. Until that answer changes, I don't think there's a point to us shooting the breeze."

"Look at us. We talk, and we're not romantically involved."

"We have to talk. We work together," I said. "Would you call me if you didn't work with me?"

"Sure," Jimmy said. "My wife will get sick of me when I retire. I'll need someone to grab breakfast with now and again just to get out of the house."

"Gee whiz, thanks."

"What about Gem?"

"What about him?" I tensed at the mention of the billionaire.

"Have you spoken with him since he got dumped at the altar?"

"He wasn't dumped *at* the altar."

"I really think you're splitting hairs with that clarification. His fiancée left him on his wedding day. That sucks."

"I think he's been taking some time for himself," I said. "You know, to heal."

The latter wasn't entirely true. I didn't have any social media accounts, and I wasn't exactly plugged into the social scene in the Twin Cities, but one of my best friends was at the center of it all. It was impossible not to catch glimpses of the various mentions of Alastair Gem on Lassie's blog, seeing as she'd subscribed me to her newsletter updates without my permission.

In another moment or three of mai tai-inspired weakness, I'd clicked on to her website to see a few articles posted from the social events of the season. I'd seen several pictures of Gem out at his clubs. He'd been surrounded by people. Mostly people of the *beautiful female* variety. According to

Lassie, he'd been spotted dining at The Carousel, the newest and hottest restaurant in the state, with a well-known Olympic gymnast as his date. When I told Jimmy as much, he raised his eyebrows.

"Needless to say, I think he's doing fine," I said dryly.

"The gymnast chick is what we call a rebound," Jimmy said, glancing at me. "Not to mention, you're the first person who says not to believe everything you read online. You're good friends with Lassie. You know she can make a story out of anything. Bonus points if there's an unflattering picture attached."

"The picture wasn't unflattering," I said. "He was looking just fine."

I caught myself a moment too late. Jimmy didn't miss my slip either. He turned to stare out the window, but I caught the little smirk on his lips as he did.

"You didn't answer my question," he said. "Have you talked to him?"

"Once," I admitted. "I don't really remember it that much."

"How many mai tais had you consumed?"

"I don't believe that's relevant to work," I said. Then I added, again defensively, "I was surrounded by love, and I had just gotten dumped. I'm allowed to make a few illogical phone calls."

"Hey, you deserved every mai tai you slurped down."

"It was late at night when I dialed Gem," I said. "Frankly, I doubt he remembers it either. I think he'd had whatever the rich-guy equivalent of too many mai tais is. We never spoke about it after the fact. Not so much as a text."

"Ah."

"It's a good thing," I said. "I need a break from everything and everyone who is not related to this current case. Speaking of, what do we have on our plates today?"

"I do believe you mean *who* do we have on our plate."

"Now who's funny?"

"Someone found a body that looks like it's been there for a few days."

"Why were we called?"

"It was sort of found in a strange place."

"Where's that?"

"The back of an ice cream truck."

"Huh?" I turned to look at Jimmy. "But it's January. Do ice cream trucks even run over the winter?"

"That's the reason the body was there for a few days without being discovered. I guess there's not as much of a rush for Dilly Bars when it's twenty below."

"I dunno. That's never stopped me before."

"Touché. Just repeating what I heard," Jones said. "The owner of the vehicle called it in this morning."

"He was just randomly checking in on his truck?"

"She," he corrected. "The woman who called it in owns a bar. I guess she'd just purchased an ice cream truck to use for the summer and parked it out back. According to the source, she uses it for some extra refrigerator storage and popped out to grab a cannister of whipped cream. She found a lot more than she bargained for."

"Huh."

"That's not all," Jimmy said. "I think the real reason we were called in is because of the family linked to the bar."

"Family? Why don't I like the sound of that already?"

"The woman who owns the bar married into the Luzzi clan."

I groaned. "A mob-related hit that involves an ice cream truck?"

"We can't be sure of anything yet," Jimmy said, "but I'm betting the chief thought this case could use some extra sensitivity in its handling."

"So he put me and you on it?" I raised my eyebrows. "I've been called many things. Sensitive's not one of them."

"Nah, but you understand how the mob works better than most. You know, firsthand experience and all. Thanks, Angelo Rosetti."

"If you were anyone else, I'd be offended."

Jimmy grinned. "I know. I sorta like that I can get away with saying stuff like that around you. Anyone else, and you'd be threatening to shoot them."

"I haven't threatened to shoot anyone in weeks."

"That's a marked improvement on your part. You're growing up there, Rosetti."

Still grinning, Jimmy looked out the window as we pulled over to the side of the road in a little section of the Twin Cities called Uptown. It was a young, hip neighborhood in Minneapolis—not an area where I'd spent a lot of time. I wasn't big on Minneapolis. I was more of a St. Paul sort of girl. Crossing the river was about the equivalent of trekking across the Sahara in my mind. Unless it was to investigate a dead body.

I parked at a meter outside of a bar named Shotz, cursing Minneapolis and its crowded streets. Sliding out of the car,

Jones and I made our way up to the door of the place and let ourselves in. At nine o'clock on a Monday morning, there wasn't much happening at the bar. A few sounds could be heard coming from the kitchen, and I assumed that would be the employees getting ready for the day.

"Let's go out back," Jimmy said. "There's an exit straight ahead. Melinda's already here."

We made our way out to the alley and immediately found signs of life. The familiar hustle and bustle of a new crime scene was evident. Yellow tape roped off the alleyway, preventing cars and walkers from coming down the road. Officers milled around the outskirts of the scene. Jimmy and I checked in quickly, then made our way over to an ice cream truck that was currently ablaze with extra lighting.

"This is one way to welcome you back, huh, Rosetti?" Melinda rose and smiled. She wore a hat with a pom pom stuck on top, a pretty peacoat, and gloves. She looked ready to attend a formal function. "You look good. How was your trip?"

"I'm glad to be back."

Melinda raised an eyebrow, then glanced at the body—or what remained of it—behind her. "Really?"

I shrugged. "There was a lot of love around me. It was fun and all, but I'm ready to be back to work."

"You're more of a death and murder sort of girl?"

"You could say that."

Melinda wrinkled her nose. "We're going to have to talk about that tonight over drinks. I want to hear all about your trip."

"Works for me. What do we have here? Any guesses at how long the body's been here?"

"Nothing conclusive yet," she said. "Judging by the state of decomp, I'd say around seventy-two hours. The lab will be able to tell us a more specific window of time."

"Can you tell anything else from a first glance?"

"The victim is male, probably in his mid-thirties. There was no identification on him of any sort. We'll check dental records to see if we can get a match."

"Any sign of how he might've been killed?"

"It's too early to say conclusively."

"What about the ice cream truck?" I asked. "How does that figure into any of this?"

"That's where you come in," Melinda said. "I'll have some more answers for you tomorrow. The woman who found the body was answering some questions for Officer Franklin when I last saw her."

"Thanks."

"Tonight?" Melinda asked. "Drinks?"

"Seven?"

"Works for me."

Jimmy and I backed out of the ice cream truck. Crime scenes didn't often make me queasy, and while I wasn't on the cusp of losing my breakfast, I didn't fancy ruining the image of ice cream trucks forever by staring at the dead guy on the floor in one. Plus, the smell of death seemed to be especially strong after my week of nothing but hibiscus flowers and fresh island air. And a little bit of tequila.

Jimmy and I made our way over to the man we assumed was Officer Franklin, judging by the fact that he was staring at a woman who was definitely not a cop. She wore bright yellow spandex leggings paired with a leopard-print top that was cropped above her belly button. Officer Franklin seemed to be having a hard time keeping his eyes on the woman's face.

"Hey there," I said, easing into the conversation. "I'm Detective Rosetti, and this is Detective Jones. We'll be the primaries on the case. Mind if we take over here?"

"Please do."

Officer Franklin all but evaporated from the scene before I could thank him. It seemed he was more than a little bit relieved to be free from the interview.

"You're the woman who found the body?" I asked.

"Yeah, I'm Meg," she said. "I own this place. And the vehicle, for that matter. Though the blood and guts sort of ruins the ice cream truck image for me. Know what I mean, bean?"

I blinked. "Um, sure. You said your name was Meg...?"

I waited so she'd fill in her last name. She just stared back at me for a very long time.

Finally, she said, "That's right. My name's Meg."

She let it sit there like I should know who she was. A one-named marvel like Madonna or Oprah.

"Okay," I said. "How long have you owned this place?"

"A few years. The ice cream truck I've only owned since October. I bought it at the end of the season for a sale." She scratched at her nose. "Then again, I'm not sure if the sale was actually because it was the end of the season or if it was because there were bullet holes in the side."

"There were bullet holes in the side of the vehicle when you acquired it?"

"Sure," she said. "I mean, you haven't really lived if you haven't owned a car with bullet holes, *amiright*?"

I glanced at Jimmy while silently marveling over the woman before us. I'd never met anyone quite like her. She seemed impervious to the fact that a murder had occurred just under her nose.

"Seems about right," Jimmy said, jumping in. "Detective Rosetti here has had a few bullet holes in her vehicle as well."

Meg reached out and slapped my arm. "Good for you, chickadee. I knew beneath that uptight exterior you knew how to let loose." Then to Jimmy, she whispered, "It's always the ones you don't expect."

"Uptight?" I squinted at her. "We've only just met. How would you know I'm uptight?"

"I read auras," Meg said. "Your aura is sort of black with some blood splotches on it."

"Because I'm a homicide cop?"

"Because that's what my psychic powers tell me," Meg said. "But underneath all that darkness is a little stripe of bright pink. You know, real sexy pink."

I cleared my throat. "Thanks for the reading. I was hoping we could talk—"

"It'll be ten dollars for the reading."

"Sorry?"

"You're right. Twenty," Meg amended. "My psychic services don't come cheap."

I cleared my throat again. "Let's focus on the murder. When did you find the body?"

"This morning," she said. "I called you guys pretty much right away."

"Pretty much?"

"I mean, I had to go inside to make a cup of coffee first," Meg said. "I knew the second you guys got here I'd be all popular, and you wouldn't let me slip away for my daily fix. If I don't get some caffeine in me before José opens up the kitchen, I turn into a raging witch. It's the withdrawals, I bet. Caffeine headaches."

"Let me get this straight," I repeated. "You went out back to the ice cream truck to—what, exactly?"

"I needed more whipped cream canisters," Meg said. "You know, for my coffee. I keep a stash of the good stuff in the ice cream truck. If I keep it in the kitchen, it always goes mysteriously missing. That, plus I have no self-control, and I keep squirting whipped cream in my mouth all day long if I keep it within reach. The health inspector told me that wasn't sanitary, so I moved my stash out back. They're real pricks, those guys. No sense of humor."

"Right." I glanced down at my notebook, not really sure which parts of this wild story were relevant and which weren't. "I'm going to try and get this straight. You went out back to get a canister of whipped cream for your coffee. You opened the truck and saw the dead body. Then you turned around and went back inside and made yourself a cup of coffee before you called the cops?"

"You make me sound like a monster," Meg said cheerily. "I mean, of course I shut the door first. Mrs. Kinders always walks her dog down the alley, and I didn't want her to catch a whiff of decomp with Fluffy."

"Very thoughtful of you."

"What can I say, I'm pretty much a saint."

"Uh-huh." I again glanced down at my empty notebook as if it would fill itself up. "Is there anything I left out of your story?"

"Yes, fine." She gave a huge sigh. "You caught me. I knew you'd be a good cop the second I met you on account of my psychic powers, but dang. You knew I was lying."

"Yes," I said cautiously. "What were you lying about?"

"I ran across the street and grabbed some doughnuts," she said. "But I have a good reason for it."

"Really?"

"Yes," she insisted. "I couldn't get at the whipped cream on account of I didn't want to disturb the dead dude in the back of my truck. Well, that put me in a real pickle because I need something sweet with my coffee."

"So you found the body, locked up the truck so Fluffy didn't catch a whiff of decomp," I said, "and then you came inside, made yourself a cup of coffee, popped across the street for a doughnut..." I paused. "Then you enjoyed your breakfast?"

"I think that's about right," she said. "Then I called the cops."

"Anything else?"

"I mean, okay, I did use the restroom first. I had to powder my nose and change into this outfit just in case the hot cops showed up. Don't get me wrong, I'm a happily married woman, but I've got a reputation to maintain."

I tried hard to digest the information. I had to say, in all my years of being a cop, I'd never met a witness quite like this one. It was hard to believe this leopard-print-wearing woman with the sweet tooth was linked to the Luzzi family.

"Do you have any idea how someone could've gotten the body in the ice cream truck?" I asked. "I assume you keep it locked."

"I'm missing a set of keys."

"A set of keys were stolen? From where?"

"From the ignition," she said. "I have so many sets of keys now that I own two cars and a bar, so I just started leaving the keys to my cars in their respective ignitions."

"So the truck wasn't locked?"

"Not exactly," Meg said. "Though I do keep the refrigerator locked. I mean, the rest of the ice cream truck was a dump. I was planning on having my man fix it up for me this spring because he's into that sort of thing. He basically drives a rocket ship."

"Huh?"

"My husband basically drives a rocket ship," Meg repeated as if the problem was that I hadn't heard her correctly. "He's very into robotics and computers and mechanical crap. He's outfitted his car so it has every fancy toy in the world in it. I'm pretty sure the seats eject."

"Right. Sure," I said, pretty sure all of that was wildly embellished. "I see what you mean."

"Since the truck was a dump, I didn't see much point in locking it," she said. "I only kept the refrigerator locked because I kept my valuable whipped cream in there. No thieves were going to get inside that lock. My husband made it. It explodes if you do the wrong combination four times."

"Okay. Good to know."

"The rest of the truck was pretty much up for grabs," Meg said. "Nobody was gonna steal it. I mean, I'm pretty much a well-known entity around here. People know not to mess with me. I've got a gun and I'm a pretty wild shot."

That part I didn't doubt. Even I didn't want to mess with this woman, and I wasn't scared of many people. I understood implicitly why Officer Franklin had been relieved to give up questioning duty upon my arrival with Jimmy.

I wasn't going to get into whether or not the gun Meg had was registered. I'd give her the benefit of the doubt for the moment. Not to mention, I wasn't trying to make more paperwork for myself just yet.

"When was the last time you'd been out at the truck?"

"I hadn't been out there for about a week or so," she said. "I don't actually like to wake up early in the mornings."

I wasn't sure how that last part was relevant. Meg sensed my confusion.

"Because I don't wake up early, I wasn't drinking my coffee here, and therefore I didn't need whipped cream," Meg said. "I only go out there for one thing."

"I see. Does anyone else have access to the truck who works at your restaurant?"

"Anyone in the entire world who knows where it's parked has access to it," she said. "I don't make a habit of having my employees go out there though. I keep it a secret. Nobody knows the code to that chamber except me. I guard it like launch codes."

"Right. Do you have any reason at all to suspect the body might've been left there as a sign?" I asked. "A warning of some sort?"

"You think someone might've targeted me and my truck by dumping a dead body there? That's pretty mean."

"Just thought I'd ask."

"Plenty of people don't really like me," she said. "I mean, I'm incredibly likeable, so I don't really understand it, but I think it's a jealousy sort of thing."

"I'm sure it is."

"I guess it could've been a sign, but it's a pretty crappy sign, don't you think?" Meg continued without waiting for a response. "I don't get it. If someone were trying to send me a message, don't you think they'd make it clearer? I totally missed the memo if there was one hidden in that dead guy."

"That is a valid point."

"I've got a lot of valid points," Meg said. "I can give you more if you need."

"You know, I think we're going to take a break for a moment," I said. "I'd like to confer with my partner. We'd also like to speak with any other members of your staff who are here. We might need to talk to you more depending on what our findings show. Would you be able to point me in the direction of your employees?"

"Sure. My main man, José, has been on vacation for the last week. I'm pretty sure that's a good alibi. He went to some resort in Mexico, and I bet you could check that out pretty easily."

"What about anyone here today?"

"Jessica's my newest hire. She's been working here a few months. Nice lady. She'll be coming in this morning. Then there's Benny, the college kid who helps out as a barback. He's here unloading a delivery and stocking shelves. He looks like a string bean, but the kid can lift pretty heavy stuff. And that's coming from me. I'm no wimp." Meg flexed her muscles as if to prove her point.

"Got it. Anyone else?"

"There's Ralph, the bartender who works most nights. Jessica switches off with him. There are a few servers we use, mostly college-aged kids, but honestly the turnover is so high I don't really bother to learn their names. We run a pretty small operation."

"Great. Thanks."

"Anytime," Meg said. "And I mean anytime. It's not often there's a murder right in my backyard. Usually that's a Lacey thing."

"A lacy thing?" I wasn't sure if I wanted to know about Meg's lacy things.

"My BFF is named Lacey," she said. "She's got a penchant for stumbling into murders."

"That would be Lacey Luzzi?" I asked. "Carlos Luzzi's granddaughter?"

"Yeah, totally. She's stumbled into so many bodies that she turned it into her job. Anyway, that's Jessica's car pulling up now. You two want a cup of coffee?" Meg leaned in and gave a wink. "I'll even give you a squirt of my finest whipped cream."

I glanced over at the ice cream truck. "No thanks. Not to mention, I think that will be considered evidence until the scene is cleared."

"Right." She winked again. "I read you. I'm gonna go talk to that cutie Officer Franklin again to see if I can get him to tell me some deets about the body. I'm pretty sure he's scared of me."

I was about to object, but Jones gave me a nudge with his elbow then gestured toward the bar. I followed him inside.

"She's a character," I said. "I got out of breath just listening to her talk."

"Tell me about it," Jimmy said. "Do you think she did it?"

"Honestly, I've got no read on her. I'm not sure that's ever happened before."

"There's a first time for everything."

Jimmy and I made our way over to the bar area. We found a tall, lanky kid who could be described as string-bean-ish. I slid onto a barstool. Jimmy took the one next to me.

"Are you Benny?" I asked. "Meg said you work here as a barback."

"If that's what you want to call it." Benny didn't stop what he was doing. He reached to replace a bottle of vodka. "I don't think that title exactly covers everything I do for her, but we'll go with it."

"What do you mean?"

"Last week she asked me to book her a manicure." Benny turned around and shrugged. "I think she thought I was Jessica. I don't really know."

"Did you do it?"

"Sure. The tips are pretty good here," he said. "Plus, she's the easiest boss ever to work for. I once didn't show up for three days straight and she didn't notice."

"Interesting," I said. "Well, I'm assuming you heard about the commotion out back."

"Yeah, the dead guy. What about him?"

"Is nobody here fazed by the fact that there's a dead body in the alley?" I turned to Jimmy. "I've never seen anything like it before."

"When you work for Meg, not much fazes you," Benny said. "This is just another day in the life working for that woman."

"Have you ever been in the ice cream truck before?" I asked. "Do you know where the keys are?"

"I only went in there once," he said. "It was a few weeks ago. The thing isn't locked. Meg keeps the keys in the ignition."

"That was common knowledge?"

"Sure. So's the fact that she's got a gun and a Taser on her person at all times. I know for a fact she's fired those things at least thirteen times between both of 'em while I've worked here. Nobody within a hundred miles of the Twin Cities would dare steal Meg's vehicle if they wanted to live the rest of their life without a bullet hole somewhere on their body or worse."

"A bullet hole somewhere on their body?"

"I mean, the chances she'd kill you by shooting you, even if she were trying her hardest, are really slim," Benny said. "She's a horrible shot. She once tried to shoot that dart board over there." Benny nodded toward the corner. Then he nodded toward a jukebox in the other corner with a broken screen. "She didn't hit it. I'll say that much."

"I am going to pretend I haven't heard about how much she fires her gun as a courtesy for your cooperation," I said. "What brought you out to the ice cream truck a few weeks ago?"

"I was out back smoking a..." He glanced at me, then at Jimmy. He cleared his throat and looked between us a few more times. "I mean, a cigarette. I was smoking a cigarette."

"Right," I said. "Definitely a cigarette."

"Meg caught me mid-smoke."

"She caught you smoking in the ice cream truck?"

"No, I was in the alley," he said, sounding annoyed, like I was missing the point. "She asked why I hadn't offered her any of my stash. Then she said we should head back to the ice cream truck for the rest of my break so long as I was willing to share."

"So you and Meg went back to the ice cream truck to smoke? There was no body in there at the time, right?"

"Nope," he said. "But there was a lot of whipped cream. We were so hungry by the time my break was over that she cracked open the case, and I think we went through a whole can just the two of us."

"She told you the code to her secret chest in the truck?"

"No way. She guards that like a launch code to an atomic bomb. She made me get out of the truck while she unlocked it."

I couldn't argue with the fact that their stories were matching up, as far-fetched as they might have seemed. I also wasn't getting any sense that they were lying. Which didn't help me with the dead body out back.

"Did you notice anyone hanging around here lately that might've drawn suspicion?" I asked. "Ever see anything suspicious out back when taking out the garbage or anything?"

He stared blankly. "You know Meg's part of the Luzzi family, right?"

"Yeah. Why?"

"We have suspicious people here all the time," he said. "It's more normal to see suspicious people than regular people at this point."

"Okay, has there been anyone who stood out to you more than usual?"

"Dude. I just lift heavy things for Meg," he said. "I don't pay much attention to what's going on around me."

"That and make her manicure appointments," Jimmy pointed out. "You're a Benny of all trades."

"If your boss let you smoke on the job and skip work at random, you'd make his manicure appointments too."

Jimmy snorted a laugh. "I guess you're right, kid. We heard there's another woman who's supposed to be arriving. Any clue if she's here?"

"Yeah. Jessica. She's in the back room dropping off her purse and stuff. She should be out in a second."

Benny went back to restocking the liquor shelves. He was just taking an empty box out of the room when a young woman entered the bar area, rolling up the sleeves of a long-sleeved shirt. She looked up at us in surprise.

"Hey," she said. "You know we're not open yet, right? We're just doing inventory."

"We're cops, actually," I said. "We're here to—"

"Is this about that expiring liquor license? Because we're working on it."

"Actually, no, we were—"

"We didn't serve those minors either. I know what they said, but they were lying."

"That's not—"

"And if this is about that health inspector dude who was here checking out our kitchens the other day, the only reason he was such a stickler was because he asked Meg out and she turned him down."

"We're not here about the bar technically," I finally interrupted. "We're here because a body was discovered in the alley behind this facility earlier this morning."

"Oh. That." She frowned. She also seemed totally unflustered. "I thought I saw some crime scene tape. Who's dead?"

I just looked at Jimmy and shook my head.

"We're working on that," Jimmy said, jumping in. "We haven't identified him yet. His body was found in the ice cream truck."

"Ew," she said. "That doesn't exactly scream Dilly Bar."

"I happen to agree," Jimmy said approvingly. "Any chance you saw anything that might have been suspicious?"

"I'm just getting in this morning," she said, gesturing behind her. "I mean, you saw me, right?"

"The time of death wasn't today," I said. "It might've been a few days ago."

"Oh, well, no. I mean, there's always something going on in the alley back there. Kids making out, drunk people peeing on the wall, homeless guys looking through the garbage. I'm not sure exactly what you want me to tell you."

"Anyone hanging around the ice cream truck?" I asked. "Anyone in the bar hanging around more than usual?"

"You mean staking the place out?" She shrugged. "Most of our clientele are regulars. They come here and stake out the place like it's their job."

"I'll take that as a no," I said. "Nothing out of the ordinary."

"Pretty safe to say that," she said. "As far as I'm concerned, it's been business as usual."

"Thanks for your time." I turned to Jimmy. "Ready?"

"How good are your cheese fries?" he asked Jessica. "I've heard about them now for a while, but I rarely make it to this side of the river."

"They're really good," Jessica said, lowering her voice and fluttering her eyelashes as if it were some trade secret. "If you promise not to report me for operating outside of business hours, I'll fry you up some right now."

Jimmy looked tempted. I shook my head.

"We're good," I said. "We have to get back to work. Thanks for your time."

"Anytime."

Jimmy and I stopped back at the crime scene to see if anything else had turned up. Melinda was still busy with the body and hadn't discovered anything of note just yet. She confirmed drinks tonight at seven, then sent us on our way, so we didn't bother her about more information she couldn't provide.

Once in the car, I sat behind the wheel for a moment in stunned silence.

"That was something, huh?" Jimmy finally remarked.

"Something," I said. "Something, all right."

Chapter 2

I spent the better part of the afternoon combing through the information we had on the Luzzi family. There were several mentions of the bar in my reading. Carlos Luzzi, the head of the family, had a very long file. I suspected I wasn't even seeing the half of it.

I found one name that made me freeze mid-read: Mindy Hartlett. For a moment, it made my heart beat a little bit harder than normal until I remembered her saying that she'd worked as a lawyer for the Luzzi family. We'd been at Wes's cabin, and she'd mentioned being on his retainer, or something of that nature.

I debated giving Mindy a call directly to get her read on the murder, but the situation was a little bit dicey. For starters, I wasn't exactly sure what time zone she was in at the moment. When she'd left Alastair Gem at the altar on Christmas Eve, she'd hopped on a plane to somewhere in Japan. From the rumors I'd heard over the last few weeks, she'd been traipsing across the globe, having given up her power suits and stilettos for linen dresses and Birkenstocks. I wasn't sure she'd welcome a phone call from her previous life.

Then there was the fact that I really didn't have any evidence that this case was related to the Luzzi family at all. It seemed to be very public knowledge that Meg not only left the ice cream truck unlocked, but that she'd left the keys in the ignition.

It was possible that someone who worked at or frequented the bar had used the place as a dumping ground. It was also completely feasible that someone had simply happened upon the truck while making their way down the alley. Maybe they'd been looking to leave the body in a dumpster and had settled on an unlocked ice cream truck instead. It seemed unfair to involve the entire Luzzi family on nothing more than a slight rumor and a long history.

"Go home," Jimmy said as the late afternoon rolled around. "You're not going to find anything helpful in there. What time did your flight get in last night?"

"Late," I said. "Very late."

"Go home and have a drink with your friends and get some rest," he insisted. "There's nothing more for you to do."

"But—"

"Even Melinda's going to be calling it a day soon, and she's the only one who can get us more information at this point. You'll have plenty of opportunities to work around the clock in the coming days once we actually have an ID on the body. Might as well get out of here while you can."

"Sure." I yawned. "Maybe I will. I'll take the file with me for some bedtime reading."

"It'll put you right to sleep," Jimmy said. "I recommend it."

"Not this file. It's pretty juicy."

"Well, are you surprised after how our morning went?"

I said goodbye to the rest of the detectives in the office and told Jimmy to call me if anything changed. Then I went home to take a shower, change, and maybe fit in a power nap before I met my friends for a drink.

Before I knew it, I was waking up to the sound of my phone ringing. A glance at the time told me it was just about 7:00 p.m. I hadn't changed or showered, though my power nap had lasted a lot longer than I'd thought. I had collapsed on my couch the second I'd walked in the door, and apparently had zonked out for a few hours.

"Were you asleep?" Asha asked.

"No," I said. "I'm on my way."

"Yeah, right," she said. "You're lucky I called you before Melinda got here. Now you can pretend you weren't sleeping."

"Yeah, yeah, thanks," I said. "I'm walking out the door right now."

I threw on some new clothes and made my way to Bellini's. The bar/restaurant/deli belonged to the Bellini family, who were related to me. My cousin Angela worked behind the bar most nights. If it could be called working, since she spent most of her time examining her nails and flirting with customers. I scooted into my table just before seven fifteen and deftly ignored Asha's smirk.

"Wow, you're even later than me," Lassie said as I joined them. "I'm always the last one here. It's sort of my signature. I'm not sure how I feel about this."

"She was sleeping," Melinda said, glancing at the menu.

"You told her?" I glanced at Asha.

Asha zipped her lips. Melinda just looked up and sighed.

"How long have I known you, Kate?" Melinda asked. "I can read you like a book. Which is why you need to tell us more about this trip that you've been avoiding talking about. What happened on it?"

"Nothing," I said. "I mean, the obvious stuff. My parents got married. Again. Sort of. The symbolic part. They did the courthouse thing before we left. My sister and Wes were newly engaged in Hawaii. I'll give you one guess how that went."

"That leaves you," Asha said.

"Lonely and single in Hawaii doesn't sound all that bad," Lassie said. "Tell me you found a friend to help you occupy some of your time so you weren't a Debbie Downer the whole trip."

"I wasn't a Debbie Downer," I said. "I just enjoyed the festivities and spending time with my family."

"How romantic," Asha quipped. "What about your other guy?"

"What other guy?"

"Jack," Melinda filled in patiently. "Have you spoken to him?"

"No. It's better if we don't talk. It would just make things harder."

"You're allowed a lapse in judgment or two," Lassie said. "Especially when your ex is as hot as Jack Russo. Then you're allowed, like, four lapses before you have to worry about being in a relationship again."

"It's not easy to 'lapse' with Jack," I said. "He's across the country from me. We tried the casual dating thing. It didn't work."

"What about Gem?" Asha asked innocently. "Have you spoken to him?"

"Why would I have spoken to him?"

"Oh, because he's your friend, and he just had his heart broken too," Asha said. "That's what friends do. They talk and bond over shared experiences."

"No. I haven't had any meaningful conversations with him." I glanced at Lassie. "Then again, according to this one, Gem has been surrounding himself with plenty of people who are willing to help mend his broken heart."

Lassie looked pleased. "You actually read my blog?"

"You subscribed me to your newsletter."

"You usually delete it without opening it," Lassie said. Then she blushed. "Yes, sometimes I check your open rates."

"I was curious," I admitted. "He is my friend. I wanted to see how he was doing. Then I saw, and I figured he didn't need help from me."

"I'm sorry," Lassie said. "It's just my job to report on the happening things right now. You know pictures can be misleading. I'm sure nothing Gem's doing right now is serious with anyone. I'm sure he'd love to talk to you."

"He has my number," I said. Then after a beat, I added, "I called him once."

Three heads swiveled to face me. I took a sip of my margarita and told them the same story I'd told Jimmy earlier.

"So, the ball's in his court," I said. "I tried to reach out."

"I'm not sure it counts if neither of you can really remember what you talked about," Melinda said. "And you know I have to ask, now that Jack's out of the picture—"

"Jack's not out of the picture," I said sharply. "For right now, maybe he is, but it's not like we broke up because there was a problem. We might get back together again."

"I think what Melinda was trying to say," Asha continued, "is just that at the moment, you're single. So is Alastair Gem."

"We've both been single before. What's the big deal?"

"I don't know," Lassie said. "It just seems like there might be some unresolved stuff between the two of you."

"Stuff?"

"Feelings. I don't know," Lassie repeated. "Maybe you should go out with Gem just to see where things go."

"Aren't you forgetting that I just broke up with my boyfriend a month ago? I think I'm allowed some time to grieve that relationship."

"You sure are," Asha said. "Sometimes the grieving process can be helped along by a little rebound relationship."

"You're suggesting I use Gem as a rebound?"

"Dude. He's a smoking-hot billionaire," Lassie said. "That's about the best rebound a girl can hope to have. Usually it's the backup drummer of some reject band or something." She paused and slurped her margarita. "Ask me how I know."

Melinda laughed. "It doesn't have to be a rebound. The two of you are friends, right? You could just spend some time together. You both went through a big life change on the same day. It wouldn't kill the two of you to have some fun together."

"Hey, now I always thought you were for Russo," I said. "Now you're changing your tune?"

"You tried dating Jack and it didn't work out. For now," Melinda said. "I have to wonder if maybe if you tried dating Gem, it would answer some questions."

"Questions?"

"Like if a relationship with Gem doesn't work out, then you wouldn't have any doubts if you wanted to resume things with Jack."

I squinted at her. "Let me get this straight. You're still for Team Russo, but now you think I need to get there via Team Gem?"

Melinda shrugged. "If you're forcing me to take sides, I guess that's one way to say it."

I shook my head. "That would imply that my breakup with Russo had something to do with Gem."

The three other women at the table stared silently at me. I stared back at them.

"Wait a minute. You all think that?" I shook my head. "Jack and I broke up before I ever knew Gem's wedding hadn't gone through. I thought Gem was married."

"But he's not," Lassie said softly, "because he couldn't go through with it either."

"Not true." I held up a finger. "Mindy's the one who left him."

"That whole engagement had problems," Asha said. When I glanced at her, she raised her eyebrows back at me. "What? I can't read Lassie's blog too?"

"You guys are nuts. This is not some huge twist of fate bringing me and Gem together. It's just two people who hit bad luck on the same day."

"Okay, then." Melinda poured herself more margarita. "Don't listen to our advice. We weren't telling you to marry the billionaire. We were just saying you could have dinner with him."

"You never turn down a free meal," Lassie said. "Plus with Gem, you know it'd be a bomb meal too."

"I can afford my own food," I said. "I'm a grown adult."

"Right. Totally not the point," Lassie said. "But I'm not going to pressure you. If Gem's still single, that always means there's a chance he'll meet me and fall madly in love with me."

"He has met you."

"Yeah," Lassie said with a sad sigh. "I'm more concerned about the falling madly in love part. That hasn't seemed to click for him just yet."

Melinda and Asha were hiding grins. I took another slurp of my margarita. I figured that since I'd technically gotten back from Hawaii very early this morning, I was allowed to sort of roll my vacation over one more day. I'd go on my alcohol-free detox tomorrow.

"Any news on the case?" I asked, changing the subject rather clumsily. "Autopsy tomorrow morning?"

"The full autopsy, yes," Melinda said, "but I had some time today after receiving the body at the lab and was able to pull dental records. We got a match. We also got a time of death."

"Why have we been sitting here talking about Alastair Gem when you have news like this?" I asked. "Why did nobody call me to tell me you ID'd our ice cream truck victim?"

"We just got the results about half an hour ago," she said. "I figured I'd see you soon enough. Plus, you were napping."

"You didn't know I'd fallen asleep," I said, sounding a little growly. "So? Who is our victim and when did he die?"

"I was right on most accounts," Melinda said. "The man's name was Garrett Landers. He'd just turned thirty-eight, and that's where I passed the background search off to Asha. Time of death was sometime Friday night. We're working on getting a smaller window, but you can start there for now. The cause of death was blunt force trauma to the head, but we don't have a weapon yet."

"So you all knew and didn't call me?"

"You were sleeping," Asha insisted. "I only had about twenty minutes to start digging into this guy, which doesn't leave me with much just yet. I'm going to do some more work tonight. Hopefully between that and the autopsy results tomorrow morning, you'll be able to get a good head start on the case before the leads get any colder."

"What'd you find?"

Asha handed me a sheaf of papers. "I printed out most of the stuff I compiled. Like I said, not much. Top-line stuff is that this guy is a local. Born and raised here. He's survived by two parents and his older brother—all of them live out in the Minnetonka area. Garrett went into the military straight out of high school. He never got a college degree, but he did fine for himself with security work."

"He was a big guy," Melinda said. "Lots of muscle."

"Here's a photo of him." Asha set a picture in the center of the table. "Before he was dead."

The photo featured a large, broad-shouldered male with a steely glint to his eyes and no smile. He had a buzz cut and wore a no-nonsense expression. He looked like the sort of man one wouldn't want to meet in a dark alley.

"He's sorta hot," Lassie said. "You know, in a bad boy sort of way. Now *this* is who you go to for a rebound." She tapped the photo. "The guy who's gonna rock your world but doesn't really care to stay for breakfast."

I blinked at her. "You know he's dead, right?"

"Well, I admit that causes some issues with my plan," Lassie said. "I'm talking in hypotheticals here."

"Was he employed at the time of his death?" I asked. "Any signs that he might've been involved in something sketchy that could've gotten him stuffed in the back of an ice cream truck?"

"His last known place of employment was a laundromat." Asha watched my reaction carefully.

"A laundromat?" Lassie asked. "Come on. There's no way this guy would work for a laundromat. I'm not a detective, but my gut's telling me there's no way this guy spent his time separating whites from darks."

"I'm going to venture a guess and agree with Lassie," I said. "Any clue if the laundromat was a front?"

"You bet it was," Asha said. "I figured you'd jump to that conclusion, so I did a little digging in advance. The laundromat's a front all right, and a badly masked one at that."

"A bad front that hasn't been closed down yet?" I asked. "That doesn't make sense."

Asha tapped a long, black-painted fingernail on the top of another sheet of paper. "The Luzzi family owns the laundromat."

"Ah," I said. "Now I understand."

"Help me out," Lassie said. "I don't know who that is."

"It's a crime family in the Twin Cities," I said. "Or they used to be. From my understanding, they've mostly gone clean lately."

"Exactly," Asha said. "From what I can tell based on my preliminary research, the laundromat is no longer an actual front for anything illegal. It's a place where people actually go to wash their clothes and whatnot."

"I still don't believe this guy worked for a laundromat," Lassie said. "I just don't see him scraping off dryer lint."

"I'm sure he was doing something else for Carlos Luzzi," Asha agreed. "Seems to me, however, that Mr. Landers' contract was terminated a few weeks ago."

"I wonder if that put a bad taste in Garrett's mouth," I said. "He could've possibly tried to retaliate against the Luzzi family after getting fired."

"He obviously didn't come out on top," Lassie said. "Seeing as he ended up in the ice cream truck."

"It's just a theory," I said. "We don't have any evidence. It's probably worth a visit to the Luzzi estate to ask a few questions."

Asha and Melinda both froze.

"You might want to wait until we get some more results before you start questioning the Luzzis," Melinda said. "I've heard it's harder to get into their estate than it is to get citizenship in the United States."

"I'm a cop," I said. "If I got scared off by every criminal I met, I wouldn't be very good at my job."

"Melinda has a fair point, though I appreciate your bravado," Asha said. "All we know is that this guy once worked for the Luzzis. That's all, and it's not much to go on especially when you're dealing with a mob guy like Carlos Luzzi."

"Our victim was dumped around three days ago, which means our leads are already over seventy-two hours old," I said. "I can't waste any more time."

"Just do me a favor and take Jones with you," Asha said. "You might not be scared, but it'd be stupid to go to the estate without backup."

"Of course," I said. "I'm not stupid."

Asha and Melinda looked at one another.

"Not stupid," Melinda said casually. "Maybe just a little too brave for your own good."

"Either way, I should probably quit on the margaritas and call it a night," I said. "Now that we're getting somewhere with Garrett Landers, I need to have a clear head for tomorrow. I'm going to go home and get some rest."

"Are you sure you want to drive?" Melinda glanced at me. "At least stay and have a few curly fries."

I glanced down, startled to see I'd sucked down an entire margarita and a half. My head was a little bit fuzzy. I guess talking about my ex-boyfriend had caused the alcohol to creep up on me.

"You're right," I said. "I'll just—"

"I can give you a ride home, Detective," a voice sounded over my shoulder.

I spun around, shocked to find Alastair Gem standing behind me. The other women looked just as shocked to see him. Apparently, we'd been so engrossed in our conversation that we'd been oblivious to the bar scene around us.

"Gem?" I halfway rose from my seat before I eased back down. My head was fuzzier than I remembered it being a few seconds ago. "What are you doing here?"

He raised a bag full of takeout. "Just picking up some dinner. I was walking by, heard the tail end of the conversation as I was waiting in line. I hope you don't mind the intrusion."

"She doesn't mind," Lassie said. "She'll go home with you."

I stared at Lassie. Apparently the margaritas had gotten to her head too. Her cheeks were flushed, and her eyes were shining.

"I mean," she said, flustered, "Kate will take a ride home with you. To her home. Where you may or may not be invited inside. Right, I'm going to stop now."

I cleared my throat. "Thanks, but my car's here. I didn't have that much to drink. I'm just going to switch to water and have some curly fries. I'll be fine in an hour."

"Let me drive your vehicle," Gem said. "My driver can follow us to your house."

"But—"

"You must have just gotten off a plane from Hawaii," Gem said reasonably. "I assume you're tired and would like to get some sleep. Take me up on the offer."

The way Gem spoke with such authority, and the way my head seemed to be swimming with tequila, I found myself unable to come up with a great counterargument.

"I don't know," I said. "I could use some curly fries."

"I ordered enough food for four," Gem said, "and I'm just one person. You'd be doing me a favor by taking some of this off my hands."

"Go with him," Lassie urged in a loud whisper. "It just makes sense."

"Go home and get some sleep," Melinda agreed. "You're exhausted. Your shirt is on inside out."

"What?" I glanced down, and sure enough, when I'd thrown on my clothes, my shirt had gone on inside out. "Why did nobody tell me until now?"

"Just go home, sweetie," Asha chipped in. "It's much safer for Gem to drive your car home tonight. Between the tequila and the lack of sleep, you wouldn't want to endanger anyone else on the road."

"Now you're just playing with my emotions," I said.

"You have emotions?" Gem said mildly. "And here I thought you were the cold-hearted detective as seen in TV shows and bad novels."

The other three women at the table hid varying degrees of sniggers and laughs. I made a face at Gem. "Yeah, fine. Whatever. You can drive my car if you're not embarrassed to be seen in it. I doubt you've been in a car that's worth less than three zillion dollars in ages."

"Three zillion dollars," Gem said. "That's very specific."

I hauled myself out of the booth. "Good night, ladies. I expect you'll call me if you get any more information on the case."

"We'll see you tomorrow," Asha said, deftly evading any sort of promise. "Get some rest. Eat some curly fries. You're looking skinny. A diet of mai tais and abstinence will do that to you."

I glared at her. "Goodbye."

I left the three women behind as I followed Gem outside.

"A diet of mai tais and abstinence?" he asked. "Half of that sounds very fun. The other half not so much."

"They think I need a rebound."

"You don't?"

"Obviously you believe in rebounds."

"Wow. Ouch. We haven't even gotten to the car yet."

Gem reached for my keys. I grudgingly handed them over. We both eased into the car. The smell of Gem's food was appetizing. He must have caught me staring at the bag because he handed it over and told me to go wild.

I didn't have enough shame to refuse. I opened the bag and peeked inside, and when I caught a glimpse of the fries, I helped myself to one.

Gem pulled out of the parking space as I munched away at my adopted snack. He gave me a few minutes to enjoy the food in peace before he glanced over at me.

"I'm glad to see you made it back from your vacation in one piece."

"What made you think I wouldn't have?"

He gave a mock frown in my direction. "Oh, I don't know. Our conversation."

"You remember it?"

"Of course I do. I wasn't sure you did."

"I thought you were ignoring me after. Not that I totally blamed you. It was embarrassing that I called you. Sorry."

"Friends are allowed to dial their friends when indulging. I didn't mind one bit."

"You didn't say anything after the fact," I said. "I thought maybe you wanted to pretend it didn't happen."

"You asked me to leave you alone."

"I did?" I jerked my gaze up at him. "What exactly did I say? I don't remember that part."

"It was late," Gem said amiably, as if the late hour had been the main problem and not the mai tais. "Just before we hung up, you asked that I refrained from contacting you during the rest of your trip."

"Oh. Well, sorry. I guess that explains the silence." After a beat, I asked, "Did I say why I wanted to make that request?"

He cast a side-eyed glance at me. "As a matter of fact, you mentioned that it was something about me making things complicated and clouding your judgment."

"Huh."

"I said the same thing. But I understand everyone grieves and heals differently. I wanted to respect your wishes."

"I think wishes, like contracts, don't exactly need to be honored when the person stating them is significantly under the influence."

Gem laughed. "Fair enough. I didn't want to take any chances."

"I appreciate that, I guess."

"You guess? Did you *want* me to call you?"

"I don't know," I said. "I guess not."

"You don't sound convinced."

"Our situation is complicated."

"Yes and no," he said. "In some ways, it's less complicated now than ever. We are both currently unattached, which means we don't have to worry about anyone else's wishes. We can spend as much or as little time together as we want."

"I just broke up with Russo," I said. "I'm not ready for anything. It's only been a month."

"I meant as friends."

"Well, that's fine," I said. "Do you want to be my friend?"

"Why would you say something like that?"

"The last time we talked, you were uncertain about spending time with me at all."

"You're referencing a conversation we had before my failed attempt at a wedding?"

"That would be the one."

"That was out of respect for Mindy and her wishes, not my own," Gem said. "I never wanted to stop being friends with you."

"Okay."

"Okay?" He glanced my way. "What does that mean? Are we friends again?"

"Do you need me to pass you a handwritten note with a box checked *yes*?" I asked. "We can be friends. But that's it. Don't get any ideas about kissing me."

Gem spluttered. It was one of the first times I'd ever seen him actually shaken.

"Ideas about kissing you?"

I realized how that sounded a few moments too late. I blamed it on the margarita. I wasn't normally so blunt, at least not with subjects like this one. And especially not in front of company like Alastair Gem.

"I just mean that I'm not looking for anything romantic at all. Full stop. Period," I said. "It's just not happening. So if that's what you were getting at, then don't waste your time. I don't want to string you along."

"You're not stringing me anywhere, Detective. I really was just asking if you'd want to have dinner." He gave me an amused smile. "We've both been dumped recently, and we're friends. It just seems like we could each use a little company."

"Seems like you've got plenty of company."

"What's that supposed to mean?"

"Lassie subscribed me to her blog."

He gave a snort. "This might surprise you, but I don't subscribe to Lassie's blog. You'll have to enlighten me on all the fun trivia she's been posting."

"I didn't actually read the articles," I admitted. "I'm not that much of a sucker. I just looked at some of the pictures."

Gem groaned. "Even better. I assume I'm the subject of some of these photos?"

"I simply noticed you seemed to have surrounded yourself with a lot of people—women especially—who seemed pretty keen on cheering you up."

He groaned again.

"Are they your rebounds?"

"Why?" Gem looked over at me. "Would you like to submit an application for the rebound position? I promise you, Detective, I'll clear the queue for you if you're asking."

"I don't believe in rebounds."

"Is that right? Why not?"

"What's the point?" I asked. "A relationship without concrete attachments and a solid future is what got me into this situation in the first place."

"What situation is that?"

"The dumped and brokenhearted one."

"Ah." Gem nodded. "But the point of a rebound is that there's no emotional attachment whatsoever. Just pure fun. A fling to distract a person from the emotional turmoil they're going through."

"You mean, a waste of time to take your mind off the person you really want to be with."

Gem made a little face. "When you put it like that, I don't think I'd like to be your rebound. Consider my offer rescinded, Detective."

"I wasn't submitting my application."

Gem laughed. The sound was full of joy, and I had to admit it warmed my heart to hear my friend sounding happy again. We relaxed, dropped the conversation, and rode the rest of the way to my place in companionable silence.

Gem parked my car in the driveway while his driver found a spot on the street. As Gem shut the car off, I glanced over at Gem.

"Thanks for the ride," I said. "You didn't have to do that. Sorry about your fries."

I handed the bag of food back to Gem. It was a lot lighter than when he'd handed it to me.

"It's for you," he said, pressing it back to me. "You need it more than me."

"You drove all the way across the city to pick up Bellinis." I thrust the bag back at him. "I'm not taking your food."

"That's not why I drove across the city."

I hesitated, letting the puzzle pieces fall into place. Sure enough, if I hadn't indulged in a couple of drinks, I would've figured it out a lot sooner. There was no way a man like Alastair Gem would drive across the city to pick up his own takeout for no reason. At exactly the spot I'd be at exactly the same time.

"Are you stalking me?" I asked. "How'd you know I'd be there?"

"I didn't. I took a chance."

"You're really trying to tell me you just got lucky running into me?"

"I wouldn't say I got lucky. All things considered."

I felt my cheeks blush. "You know what I mean."

"That's actually not what I was referring to," Gem said, amused. "I simply don't believe in luck."

"No?"

"No. I believe in reasonable deductions. I didn't make millions of dollars based on luck. C'mon, Detective. You just got off a plane last night. Your girlfriends would have missed you and wanted to talk. You probably wouldn't have a ton of work seeing as it was your first day back, so you wouldn't mind their invitation out—especially since you probably didn't have much food in your refrigerator at home."

"That's all true. Especially the food in the refrigerator part, but unfortunately that has nothing to do with whether or not I've been on vacation. That's just the state of my refrigerator on any given day."

Gem shrugged. "You're only helping to prove my point. I took a reasonable guess that you might be out and about.

I could've been wrong. You could've been hot on a case, and in that circumstance, the only thing I would have been out was an hour of my time. But I'd have gotten a good meal in exchange. I considered that a worthy enough risk."

"I'm going to have to start calling you Detective."

"Or just start calling me."

I rolled my eyes at him. "Do pickup lines like that actually work?" I held up a hand. "Oh, wait. You're Alastair Gem. You don't even have to speak to get women to flock to you."

He cleared his throat. "Not every woman."

"I'm glad to see you looking happy, Gem," I said earnestly. "It's nice to hear you laughing again. I know how much you cared about Mindy."

"Thank you. I hope the same is true for you."

"I suppose I'll get there. Maybe I'll have to test out your methods."

"My methods?"

"Rebounding seems to have worked well for you," I said. "Maybe I'll have to give it the old college try."

Another throat clear sounded from Gem. "Can I submit my application?"

"No."

"You didn't even take time to think about it."

"You're not a rebound," I said. "You said it yourself. Rebounds are where you're unattached to the other person. You and I are already too attached for that to work."

It took me a long moment to figure out why Gem looked so happy with the rejection. When it hit me, it was my turn to groan.

"Don't get a big head," I said. "We're more attached like, I don't know, lint to a shirt. We sort of just stick to one another for no reason."

"There's a scientific reason lint happens," Gem said. "But I'm more concerned with the fact that you compared me to lint, so I'm not going to dwell on this argument."

I grinned. "You're not lint, Gem. I'm a little intoxicated."

He pushed the bag of food across the seat toward me one final time. "Dinner's on me."

Gem and I climbed out of the car, and he locked it. Then he handed me the keys, lingering a second too long. My breath felt tight in my throat. It didn't feel right, but it didn't feel totally wrong. Before I could contemplate what that meant at a deeper level, I took a step back, opened the take-out bag, and popped another fry into my mouth. Then I raised the bag in a cheers.

"Thanks," I said. "I'll see you around."

"See you, Detective."

I headed up the front steps and let myself into the house. I found Jane waiting for me. She glanced out the window behind me as I entered the living room.

"You didn't want to invite him in?" she asked with a wiggle of her eyebrows.

"Shouldn't you be out with your fiancé?"

"He's working. I'm bored. And you have food." Jane crossed her legs on the couch. "What do you say to a rom com and ice cream and this delicious bag of goodies you brought me?"

"I'm tired."

"You have a broken heart. You just spent a week around couples in love," Jane pointed out. "You need to binge. Plus, I can smell the margarita on you. You'll feel better in the morning if you eat something first."

"I don't know. I'm not sure I'm up for more talking."

"No talking," Jane said. "Miss Congeniality?"

Chapter 3

By 9:00 a.m. the next morning, I'd showered, downed a cup of black coffee at home, and popped by my mother's café to grab a latte to go. When I reached my desk, I was feeling pretty good, considering the first item on my agenda was to visit a well-known mobster to ask him a few prickly questions about his former employee.

"How was your night?" Jimmy asked as I reached my desk.

"Why?" I snapped. "Who told you something?"

Jimmy raised his hands. "I don't know anything. I was trying to make small talk so you wouldn't notice I ate your doughnut."

"Trust me, I put away enough curly fries last night to keep me full until Wednesday."

"Sounds like you had a more exciting night than I did."

I rubbed at my forehead. "I'm too old to be exciting."

"Ah," Jimmy said. "*That* sort of exciting."

"It was eventful," I admitted. "I went out with the girls. Then Gem gave me a ride home. Long story."

"Did you ask him to put in a good word for us?"

"A good word? With who?"

"We're going to talk to the Luzzis in an hour," Jimmy said. "I guarantee the guy knows who they are."

"Oh."

"Not to mention Alastair Gem's ex-fiancée worked for them," Jimmy added. "I'm just saying there's a chance a kind word from a powerful man like Gem could help us out."

I shook my head, remembering what had happened last time I'd asked Gem for help. His club had gone up, literally, in flames, and two innocent people had died.

"I'm not asking him for favors," I said. Then I revised, "Unless I can't help it."

"He's happy to do it. All I was thinking was that he might put in a kind word for us. Smooth things over."

"I'm the cop," I said. "I did my job just fine before Gem came into my life. I don't want to start using him like a crutch."

"Don't want to start mixing business and personal?" Jimmy crooked an eyebrow. "Is he in the personal portion of your life now?"

"You're not," I said pointedly, "so butt out. I'm not asking him to call the Luzzis for me. Let's get going. With any luck, we can catch the family before they get started for the day."

Jimmy and I made our way to the outskirts of St. Paul. The Luzzi family home was an estate in the most grandiose sense of the world. It was located between both downtowns but still set off from the main suburbs in its own little kingdom. The front lawns were sprawling with intricately designed landscaping and decorations behind ornately carved, intimidating fences.

We pulled up to the front gates and were stopped at a guard tower. I rolled down my window and spoke to the oversized gentleman stuffed into the little booth. He looked just as scary as the picture of Garrett Landers, and I had a lightning quick thought that maybe Garrett had been sitting here just a few weeks back. I wondered if this guy here knew what had happened to his coworker.

I introduced myself and Jimmy. "We're here to ask Mr. Luzzi a few questions."

"Carlos Luzzi?" The guard looked at me as if I were nuts. "Do you have some sort of a warrant?"

"It's more of an informal—"

"He wants his lawyer," the guard said. "You'll have to work through her."

"Are you talking about Mindy Hartlett?" I asked. "Because she's not even in the States at the moment."

"I'm not privy to the details of Mr. Luzzi's team of lawyers. All I know is that you'll have to get through them first."

"If I could just—"

"Sorry," he said. "You'll have to come back a different time. He's busy."

"You didn't even check with him."

"Doesn't matter. He wants his lawyer."

"I just need a few minutes—"

"It's fine," Jimmy said under his breath. "Let's pull out of here. I have a different idea."

"A different idea?" I gave Jimmy a skeptical look. Then I shot a scowl at the guard and reversed out of the gated driveway. "What's this brilliant idea? This place is locked down tighter than the Pentagon. They're going to make it incredibly difficult for us to get any face time with the family at all."

"You're not the only one with Alastair Gem's number," Jimmy said. "With how often you get in trouble, we exchanged digits a while back."

"So you guys could keep tabs on me? Talk about me behind my back?"

"You got a problem with that?" Jimmy held the phone to his ear. "Don't give me that look. You'd be calling him yourself if you weren't so stubborn."

"I'm not stubborn. I just don't think we should be involving Gem in matters that don't concern him."

"He considers it a donation to a good cause," Jimmy said. "Who am I to prevent him from doing good deeds? Yes, Mr. Gem. How are you? This is Detective Jimmy Jones."

I could only hear bits and pieces of Gem's voice from the other end of the line. I had to puzzle together what he was saying from Jimmy's side of things.

"Yeah, she's fine this morning. Little bit of a headache, but she doesn't smell like tequila, if that's what you're asking."

I scowled at Jimmy. He grinned back at me.

"Say, I was hoping to ask you for a little favor. Feel free to shut me down if you're not comfortable with it." Jimmy waited for a response, then he continued. "We're outside of the Luzzi gates right now, and the old man's lawyering up. The thing is, I don't personally think Mr. Luzzi is responsible for anything in our case, but talking to him could help us out. I was wondering if you might be so inclined to let him know how much we'd appreciate his cooperation on this little matter."

I couldn't read Jimmy's face as Gem spoke on the other end. Then Jimmy hung up without another word.

"He said to give him five minutes," Jimmy said. "Then we can pull back around."

I harrumphed. I seriously doubted this would work. Gem was a billionaire, not a miracle worker. A man like Carlos Luzzi didn't talk to cops without an army of lawyers surrounding him. That was why people like Carlos Luzzi never ended up in prison.

"Five minutes," Jimmy said when the clock ticked over. "Pull back around."

"This is stupid."

"What is?" Jimmy asked. "Stupid because you don't think it'll work or because you do?"

"Both. Either." Still, I wasn't about to waste an opportunity when it came to my job. Not when it came to finding a murderer and putting him behind bars. If this worked, it might be our one and only time to question Carlos Luzzi without a lawyer present. That sort of rainbow opportunity didn't come around often.

As I pulled back up to the gate, 90 percent of me expected the guard to look at me like I was an idiot, then pull out a gun and threaten that we leave and never come back. I wasn't even sure I'd blame him.

Instead, I didn't even have to say a word. I barely had to touch the brakes. By the time the guard glimpsed the front of the car, the gates were already opening. He just stared without saying a word as I pulled through.

The gates closed behind us. I didn't take a breath until the actual Luzzi home was within our sights. Then I expelled that breath and found Jimmy grinning next to me.

"I'm just saying," Jimmy said, "you're welcome."

"Come on," I said. "Let's move before we overstay our welcome."

Jimmy and I headed up the front path to the door of the intimidating Luzzi estate. There was a walled enclosure around the place, and I caught glimpses of security guards slipping in and out of my peripheral like shadows. On the surface, it looked like a beautiful, old palace. If I didn't know any better, I'd think it to be a museum of some sort. Maybe someday it would be. The home of the famous mobster Carlos Luzzi.

I was quite surprised when the front door opened without warning, and an older gentleman with shockingly white hair and a kind smile stood waiting for us. When he greeted us, it was with a quaint English accent.

"Good Morning, Detectives," the man said. "My name is Harold, and I'd be happy to assist you today. May I take your coats?"

I slipped off my jacket and handed it over. As Harold reached for Jimmy's coat, I muttered to my partner, "Have we stepped into a book or something?"

Jimmy just snorted and gave a shrug of agreement.

"I assure you this is very real." Harold turned around and gave me a smile. "I received a message that the two of you are here as guests of Carlos Luzzi. May I show you into the kitchen?"

"We just need to speak to Mr. Luzzi for a few minutes," I said. "Wherever is convenient for him."

"He's having his breakfast. I'm sure he'd like you to join him. Right this way."

Harold gestured for us to follow him down the hallway. We reached some sort of grand-entrance-type room with a big set of stairs and fancy décor. He kept right on marching down a narrower hallway off to one side. As we entered the walkway, I started to examine the art on the walls. Or what seemed to pass for artwork. The farther we moved down the hallway, the more I realized the theme. There were all sorts of arrest warrants and mug shots posted proudly in frames, like most people posted family portraits or their children's glamour shots.

"As guests here by Mr. Luzzi's voluntary invitation," Harold started when he saw me looking at the pictures on the walls, "I'd advise you to avert your eyes from the Hallway of Infamy as a courtesy to Carlos."

I swallowed and nodded. Jimmy seemed like he was finding it hard not to laugh.

At the end of the hall, Harold pushed open a swinging door and led us through. Inside, I was surprised to find a warm, smallish kitchen that didn't fit into the rest of the grandiose décor of the house. A family-style picnic table sat against one side of the eat-in space. The walls were a sunny shade of light yellow.

The quarters were somewhat cramped, especially since a woman was standing at the stove, whirling around the room like a tornado. Spoons and ladles sat on just about every spare countertop. A pot of something that smelled delicious simmered on the stove. Over on the table sat a stack of waffles at least eleven inches high. Just visible behind the stack of waffles was the man we'd come to find.

Carlos Luzzi raised a teeny tiny espresso cup to his lips and took a sip. He stared at us without a word. It was a moment before the woman at the stove noticed our presence over the sound of her own mutterings and curse words at a recipe that seemed to be not quite working as she'd anticipated. When she saw us, her eyes widened in surprise.

"You're here already!" the woman said. "Thank goodness. Someone needs to make a dent in that stack of waffles. Take a seat, will you? Thanks, Harold. You're free to go, but you must take a plate of waffles with you."

I glanced at the butler who glanced back at me and raised his eyebrows as if to say it was better not to argue. He helped himself to a modest two waffles, a scoop of strawberries, and a dollop of whipped cream before he let the swinging door close behind him.

"Well, sit, sit." The woman at the stove wielded her ladle like a sword. "You both seem like capable adults. You can talk and eat at the same time, can't you?"

I cleared my throat. "Thank you, ma'am, but we're actually on the clock—"

She waved a hand. "I'm Nora. You obviously know my husband, Carlos, which means you're friends of the family. Sit down."

"They're not friends," Carlos muttered. "They're detectives."

"Ooh la la," Nora said. "Law enforcement. We haven't been questioned in a good long time. Even more reason to impress you lot so you don't believe we've gotten into any trouble. We haven't lately, have we, dear?"

Nora moved across the room in a swish of pink apron and gave her husband a squeeze around the neck.

"Right, dear?" she insisted, a little louder. "No trouble at all."

"No trouble," Carlos choked out. "Sit."

I took the command to be for Jimmy and me. We both did as he said and took a plate. I couldn't see Carlos's face over the stack of waffles until Jimmy unloaded a couple onto his plate. Then I caught a glimpse of Carlos's eyebrows.

I unloaded a few more waffles onto my own plate and caught a glimpse of the mobster's nose. One more waffle let me see his mouth. Next came the syrup that was generously poured for us by Carlos's wife. My waffles were drowning in syrup. I squinted closer at it. My syrup seemed to be full of glitter.

"Sparkly syrup," Nora said proudly. "Limited edition. I ordered three hundred bottles. Apparently I bought the store right out. My great-granddaughter Bella loves it."

"Very nice," I said, feeling shocked all over again at the sparkling reception we'd gotten inside the home of a very well-known and greatly feared ex-criminal.

"Thank you for having us," I said, directing the conversation at Carlos. "We appreciate your cooperation in this investigation."

He made a noise in his throat. It was obvious his arms were being twisted: one by Alastair Gem and the other by his wife. Carlos would rather be anywhere other than sharing a stack of waffles with two detectives.

"The reason we're here is because we found the body of a man named Garrett Landers recently."

Carlos's eyes stared at me. He was very intimidating. I glanced at my waffles for support.

"We have it on record that his last place of employment was working for you," I said. "The report mentioned a laundromat, but we both know that's not true."

I let the insinuation hang. Carlos was smart enough to realize that I didn't believe Garrett had worked folding laundry for a second. He still didn't offer anything, and I was beginning to think that Gem's favor was going to be a huge bust. All we were getting out of this was an inside tour of Casa Luzzi and a few inches added to our waists with the sparkling syrup.

"Can you confirm if Garrett Landers worked here?" I finally asked directly. "And if so, in what capacity?"

"I'd like my lawyer present," Carlos said. "I understand this is a favor for Alastair Gem, but I won't compromise myself in a murder investigation without a lawyer."

"Oh, honey," Nora said, "you know Mindy is frolicking braless around Bali or riding a camel through Egypt right now. Don't bother her."

"I have other lawyers," Carlos said irritably. "Any of them would do just fine."

"Just help these nice people out," Nora said. "A man who likes my waffles that much can't be out to get you."

I glanced over at Jimmy's plate, surprised to see it was completely empty. Not a drop of glitter left. He gave a salute to Nora, who blushed furiously. The disappearing food surely explained his silence.

"Best breakfast I've ever had," Jimmy confirmed. "I'm not sure we've properly introduced ourselves. I'm Detective Jimmy Jones, and this is Detective Kate Rosetti. We don't actually believe anyone here did anything wrong. We're just here trying to get a lead on Garrett and where he might've gone after he left here."

"Rosetti?" Carlos's eyes fixed on me. "Do you know Angelo?"

I swallowed hard. "You know my father?"

"I'll talk to her." Carlos didn't look away from me for a second. "I'll talk to you alone."

"Carlos, don't be ridiculous," Nora said. "You can't kick this fine gentleman out of my kitchen."

I made eyes at Jimmy. He seemed to understand. We were here on thin ice. One crack, and we'd lose any chance of a lead we might hope to get.

"It's not a problem, ma'am," Jimmy said. "If you don't mind, I'll take another bite of food and go see if that butler would like company while he eats."

"What a lovely idea," Nora said. "I'm sure Harold would like to chat with you."

I could see where Jimmy was going with his plan, and it was a good one. Sometimes we learned more information from the staff than the owners of a place like this. A butler? He'd know some things that went on under the radar that could be more useful than whatever calculated answers Carlos Luzzi gave me.

"I'll walk you to him," Nora said. "I'll bring him another cup of coffee. Harold always says he doesn't want one when I make it, but he always drinks it when I leave it out."

Once Nora and Jimmy vanished down the Hallway of Infamy, I turned back to Carlos. I pushed the waffles to the side and leaned my elbows on the table.

"Are you going to talk to me now?" I asked. "Because I'm a Rosetti?"

"I like your dad. Real family guy."

I wasn't sure which sort of family Carlos meant. The regular kind or the kind with a capital "F." "He was in prison most of my life."

"He did the right thing by serving his time like a man."

"You've never been to prison."

"I'm different," Carlos said. "Not necessarily in a good way. But that's not what you're here to talk about, is it?"

"Look, I don't think you killed anyone," I said. "At least not lately. From what I've heard, you're out of the business. Not to mention, I know Mindy. I haven't spoken to her yet, but I'm sure she'll vouch for you too."

Carlos gave me a slow nod.

"But I got a call this morning about a dead body in the back of an ice cream truck, and it's my job to figure out how he got there. I don't have much to go on," I admitted. "The biggest lead we have is that he worked for a bogus laundromat front under your name up until recently."

"If you'd ever done your laundry there, you'd know it's not bogus," Carlos said, his expression deadpan. "We run an exceptionally high-quality service. The best in the Twin Cities. We've even started airing commercials on the radio."

"Right. Yeah. Okay. And you had to hire an ex-military guy to work there?"

"I don't discriminate."

"Uh-huh." I nodded again. "I know how this works. Like you said, I'm a Rosetti. Did you invite us in to waste my time?"

"I didn't invite you in," Carlos said. "I thought this was a stupid idea. An acquaintance of mine asked for a favor. Nora overheard and wouldn't let me say no."

I sighed. "I'm good friends with Alastair Gem. We promised him that we didn't think you were guilty of anything. You don't have to trust me, but you should know that

I would never betray my friend like that. It's not in my blood. We're just here to talk."

Funnily enough, my honest statement seemed to have hit home with the mob boss. He looked at the ceiling, then sat back in his seat.

"He worked here," Carlos confirmed. "He reported to my chief of staff, Anthony."

"Did you hire him or did Anthony?"

"Anthony," Carlos said. "But I know everything that goes on here. I met Garrett. He didn't last all that long here."

"I'm under the impression he was terminated," I said, then realized how my words sounded. "I mean, his contract was terminated."

"That's what happens when you try to steal from me."

"Garrett tried to steal from you?"

Carlos nodded.

"Can I ask what he tried to steal?"

"No."

I looked down at my plate, wondering if the goods that Garrett had tried to steal might have been stolen goods in the first place. I decided I didn't want to know. Honoring Jimmy's promise to Gem and all.

"Fine," I said. "Is it possible that someone from your staff took things a step too far and went after Garrett as revenge?"

"No."

I blinked. "You're telling me there's zero percent chance? That's a pretty confident show of your staff."

"I only hire the best. I fire anyone who doesn't make the cut," Carlos said. "We run a tight ship around here. Like family."

The way he said *like family*, however, had a bit of a dark edge to it. I tried not to shiver.

"A family that loyal," I mused, "might want to protect you."

"A family that loyal would understand that would be stupid," Carlos said. "It's not easy to find good men—and women—" he added, with a glance in my direction—"to work for you. I would be very angry if one of my staff murdered someone as disposable as Garrett Landers and risked jail time. He's not worth my losing a member of my staff to the prison system."

I refrained from making a surprised face. It wasn't exactly the logic that shouted to me that Carlos Luzzi was innocent, but I was starting to see that Carlos followed that same criminal code as my father, and even Alastair Gem, on occasion. It was starting to make sense to me in little bits and pieces.

"He was fired. Enough said, point proven," Carlos said. "The second he was escorted off the premises, he was dead to me."

"Poor choice of words," I said, trying for a joke.

It didn't work. There was no smile on Carlos's face. I cleared my throat.

"Do you know of anyone else who might have wanted to harm him?"

"Anyone else who knew him."

My confusion was obvious to Carlos. He continued without prompting.

"A man who will try to steal from me will steal from others," Carlos said. "I don't doubt he crossed several other paths. It was just a matter of finally crossing the wrong path."

"I'd say it was a wrong path," I said. "He ended up dead in an ice cream truck."

"Is the only reason you're here because he worked for me?"

"That and because the ice cream truck belonged to a member of your family."

"A member of my family?" Carlos squinted. "I don't think anyone here owns an ice cream truck."

"Does the name Meg mean anything to you?" I let it hang there, once again, like Oprah or Cher. Judging by the five shades of pale Carlos's face went through, that single word meant something to him.

"She's not a member of my family."

"Technically, she is," I said. "She married in."

"She's not blood related," he clarified. "That's an important differentiation."

"Neither is Anthony," I pointed out. "He married in."

"He's related."

"Okay, then," I said, sensing Carlos had his own system by which he declared who was family and who wasn't. "I see. Well, the body was found in Meg's ice cream truck outside of her bar. That gives us two links back to the Luzzi family."

"That one doesn't count," Carlos said. "I don't vouch for anything that woman says or does."

"Can I ask why?"

"Have you met her?" He stared at me blankly.

"Okay, I understand," I admitted. "But could she have murdered someone?"

"She once shot the wheel of my car with her weapon still in her purse," Carlos said. "She forgot it was loaded. It'd be a miracle if that woman *hasn't* killed someone."

"How about on purpose?"

"I don't know what goes on in that woman's mind."

It seemed Carlos was allergic to referring to Meg by her name. It was "that woman" for him or nothing.

"I just find it very coincidental that his body was found outside Meg's bar, and his last place of employment was here. Could another ex-employee have run into him who might've been holding a grudge?"

Nora brushed into the room then. She gave a little full-body, exaggerated shiver. "It's sort of sexy seeing my husband being interviewed by the cops, even though I know he's innocent. I mean, I've always had a thing for bad boys."

I glanced away as she walked over to Carlos and gave him a smooch on the cheek. Then she turned to me.

"Are you still talking about Garrett Landers?" Nora asked. "He's a thief. I fired him for stealing my nice china. It's got real diamonds embedded in the teacups. I invited him to eat some eggs one morning, and I was using the nice china to serve coffee, and I think he got a little greedy."

"You said you fired him." I turned to Carlos. "Is that not true?"

"He's just covering for me," Nora said. "Plus, we've been married so long that it doesn't matter who does something, technically. We're a unit. I fired him, and Carlos backed me up."

I took Carlos's lack of response as confirmation that his wife's statement was accurate.

"It's so sweet, him always trying to protect me," Nora said. "But I don't need to be protected. I've got my own gun. Meg and I have been practicing at the range lately. I keep inviting my granddaughter Lacey, but she says she's too nervous to be in the room with two guns and me and Meg at the same time."

After the purse-shooting incident as reported by Carlos, I couldn't say that I completely blamed Nora's granddaughter for keeping away. I was hoping that Nora was currently unarmed except for the ladle she'd picked up upon her reentrance to the kitchen.

"Where'd they find his body?" she asked. "Did his girlfriend do it?"

"Girlfriend?" I asked. "Do you know who his girlfriend was?"

"No, but when I fired him, he tried to tell me he was just trying to get his girlfriend a birthday present."

"He could've been lying," I said. "Just trying to get your sympathy."

"He wasn't lying," Nora said. "I have great instincts. Garrett Landers had a girlfriend; there's no doubt about it. Not to mention, it helps confirm my instincts because I actually saw him get picked up by a woman recently, and the kiss she gave him when he got in the car—let's just say I'm certain that wasn't his mother."

"Gotcha," I said. "How long ago was that?"

"A few days before he was fired. A couple of months ago. I don't remember the exact date."

"Thanks," I said. "Did you get a good look at this woman? A name, maybe?"

She shook her head. "Sorry. I'd forgotten my binoculars. I wasn't ready to spy, and these old eyes aren't what they used to be."

"I understand," I said. "Thank you so much. This has been very helpful."

"You never did say where you found the body," Nora prodded. "How'd he die?"

"We're not certain about the details of his death yet, but he was found in an ice cream truck outside of Meg's bar."

Nora inhaled sharply. "Meg told me she accidentally shot her dumpster the other day. You don't think she accidentally killed him, do you?" Nora's eyes widened. "If he was in the dumpster, maybe the bullet grazed him, and she tossed him inside."

"Nora," Carlos said sharply. "I'm sure the detective doesn't need help coming up with theories."

"I make for a very good couch-detective," Nora said. "I like to read books. I can usually figure out whodunnit well before the end. Well, sometimes I skip to the last chapter to peek, and that helps me figure out whodunnit even faster. But I mean, if you already have the answer right in your hands, why work hard to get it? That's just silly, if you ask me. I'm working smarter not harder."

I didn't bother to tell Nora that the point of a book or a movie was to actually experience it from beginning to end. I suspected the logic might be lost on her. I just appreciated her candor.

"I doubt that's what happened," I said. "I doubt she could've lifted the body by herself."

"Meg's pretty strong," Nora said. "Especially after a shot or two of tequila. I once saw that woman, well, I'm not going to tell you because it was technically against the law." Nora's eyes shifted toward her husband. "But we were in Vegas at the time. So maybe it wasn't illegal there."

Carlos cleared his throat again as if he'd developed a pesky cough that wouldn't quit.

"You're right," Nora said. "I doubt it was her. And the dumpster thing might have been a superlative. I'm not sure she actually discharged her firearm. You should probably forget I told you that on account of I'm not sure if it's registered."

Carlos glanced at me. "Should I call my lawyer?"

I shook my head. "Don't worry about it. I'm only interested in Landers' murder. I think his girlfriend is a good bet to check into for now. Do you mind if I give you a call with any other questions?"

"Call me anytime," Nora said. "Can I program your number into my phone? I'll text you next time I'm making waffles. Also, if you're on *Words with Friends*, I'd love for you to be my friend. I got a new username after they booted my last one off the service. It's HotItalianMama69."

"I don't play," I said apologetically. Then I slipped my business card to Carlos. When Nora stared at me, I slipped her one too. "But good luck with your games."

I rose from the table.

"Before you go, take a taste of this," Nora said. "I know it's still breakfast time, but honestly, this sauce needs to simmer for over ten hours before it's any good. Do you think it's too salty?"

I found a long-handled, wooden spoon pressed to my lips. The only thing I could think of to do was open my mouth and smile.

"Delicious," I said, finding an entire bay leaf inside my mouth. I felt Carlos's glare on my back and knew there was only one answer. I chewed the inedible bay leaf slowly, tucking it into my cheek to discard later. "I think it's perfect."

"Oh, good. Well, thanks for your help, dear," Nora said. "Call us anytime. You've been such lovely company."

Carlos didn't seem to agree, but I was simply relieved to have survived a visit into the Luzzi estate. I followed Nora down the hallway laden with mugshots of various Luzzi family members and one odd spelling bee championship certificate before she pointed me in the direction of the front door. I could see Harold and Jimmy chumming it up, both holding mugs of coffee.

We said our goodbyes, then returned to the car. I spit out the bay leaf I'd been saving once I was safely away from any prying eyes. Jimmy stared at me. I told him not to ask.

"Did you get anything interesting out of Carlos?" Jimmy asked as I turned the key. "Besides a stomachache?"

"Breakfast was interesting," I said. "There's a chance Meg, the witness, accidentally shot him. If Garrett Landers was laying around in a dumpster when her weapon went off, that is."

"Huh?"

"Yeah, that's what I thought," I said. "On another note, it seems like Garrett had a girlfriend. Nora saw a woman pick up this guy a few days before he was let go. They made out in the car. Then a few days later, Garrett was caught trying to steal some china from the estate—supposedly for this girl-friend—and that's why he was fired."

"Seems our man Garrett had a hard time working legitimately. As legitimately as it gets when you work for the Luzzi family."

"What do you mean?"

"I got talking to Harold, and it seemed like Garrett was trying to poach people out from underneath Carlos's grasp after he got fired. Seems like it might've been a revenge move."

"You mean other employees?"

"Two additional employees quit within a month of Garrett's firing. They were buddies of his. Turns out they went to work with Garrett. They were promised some big payoff if they abandoned the Luzzi ship."

"Did Harold know what sort of payoff they were promised?" I asked. "Or for what sort of job?"

Jimmy shook his head. "Seemed like the sort of job that wasn't talked about too much to outsiders."

"Did you get any names?"

"Yes. A guy named Jelly and a guy named Pound."

I looked over at him. "Really?"

"I don't know," Jimmy said. "I didn't get a chance to press. I'm assuming they're nicknames."

"No kidding."

"What sort of bodyguard is named Jelly?" Jimmy asked. "Not the most intimidating sort of name."

"I guess we should go ask him ourselves. Then we can pay his buddy Pound a visit while we're at it. Asha should be able to connect the dots. While she's at it, she can look for a girlfriend."

"I think that's a good idea. In the meantime, I vote we head back to the precinct."

"Something you need to do?"

"Yeah," Jimmy said. "Let's just say those waffles aren't sitting right."

"Thanks for taking one for the team."

"That's what they pay me for," Jimmy said. "You're gonna miss me when I retire."

Chapter 4

"You survived," Asha said as I made my way to her desk. "I will pretend I wasn't worried about you."

"Gee, thanks," I said. "We did have Gem's blessing, which gave me a little peace of mind. Did you find anything on Landers?"

"Some. Where should I start?"

"We've got a couple leads," I said. "Seems like Garrett was stealing employees out from under Carlos Luzzi."

"He wouldn't have appreciated that."

"No, and he strategically didn't mention that little fact," I said. "We found that out when Jimmy talked to the butler."

"Where is Jimmy?"

"The bathroom," I said. "It'll be a while. Don't ask."

"I wasn't going to. What else?"

"Carlos's wife seems to think that Garrett was seeing a woman. A girlfriend."

"Was he *ever*." Asha raised her eyebrows. "I'm pretty sure he had three women who all thought they were his girl-friend."

"Man, this guy knew how to get himself in trouble." I started ticking off tallies against Garrett on my fingers. "He goes to work for a mobster. His résumé says he works for a laundromat. He tries to steal precious china from the mob-ster's wife. Then he gets fired, and if that's not bad enough, he tries to poach precious employees from his former boss. A very dangerous boss, I might add."

"Sounds like it was only a matter of time before he saw the inside of an ice cream truck," Asha said, "and I don't mean that in a good way."

"You don't say."

"Now he's got three girlfriends?" I remarked. "Any one of them had motive to kill him. Jealousy."

"Or it could have been all of 'em."

"Or it could've been Carlos Luzzi, or more accurately, one of his employees."

"I'd agree."

"Or it could've been one of the two employees that he poached from Carlos," I added. "Apparently, Garrett promised Pound and Jelly a big payoff. If Garrett didn't follow through, I'd bet those guys would've been really steamed to have lost out on their job for nothing."

"They'd have been super mad," Asha agreed. "Carlos wouldn't have taken kindly to them leaving either, making those two practically unemployable within their circles. They'd have been counting on that payday Garrett promised them."

"We're not short on motive this time around," I said. "Though I'm not sure if that makes this case easier or harder. It seems everyone who met the victim wanted him dead."

"Did you get names on the two guys with the dumb nicknames?" Asha asked. "You can start on the girlfriends while I try to dig around on them. Specifically, if Garrett reneged on his promise or pulled through with the payoff."

"All we got were the names Jelly and Pound."

"And now I'm thinking about cake and doughnuts." Asha sighed. "I'll see what I can find. Here's the stack of info on the girlfriends. Go wild."

I took the stack of papers and made my way to my desk. I settled in to read with a cup of tea. I had made it through two cups of tea and about an hour's worth of reading material by the time Jimmy returned. He was still sweating.

"I think that woman poisoned me," Jimmy said. "Do I need to go to the hospital?"

I winced. "It's that bad?"

"I've got a stomach of steel," Jimmy said. "Something about those waffles wasn't right. I'm a disaster."

"Are you able to continue working? You can take the afternoon off if that's easier."

"I'm all good," he said. "There's nothing left in me."

"You're sweating a lot."

"I'm good."

"You sure you don't want to go to the doctor?"

"Where are we off to?"

"It's a game of Russian roulette." I tossed Jimmy three sheets of paper, each one featuring a photo of a different woman. "Those are three of Garrett's girlfriends."

"Yikes. Any clue which one picked him up from the Luzzi estate?"

"I figure we can ask them when we see them."

"Let's go," Jimmy said. "I need to take my mind off the fact that I might've gotten poisoned by a mobster's wife."

"Is that why you're not going to the doctor? Because you're afraid word will get back to Carlos, and he won't be happy about you accusing his wife of poisoning?"

"No comment," Jimmy groaned. "Let's just go."

I played a quick game of eeny, meeny, miny, moe with the three girlfriends and landed on a woman named Dominique Albertson. She lived about ten minutes from the precinct. I quickly volunteered to drive mostly because I didn't trust Jimmy's state of mind. He seemed a little distracted. And oh-so-sweaty.

We made it to Dominique's place in downtown St. Paul. She lived in a new high-rise that'd gone up across the street from a little Italian deli I happened to frequent. Jimmy and I found her name on the door buzzer and rode the elevator to the fourth floor.

We headed down the hallway and knocked on the door that'd been listed under her name in the directory. She answered quickly.

"Hey," she said, seeming unsurprised to see us, even though we'd given her no warning we were coming. "Who're you?"

"Detectives Rosetti and Jones," I said, pointing to myself then Jimmy. I made sure to keep myself mostly in front of Jimmy, who looked like he was having trouble standing up straight. "We're just here to ask you a couple of questions about a case we're working. Do you have a few minutes?"

"Okay," she said.

Dominique seemed entirely too relaxed about the fact that there were cops at her door. I had to wonder if it had happened before, or if she was just so confident nothing was wrong that she wasn't bothered in the slightest.

"Nice view," I said, once she let us into her living room. I nodded to the restaurant across the street. "I love Cossetta's."

"Yeah," she said with a shrug. "Their focaccia is okay."

I wanted to tell her it was more than okay, but I didn't want to get into an argument with one of our suspects over bread. I had bigger fish to fry.

Jimmy eased himself onto a couch without permission. Dominique gave him a little frown. I sat as far away from Jimmy on the couch as I possibly could. Dominique took a high-backed seat across from a glass coffee table.

Her apartment was small but neat. It felt bigger than it was, probably due to the minimalist design. There were lots of white walls and cream furniture. Black-edged appliances gave a sharp look to the space.

Even Dominique herself looked like she belonged in the heart of downtown. She was wearing a black pencil skirt and a white blouse. High heels sat abandoned by the door, along with a bright red purse. Her nails were long and a pretty shade of peach. Her hair was pulled into a tight ponytail that swished a tiny bit when she turned her head.

"Thanks for letting us have a few minutes of your time," I said. "We're here because of the man we believe you've been dating. Garrett Landers."

Her eyebrows raised slightly, but she didn't say anything.

"Can you confirm that?" I asked. "Are you seeing him?"

"Yeah, he's my boyfriend."

I glanced at Jimmy. "Are you aware he's been missing for a few days?"

She shrugged. "I'm not his keeper. We trust each other. It's not like I have GPS tracking on his phone or something. He'll call me when he's not on a job."

"What sort of jobs does he work?"

"I don't know," she said. "Random jobs. Security and stuff. Like I said, I'm busy with my own career. I'm a real estate agent, and I pay my own bills. I don't *need* a man. I just like having one around."

"I see," I said. "Are the two of you exclusive?"

"Now you're just getting personal. What's this about?"

"This is actually about a murder investigation," I said. "I'm sorry, Dominique, but Garrett's body was found yesterday."

She blinked. "His body?"

"His body was found behind a bar in Uptown."

"He's dead?"

I nodded again. "I'm sorry."

She sat back in her seat. "The bastard."

"Sorry?"

"I told him he had to be careful." She cursed. "He thought he was Mr. Tough Guy, but he was a teddy bear inside. I told him he shouldn't be working all those dangerous jobs. I told him it'd get him killed. So selfish of him."

"Getting killed was selfish?"

"We loved each other," Dominique said. "We were going to get married. I told him I'd never forgive him if he went and got dead on me. Now I'm all alone. What am I supposed to do about that? I wasted two years of my life dating him, and now I've got to start all over? I don't have time for that. I have a timeline to keep. I'm thirty-two. If I'm going to have two kids, I need to get moving."

I swallowed, trying to digest this reaction. It was one I'd never gotten before, that was for sure. There was a very good possibility this was a side effect from serious shock. There was also the distinct possibility that this woman just took a different view on love than one I'd ever seen before.

"It's very unfortunate," I ventured. "I'm sorry we have to ask you questions under these circumstances, but we are trying to find out who killed your boyfriend. Do you know why he might've been in Uptown?"

"Like I said, some job probably. I didn't ask too much. He had some sketchy friends."

"You didn't mind him having sketchy friends?"

"They were *his* friends," she said. "He had his own place, his own job, his own friends. Just because we were gonna get married didn't mean we had to combine everything."

"Right," I said, though I was pretty sure that was what getting married actually was all about. Combining stuff like friends and households. "Did he have any enemies?"

"Are you not listening to me?" Dominique retorted, sounding annoyed at the nerve I had to be questioning her. "I told you I didn't pry into every little detail of his life."

"Okay, maybe we should talk more about your relationship," I said. "I'm obviously not understanding. You said you dated two years? How often did you see him?"

"Every couple of days. He'd come by my place usually. His place is a pigsty. He's not big on cleaning."

"So he'd stay with you a few nights a week. What about—"

"I didn't say that," she said. "He didn't really sleep over. I like my bed mostly to myself. He hogs the covers. I usually kicked him out around two in the morning. He didn't care. Sometimes he went out with his buddies actually."

"Interesting. But you guys were going to be married?"

"We had already browsed rings. He was supposed to buy me one and propose on Valentine's Day. We were gonna get married Fourth of July weekend because my cousin Jenny's back from her trip abroad. Ask anyone. I'm already getting the Save the Dates printed."

It seemed a little premature to me to have Save the Dates printed before an engagement ring, but I was newly dumped and single, so what did I know? I glanced over at Jimmy, but he was too busy mopping his forehead with a napkin from Chick-fil-A to care about much of anything.

"Sounds like your plans were pretty set. Can I assume that means the two of you were exclusive?"

"In our relationship?"

"Yes."

"Duh." She stared at me like I was an idiot. "That's what getting married means. You are with one person for the rest of your life."

"Of course. I'm just confirming."

"You think he was dating someone else?" She shook her head. "He was whipped. He needed me."

"As in, he loved you?"

"Sure, that too," Dominique said with a flick of her fingers. "But I meant financially. Garrett had the mindset of a serial entrepreneur but the work ethic of a couch potato. He'd basically try a bunch of different jobs that would pay a little bit for a while. Some of his more dangerous jobs even paid pretty good, but then he'd just blow the money thinking he was rich. He'd always come back to me needing money."

"And you gave him money?"

"Duh," she said again. "We were getting married. We shared stuff."

Dominique was a mess of contradictions, but she didn't seem to see how any of the things she was saying didn't match up quite right. I could see how she made for a great real estate agent. I was ready to believe her, and I knew logically that half of the stuff she said didn't make sense.

"Did he owe you money when he died?"

"He's owed me money since the day we met. It's just cash. You know, the cost of having a husband. He could be stupid and wasn't a very good businessman, but he loved me. I'm very talented at my job and make more than enough money. Look at me. I'm doing just fine for myself. It's not like I kept track of the money he needed to use."

"There's no one else you can think of who might know how he ended up in Uptown? Or anyone else who might wish him ill?"

"Sorry. Not really."

"Did you ever happen to pick him up from any of his jobs?"

"No," she said. "When would I have time to do that?"

"I'm going to give you my card," I said. "Please call us if you think of anything else. We'll be in touch if anything comes up."

She took the card, but judging by the way she palmed it without even looking at it, she wasn't going to be giving anyone a call. I rose, helped my partner to his feet, and headed for the door. As soon as we got in the elevator, I turned to Jimmy.

"Is she a psychopath? Or just totally self-absorbed?" I shook my head as Jimmy keeled over. "I get the impression she really believed what she was saying, but it didn't make sense. She doesn't mind giving her boyfriend money, but she won't let him sleep over? I don't understand the sort of relationship they had."

Jimmy grunted.

"Of course, she could be lying," I mused. "Maybe she was actually annoyed about the money situation. It'd be motive to kill him. She didn't exactly seem heartbroken. I understand people deal with shock and grief differently, but she didn't even flinch."

"Uh-huh."

"Are you sure you're okay?"

Jimmy winced. "Who's next on our list?"

I glanced down. "The tattoo artist is the closest. Actually, we can walk to her place of work from here. Do you think you can handle it?"

"I'm good," Jimmy squeaked. "Let's go check out some ink."

Chapter 5

Our victim's second girlfriend's name was Ellen Strand. Apparently her place of employment was a mere seven blocks from Dominique's apartment. Our victim was playing dangerous by dating several women within a mile radius. Either he wasn't cautious at all, or he just didn't care. I didn't have a good enough read on the guy to have a guess as to which it was.

According to Jimmy's face, seven blocks was just too far to walk today. I didn't argue, seeing as it was cold outside, and I was looking for an excuse to be lazy. We drove, and I parked in the small lot behind the tattoo shop. We headed inside beneath the sound of a jingling bell over the front door.

"Hey, I'll be right with you," a woman called. "Take a seat."

Jimmy seemed happy to oblige. I remained standing, glancing at the images on the wall. Mostly photographs of different tattoo artists beaming next to their finished masterpieces on their clients.

After a few minutes, a woman appeared from the back of the shop wiping her hands on a towel. She had blonde hair that was tossed up in a loose, shaggy bun. She had a plump figure slightly accentuated by what I guessed were the beginnings of a baby bump. She wore a loose tank top that left her sports bra visible underneath, along with a pair of black leggings.

"Howdy," she said. "First timers?"

"You could say that," I said. "We're actually detectives here to ask you a few questions."

"A few questions?" She froze. "About what? Everything here is above board. We're properly licensed. We've never had one complaint. Well, one complaint, but I fired Hank because of what happened last year. I swear I didn't know what those Chinese symbols meant that he tattooed on that woman."

"It's not about that. We're just here to ask you a few questions about a man we believe you knew. Does the name Garrett Landers mean anything to you?"

"Uh, yeah," she said. "We dated for a bit."

"Dated for a bit?" I repeated. "Were you currently together?"

"Sort of. He's my baby daddy."

"Oh, well, congratulations." I shifted awkwardly. "Then I'm terribly sorry to be the bearer of bad news. The truth is that we found Garrett's body yesterday. I'm so sorry."

"He's dead?" she asked in a way eerily similar to what Dominique had said a few moments before. "*Dead?*"

"I'm so sorry for your loss."

She burst into tears. I was almost relieved to see such a normal reaction after the last interview. I was starting to think I'd done something wrong. Tears, sorrow, distress over the loss of a loved one—that I could understand. I couldn't quite understand the indifference of Dominique, which bothered me because I also couldn't understand if it pointed to guilt or something else.

"I'm sorry," I repeated. "I understand this isn't a great time to ask questions about your relationship with Garrett, but we're currently investigating his death, and it would be very helpful if you would talk to us."

"Wait a minute. You think he was killed?" She wiped at her eyes. A bit of mascara and eyeliner streaked to the side of her face. "Sorry about my reaction. It's the pregnancy hormones."

"It's completely understandable," I said. "Losing a loved one is never easy. Would you like to sit down? Can I get you a glass of water or something?"

She shook her head. "I'm working on Bill in the back. If you want to talk, maybe you can come back while I work. He's got to get going, so I'd like to finish up for the day."

I frowned. "We might have to ask you some sensitive questions. It might be better if we could talk somewhere private."

She shook her head and waved. "Bill won't care. He's a regular. He knows everything that goes on here anyway. It's better if I'm distracted."

"Are you sure you don't need to take a moment? I know this is shocking news."

She sniffed. "Now I'll have more bills to pay than ever, so I should keep working. Bill's one of my best clients. He'll understand."

"More bills to pay than ever?"

She pointed at her stomach. "Baby. No daddy. That means I'm a single mom now."

"Right. Sure, okay," I said. "We can talk in front of Bill if that works for you."

I followed Ellen to the back of the tattoo parlor. Jimmy shuffled after me. There were a couple of chairs in the corner that we awkwardly took as Ellen eased next to her client.

"Hey, Bill," she said softly, "these guys are cops. They're here because someone killed my Garrett. They want to ask some questions. I told them they could do it while I worked. You mind?"

Bill shook his head. "Go for it. I need to pick up the kids before my shift, so I gotta get out of here on time."

"Bill's getting a unicorn added to his art today," Ellen informed us. "His daughter's fourth birthday is coming up, and she requested it. Like a present."

"A permanent present," I said. "Are you sure she'll still like unicorns when she's eighteen?"

"That's none of your business, is it?" Bill mused, closing his eyes as Ellen set to work.

"Nope, sorry," I said, scanning his large form and the wide array of artwork already printed on his skin. "Carry on. Ellen, could you tell me about your relationship with Garrett Landers?"

"Sure." Ellen leaned forward to focus on her work. "I've known Garrett for almost a year. He came in here to get his first tattoo. It was pretty much love at first sight."

"So you'd say the two of you were in love?" I asked. "Were you exclusive?"

"Maybe love was the wrong word. It was more like lust at first sight, but a little bit more."

"A little bit more?"

"We actually liked hanging out with each other. I mean, we were mostly attracted to one another physically, but it wasn't totally a no-strings-attached fling. We spent a couple of nights a week together."

"Did he sleep over at your place?"

"Yeah." She stared blankly at me. "That's what spending the night together means."

"Ever go to his place?"

"Not really. He was a slob. I've been there, if that's what you're asking, but it was like Dude Central. No way a lady would want to spend any time there."

I was beginning to wonder if Garrett's sloppy status as a bachelor was actually a well-crafted persona to ensure that none of the women he was dating ever wanted to spend much time at his place. It would help eliminate the risk of being found out. I imagined Dominique wouldn't have been happy if she'd popped over to her boyfriend's house only to find Ellen's underwear in the laundry. This way, Garrett kept all extracurricular activities at the women's respective homes.

"So you were exclusive, then?"

Ellen's gaze flicked toward me as she paused in her work for a moment. "Why does that matter?"

"Just trying to get a feel for your relationship."

"Do you really think he was murdered?"

"I'm afraid the evidence points to it," I told her. "The reason we're prying into your personal life is to try and understand if there might have been someone who wanted to cause Garrett harm."

"I don't see how our relationship status had anything to do with it."

"Please just answer the question," Jimmy said, leaning against a wall for support. Usually the patient one in our partnership, he seemed eager to get out of the tattoo parlor as soon as possible. "We're sorry for your loss, but the best thing you can do to help Garrett now is to cooperate."

"Sheesh," she said, turning her gaze to me. "I was just asking."

I wasn't used to being the nice cop. I cleared my throat and smiled at her. Usually this was where Jimmy swooped in and uttered some calming words. Fortunately, Ellen busied herself with her work, and I was spared having to voice the appropriate sentiment.

"No, I guess you wouldn't say we were exclusive," she said. "Garrett wasn't that sort of guy."

"What do you mean?" I asked. "He didn't want a commitment?"

"It's not even that," she said. "I mean, I guess it's that a little bit. He was the sort of guy to keep his options open. I didn't really care about that, to be honest."

I found my eyebrows inching up. "You didn't care that the father of your child was seeing other women?"

"You don't have to be so judgmental. I would think you of all people would understand."

"Me?" I felt my voice go a little squeaky. "How would I understand?"

"You're a female and a cop. You're obviously successful. You don't need a man."

"Amen," Jimmy said. "She knows that. A little too well, if you ask me."

Ellen ignored him. "Same here. I own this place. I built it from the ground up. Bought it a year ago. I've got my own house, my own clientele, my own life. I wanted a baby."

"And Garrett was the solution to the other half of your problem?"

"It was cheaper than going through some clinic to get a donor. Plus, I knew the guy," she said. "He was a looker. His IQ wasn't great, but the baby's a girl, so I'm pretty sure she'll take after me in the brains department."

I wasn't sure that Ellen had the best handle on genetics, but I let it fly.

"Did he know?" I asked. "Was Garrett okay with being the father?"

"Do you know how babies are made?" Ellen asked, and Bill snorted. "I'm pretty sure he enjoyed himself in the process."

"Did he know you were pregnant?"

"Yeah," she said. "I wasn't trying to dupe him, if that's what you mean. I promised him I wasn't going to come after him for child support. This is my baby. Not his. I made that crystal clear. I'm thirty-six, and I'm not sure I'm ever going to get married. Did you know I'm already considered at an advanced maternal age by my OB/GYN? I'm having a geriatric pregnancy at freaking thirty-six years old. You'd think they could come up with a kinder term for it. It's not like I've got gray hair and wear granny panties."

"Okay," Jimmy said uncomfortably. "When's the last time you saw Garrett?"

"I dunno. A few weeks ago."

Again, I was surprised. "I thought you guys spent the night together several times a week."

"That was an average. It was also in the earlier stages, you know, when we were busy doing the stuff needed to make a baby." She expelled a breath. "Once he did his part, I sort of didn't care that much about keeping up our relationship. Plus, I've had awful morning sickness and constipation. I've barely been able to pull my head out of the toilet for the last fourteen weeks—it's not sexy. Do you have kids?"

"No," I said, feeling quite grateful for that fact at the moment. "So your relationship cooled off a bit. Do you happen to know who else he might have been spending time with?"

"Sure. Some girl down the street named Dominique, and another gal he met more recently named Jessica."

"Jessica?" I asked. The name of the third girlfriend we'd been given on Asha's list was Marissa. I had to wonder if Ellen had simply gotten the names confused, or if there were more women than we'd even expected. Could Jessica be a fourth girlfriend? "Do you know anything about Jessica?"

"Nothing interesting. I just heard the name a few times."

"I see," I said. "Do you know what he did for a living lately?"

"He used to be some thug," she said. "I think he got fired. I don't know. But if you ever met that guy alive, you'd know that he had to do a physical job seeing as having brains wasn't his forte."

I was wondering more and more why Ellen had wanted to procreate with a man she barely seemed to like. I had to wonder if it was really just for the sake of convenience, or if there was something beneath the surface of her tale.

"And the other women, did they know about you?"

"Oh yeah," she said. "We all knew about each other."

If Ellen said they all knew about one another, then I was stumped. Ellen had listed Jessica and Dominique as Garrett's other girlfriends, but what about this Marissa from Asha's list? Not to mention the fact that Dominique had seemed quite put off at the idea that her boyfriend might've been seeing someone else. Someone was lying. Either Dominique lied about thinking her boyfriend had been exclusive, or Ellen was lying about them all knowing one another.

"Actually, we just spoke with Dominique," I said, watching Ellen carefully for a reaction, "and she insisted that Garrett was being faithful to her."

Ellen just snorted. "I always knew that woman was a liar. I told that to Garrett, but if you ask my opinion, he just liked feeling fancy. That woman bought him stuff. Not like me. I worked hard for every penny I made. I'd feed the guy breakfast then kick him out. I didn't write him checks for his stupid entrepreneurial ideas. I didn't get a handout for starting my business, so why should I give him one?"

"Dominique knew about you?" I asked. "Are you positive?"

"Dude. I had lunch with her last week," Ellen said. "Yeah, she knew. That's how we met. We're not stupid. A guy can't have three girlfriends—three smart women—and not get caught. Especially someone like Garrett. He wasn't exactly sly."

"How long had you known about each other?"

"A few months," she said. "Right around the time I got knocked up."

"How did you react when you found out?"

"I couldn't care less," she said. "I had my positive pregnancy test and my baby girl. I didn't really care what Garrett wanted to do with anyone else."

"Right. What about the others? This Dominique and Jessica?"

"I've actually never met Jessica. I just heard about her through Dominique. Dominique's a little bit of a stalker," Ellen admitted casually. "She thought she was going to get married to Garrett. I told her she could have him. I think that's why she liked me."

"Did Dominique ever meet Jessica?"

"Not that I know of. I mean, if she did, it wasn't something she told me about. At best, I'm guessing she stared at her through binoculars across the street or something. That's the sort of creepy thing Dominique would do. Not that I blame her. After all, she really thought they were gonna get married. If I thought me and Garrett were gonna get married, maybe I would've cared more."

"Did Garrett know that the three of you knew about one another?"

"Bless his heart, no." Ellen gave a dry laugh. "He thought he was God's gift to women. He really believed he was being sneaky. We thought it'd be easier to let him keep on thinking that."

"Easier to manipulate him, you mean," Jimmy said. "What did you get out of keeping a relationship going once you had your baby?"

"Man, your partner's testy today, isn't he?" Ellen said to me. "A woman's got hormones during pregnancy. I still had needs. He was good for a call once in a while to scratch that itch, if you know what I mean. I'm starting to show now. Most guys think it's weird to date a woman pregnant with another dude's kid."

"I wonder why," Jimmy muttered.

"Do you think it's possible Dominique wanted to cause him harm?" I asked, steering our conversation back to the investigation. "Could she have been responsible for his death?"

"No. She loved the guy. She wouldn't have killed him. She's a liar and a stalker, but I think that's about it. She's more bark than bite."

"What about Jessica?"

"Don't know the girl. Never met her. Just heard the name."

"What about work or other friends or acquaintances?" I asked. "Do you know of anyone else who might've wanted to cause Garrett harm?"

"We didn't have a ton of talking in our relationship," she said. "I had a job to do. We were naked a lot of the time. I mostly just knew when he was out of a job because he hung around in the mornings a lot longer. Sort of annoying. He did seem to have some sort of work lately though. He didn't even try to booty call me in the last few weeks. Either he picked up a new girlfriend, or he was working, but I bet it was the latter."

"Okay, well, thanks for the information," I said. "Please let me know if you think of anything else that might help in our investigation. We'd really appreciate it."

"Sure."

"Bye, Bill," Jimmy said. "Nice unicorn. It's looking good."

"Thanks, man."

We left the tattoo parlor and headed to the car. Once we were inside, Jimmy glanced over at me.

"Interesting," he said. "Not only did this guy have multiple girlfriends, but at least one of them is lying."

"Not to mention their relationships were all weird," I said. "You have one lady who didn't care about the guy except that she wanted a baby. Then you've got the other lady who's printing out wedding invitations before she's got a ring."

"Not to mention the fact that Dominique was lying to us," Jimmy said. "If what Ellen said is true, and I don't see why she'd lie about something we could verify as easily as a lunch date, then Dominique was telling us a tale. She knew about the other women."

"Especially if she was the one stalking the others," I added. "The question is if she was lying just because she thought it would make her look guilty, or if she was lying because she's actually guilty."

"Are we stopping back at her place?" Jimmy asked. "Or are we moving on to the next?"

"I vote we give her a little time to stew. Let's finish our visit with the other girlfriends and go from there. It'll be interesting to see if the rest of their stories line up."

"Sounds good."

"How's your stomach?"

"I'm hanging in there."

"You look like you're on the verge of passing out."

"I haven't passed out yet, have I?"

"All right, then we'll pay a stop by Marissa's next," I said. "I'm going to call Asha and give her Jessica's name and see if she can link any connections to this woman. It's interesting

Asha didn't turn her up in a search. I do have to wonder if it could be the same Jessica we interviewed yesterday."

"The one from the bar?"

"Running into two Jessicas in two days on the same case? It's a little coincidental. If she's the mystery fourth girlfriend, that could change things. She might've found out about the other three and was a little mad."

"Justifiably so," Jimmy added. "There's a motive built right in for her. Not to mention opportunity, seeing as the body was dumped right behind the bar where she works."

"Let's see what's behind Girlfriend Door Number Three."

Chapter 6

On the drive to Marissa's place, I called Asha and gave her the quick rundown on the two girlfriends we'd already visited as well as the mystery fourth girlfriend. I asked if the name Jessica rang any bells for her.

"I saw the name from your interview report from yesterday," she said. "But I didn't find any specific connections between her and Garrett in my searches."

"What sort of searches?"

"Phone records, financial transactions, GPS location check-ins where available," she said. "Usually that'll turn up any sort of casual relationship."

"But if Jessica was a newer girlfriend," I mused, "and they met at the bar, you might not have turned up anything. Say they'd only gone out a few times. They could've made arrangements in person to meet up later. If they weren't seriously dating, they might not be buying each other dinner or hanging out in public yet."

"It's very possible that could be a scenario," Asha confirmed. "My searches wouldn't have connected the two in any meaningful way. The closest I would've gotten was to think that Garrett was a customer at the bar where Jessica worked."

"Interesting. It's a working theory."

"Well, it would've been convenient for her to stash the body in the ice cream truck," Asha said. "She would've known the keys were in there. She'd also have known that Meg didn't check on the truck all that often. She could've been out and back before anyone noticed during one of her shifts, giving her the perfect alibi."

"That's exactly what I was thinking." I glanced at the house ahead of me. "We're just coming up to visit Marissa's place. I'll give you a call later. See what you can dig up on Jessica."

"Will do."

Jimmy and I climbed out of the car and paused on the sidewalk outside of a small brick building. The building itself had seen better days, but it blended in naturally into the West Seventh neighborhood. A handwritten sign out front read Business through the Front, Party through the Back.

"Do you think Marissa works here?" I asked. "And lives in the back?"

"I don't want to think about another meaning," Jimmy said. "So let's go with that. My brain's not operating on all cylinders just yet. Half my brain cells are dedicated to keeping the waffles down."

"Right. I'll take the lead on this."

I went to the front door and knocked. After five minutes of intermittent knocking and peering through the glass, I surmised that nobody was coming to the door. I made my way around the back and knocked again. It only took two minutes before the rear door opened.

"Hi, are you Marissa?" I asked. "I'm Detective Rosetti. This is Detective Jones."

Marissa had dark hair she'd tied in a loose, messy bun. She had on a matching tracksuit and held a cup of coffee in her hand. It looked like we'd interrupted a lazy morning at home.

"Yeah, that's me," she said. "Why are you here? You need a warrant. I know my rights. I'm a PI."

"You're a PI?" I asked. "Really?"

"Why do you say it like that?"

"I was just verifying," I said. "You mean PI as in private investigator?"

"That's what it stands for, Detective," Marissa added with a touch of sarcasm. "Okay, I don't totally have my license yet, but I'm working on it, and when I get it, I'll be unstoppable. I already got clients lined up. My brother's girlfriend's sister thinks her boyfriend's sister is getting cheated on. I'm gonna get to the bottom of it."

"We're not here about that," I said. "We're actually not here to search anything. We just wanted to talk to you."

"Off the record?"

"Sure," I said. "Did you know a man named Garrett Landers?"

"Why?"

"We may have information that would be of interest to you."

"Look, I know about his criminal record. It doesn't mean he can't be a good employee. I believe in second chances."

"Employee?" I asked. "Garrett was your employee?"

"Not really. I mean, not technically. Not yet. Remember what I said about not quite having my license yet? I was planning to hire him just as soon as things got legal. He was helping me out a little bit. We were going into business together."

"Were you dating?"

"You need to learn a little bit about personal boundaries," she said. "I don't talk to random strangers about my love life."

"I'm sorry, but we found Garrett's body yesterday," I said. "We're just trying to notify anyone who might've been important to him about his death."

Her eyes widened. "You really think Garrett's dead?"

"We know he's dead. We found his body."

"Holy moly. A real live murder case delivered right to my doorstep. I can barely believe it."

"So were the two of you dating?" I asked. "Or business partners?"

"We weren't dating," she said. "We made out a couple times, and then we both decided it wasn't for us. But I liked him well enough as a person, and he had the experience I was looking for, so we were going to go into business together."

"Do you mind if we come inside?" I asked. "We'd like to discuss this in a little more depth. You might be more comfortable sitting down."

"Okay. Come around the front then. This is professional, not personal."

Marissa closed the back door in our faces. Jimmy and I made our way around to the front of the house. I knocked again. A few seconds later, Marissa answered, looking a little more excited. I had to wonder if her excitement was over the prospect of a murder investigation, seeing as it didn't seem totally appropriate for her to be so thrilled over the death of her supposed business partner and friend.

Marissa led us into a threadbare front room with an old mustard-colored couch that looked like it had been hauled in off the street corner. A couple of mismatched chairs sat around, and a table on wobbly legs balanced in the center of the room. Marissa sat behind an oversized mahogany desk that looked like it'd been mauled by a rabid raccoon.

"Okay, so how does this work?" she asked. "Do you want to work together on the investigation, or should I work separately and we can compare notes?"

I glanced at Jimmy. "Actually, this case falls into our jurisdiction at the TC Task Force. We'll be handling the investigation."

"Well, I'll consult then. Free of charge, of course, since my license is pending. And by pending, I mean that I still have to sign up for the class and pay for it and all that stuff."

"We can discuss that later," I said vaguely. "Can you tell me a little more about your relationship with Garrett?"

"Sure. We met at a club. I was going inside, and he was the bouncer outside—a real Cinderella story. We both got a little drunk that night and made out. He got fired for it. I felt sorta bad for that and gave him my number."

"Did he call you?"

"Yeah, we met up when we were both out, but we never made it to the next step. Just bought each other a few drinks. He's not really my type. I guess I'm not his either. We agreed not to smooch anymore, but it's not like I thought he was a bad guy or anything. I was thinking about starting my PI firm, and I thought he'd be a great first employee. You know, he was a big guy, lots of muscle, questionable morals. If I needed to intimidate someone or whatever, I thought he might be able to help."

I hesitated to comment on the illegality of her intimidation techniques she planned to use in a professional environment. At the last second, I kept my lips zipped. I needed more information out of her before this conversation devolved into an argument.

"Was he an actual partner in the business?" I asked. "Or were you hiring him on as a contractor?"

"I wanted to do a contractor-type role, but then he told me he wanted to be a full partner. I told him he'd have to come up with five grand to contribute to start-up fees. He said that'd be fine. He was supposed to get me the money by next week."

"He never got you the money?"

"No," she said. "I knew he didn't have a ton of cash on hand, so I figured he had to, you know, do stuff to get the money. I wasn't expecting it for a few more days."

"I see. And you wanted him to be a business partner?"

"Sure. More start-up capital. Another helping hand around here. I told you, I've got clients lined up and waiting for when I get all my ducks in a row. I didn't doubt we'd make a good run of it. Plus, he didn't bother me much. He just did his stuff and left."

"Did you guys talk?"

"We were going to be business partners. Sure we talked."

"Did you ever discuss personal things?"

"A little bit. He didn't talk much about family. He wasn't married."

"Were you aware he was dating other women?"

"I told you, we were never a thing. I didn't care that he dated people. I'm dating other people too. It wasn't a secret between us."

"Do you happen to know the name of his girlfriend?" I asked, curious which one he would have mentioned to Marissa.

"He had a couple," she said. "He wasn't serious with any of them. Well, he didn't want to be. There was that one witch who tricked him into getting pregnant."

"Do you have a name?"

"She runs a tattoo parlor, I think. I can't remember the name. Ellen or something. Something totally normal that I didn't expect, considering her career."

"How do you know she was a witch?"

"I told you, me and Garrett talked about things. It was easy because we weren't tempted to get involved in a complicated relationship. We were just business partners, and I guess a little bit friends, so we could be honest."

"What'd he say about Ellen?"

"He kept trying to keep things casual, and she wanted him to commit to her and be all serious. She kept asking if he'd move in with her. When he tried to break things off, she went a little nuts. Then she told him she was pregnant."

"What was he planning to do about the baby?"

"Ellen was obviously planning to keep it because she thought the baby was her ticket to finally getting Garrett to pop the question to her and settle down. Garrett wasn't going to marry her though. Would you marry a psycho who tricked you into a relationship?"

"That sounds pretty unfair," I said, trying to keep her talking while silently noting the inconsistencies between Ellen's story and Marissa's. "You said he was dating other women. Did that stop when he found out Ellen was going to have a baby?"

"No. Like I said, Garrett wasn't going to marry Ellen. He wasn't the settling-down type. There was a girl, Dom, who's pretty psycho too, just in a different way."

"What sort of way?"

"That girl stalks everyone Garrett ever looked at the wrong way. I'm pretty sure she came in here pretending to be a fake client just to meet me and see who I was. I bet she wanted to see if I was encroaching on her man. I definitely wasn't, so I set her straight."

"You told her you weren't dating him?"

"Yeah. I told her to get a life because Garrett wasn't interested in getting married to her no matter how many wedding invitations she printed off. She's on her third round of Save the Dates because the saved date keeps passing."

"Yikes."

"I'm telling you, that man's got a type. Or, I guess, he had one." Marissa scratched at her messy bun. "Except for me. I guess that's why we didn't work out. I was too normal for him. We made better friends than lovers. He preferred to date the psychos."

"Gotcha. Well, this has been very interesting," I said. "Do you know about a woman named Jessica?"

"No. Should I?"

"Just curious. Since the two of you were close, do you happen to know anything about his personal life aside from the dating aspect? Anything specifically that might have gotten him killed?"

She bit her lip. "I guess if he was doing something to get the five grand for start-up funds and it went sour, that could've gotten him in trouble. Crap. I hope that's not the case. That would mean his death was my fault."

"No. Of course not," Jimmy reassured her. "You just asked for him to contribute to start-up costs. You didn't force him to do anything illegal."

"I suppose you've got a point," she said. "So can you use my services? Seeing as I knew Garrett possibly the best, don't you want me to help on the case?"

"We actually work better when operating within our own department," I said. "We've sort of got a system."

She nodded knowingly. "You think I'm a suspect."

"Unfortunately we have to treat most people in Garrett's life as suspects until proven otherwise. Plus, it's just a general rule that we don't comment on active investigations to civilians."

"But I'm not a normal civilian. I'm gonna be a PI soon."

"Thanks so much for your help on the case," I said. "We'll be sure to let you know if there's anything else you can do for us. In the meantime, best of luck with your business."

"Thanks," she said. "Can I use you as a reference on my website?"

"Um, I don't really do that sort of thing," I said, glancing at Jimmy, hoping he'd save me. He mostly just mopped his forehead.

"Any chance you have public restrooms?" Jimmy asked. "Seeing as you're a business and all?"

"Sure, through the door. Hold the handle down for three seconds when you flush. There's a plunger in there if that doesn't work. Change the toilet paper roll if you use the last of it."

Jimmy disappeared around the corner. I said goodbye to Marissa and stepped out front. While I had a moment alone, I glanced down at my phone. Then I called a number I hadn't had any intention of calling so soon. But for my partner, I'd do just about anything.

"Hello?" Carlos's voice sounded gruff and unfriendly on the other end of the line.

"Hi, Mr. Luzzi," I said quickly. "This is Kate Rosetti. I have a quick question to ask you."

"I answered everything already. I don't know anything more."

"I'm afraid this is of a more personal nature."

Silence sounded on the other end of the line. I took that to mean I could try my best and see what happened.

"Is it possible that your wife poisoned my partner with her waffles?" I asked. "I'm only asking because I'm concerned about his health. See, Jimmy Jones is a good guy, and he's on the verge of retirement. He and his wife are looking forward to having some time together to travel the world and eat Sunday brunches. I'd hate for him to die before he got to spend time with her. Could you just tell me if I need to take him to the hospital?"

I realized I sounded like an idiot, but I wasn't totally sure how to handle the situation. I wanted to be sensitive and deal with the potential poisoning as under the table as I could. I hoped that because my name was Rosetti and tarnished with mob connections that Carlos Luzzi trusted me a little more than the average cop.

When he cleared his throat, I thought that was all he was going to do. Then, when he spoke, I was surprised to find he sounded a little bit sheepish.

"How many waffles did he eat?"

"I don't know," I said. "Like four?"

"My wife is very hit or miss with her cooking," Carlos said. "This morning was a miss. I guess your partner didn't get the memo. I apologize."

"So he's not poisoned?"

"Nora lost her glasses last week, and she's been substituting the wrong ingredients ever since. She refuses to admit she can't read a label. Yesterday she put a laxative in someone's coffee instead of sugar."

"Well, that would make a lot of sense," I said. "It matches with my partner's symptoms."

"I apologize. And I would appreciate if this didn't get back to my wife. She's having a hard time accepting the fact that she needs a stronger prescription."

"Of course. On a similar note, I'd like a favor," I said, feeling a bit daring. Carlos seemed to be in a more reasonable mood than I suspected he was normally. "I'd like the opportunity to speak with your chief of staff. Anthony."

"I'll arrange it."

I felt my eyebrows raise in surprise. "Great. Thank you."

"I'll have Harold set up a time."

"Thank you," I said, but the phone had already disconnected.

Right around then, Jimmy reappeared.

"Everything okay?" he asked.

"I should be asking you that."

He just made a low whistle that told me not to mention it.

"I got us an interview with Anthony Luzzi. Carlos's right-hand guy."

"How'd you do that? Gem?"

"Nope. I've got my own ways."

"Is it because your name's Rosetti?"

"Sure. We'll go with that."

Before I could chat with Jimmy about our plan for the remainder of the day, my phone buzzed. I answered it, expecting to hear Asha's voice on the other end of the line with an update. It wasn't Asha.

"Are you free tonight, Detective?"

"Gem?"

"Yes," he said. "That is my last name. "

"Why?"

He sighed. "I was hoping you might be interested in grabbing dinner with me."

"I don't know. I've got a case I'm working on, and..." I hesitated. "Hold on a second."

Jimmy was making funny hand signals at me. I held the phone away from my ear and waited for him to explain.

"Go on," Jimmy said. "Make your dinner plans. We've got all the girlfriends interviewed. We'll hit Jessica and Dominique tomorrow morning. I'm gonna have to call it an early night for reasons I'd not like to discuss in detail. There's nothing urgent tonight."

I held the phone back to my ear. "Gem?"

"Great, so that's a yes?"

"You heard all that?" I made a face at Jimmy. "I guess I'm out of excuses. Fine. But so long as you know it's just dinner. Nothing fancy, please."

"Of course. I'll pick you up at six."

"Where are we going?"

"I'd like to surprise you, if that's acceptable."

"It's fine, but I need to know what to wear."

"Something comfortable."

"Gem, for me comfortable is an old T-shirt with no bra. You're going to have to be more specific."

He made a little gargled sound in his throat. "I think that would be lovely."

"I'm serious. What's the dress code?"

"Something you might wear to a wine bar. I figured we'll have a little wine and some appetizers. Nothing crazy."

"I can work with that," I said. "I'll see you later."

Once I'd hung up, I faced Jimmy. He was staring at me expectantly.

"Are you back in the dating pool?" he asked. "Is this your first date?"

"It's not a date," I snapped. "I was very clear about that. We're just having dinner."

"I'll believe that when I see it."

"You're ridiculous."

"Look me in the eyes tomorrow and tell me it wasn't a date," Jimmy warned. "Then maybe I'll believe it."

Chapter 7

The rest of the afternoon passed quickly at the precinct. I caught up with Asha and Melinda, neither of them having turned up any pressing leads that could possibly get me out of my dinner non-date with Gem. I finished a few reports and sent the chief my updates. Only when I glanced at the clock and saw it was already after five did I officially start to panic.

"What if it's a date?" I stood before Jimmy's desk.

He'd had his head down most of the afternoon. I wasn't sure who he thought he was fooling that he was getting any work done. Or it was very possible he didn't care about fooling anyone at all. A napkin stuck to his forehead as he raised his head, and he gently peeled it off.

"Of course it's a date." Jimmy groaned and looked at me. "A guy doesn't ask a woman out like Gem did without thinking there's some sort of date attached."

"I told him specifically—"

"Look, y'all can pretend it's not a date if you want. Whatever makes you feel better. You're both single and unattached. Do whatever makes you happy."

"But I don't want it to be a romantic thing."

"Do you think he wants it to be?"

I hesitated. "I don't know. I was very upfront with him about my not wanting to get into anything."

"Gem didn't make a billion dollars by being rash."

"Huh?"

"He's patient," Jimmy said. "He could be playing the long game."

"Now I'm a game to him?"

Jimmy wiped at his forehead with the crumpled napkin. "I didn't mean it in a bad way. I just meant that if he likes being around you, he'll be patient. It's the respectful, gentlemanly thing to do. There's an art to keeping a person close but not pressuring them. My guess is that's what Gem is trying to do."

"So I'm leading him on."

"Do you want to go or not?" Jimmy asked. "If you don't want to go, don't go."

"I do want to go. As friends."

"Sure. Let me know how that works out."

"Are you a person that believes men and women can't be friends?" I asked. "What about you and me? No offense. I love having you as a friend, but I think it's mutual that we're not interested in one another."

"It's different. We're colleagues and in way, way different stages of life." Jimmy sat back at his desk and mopped his nose. "Plus, you've seen me like *this*. Nobody wants to date a person they've seen looking like this."

I gave him a sympathetic smile. "It's not you, it's me."

Jimmy cracked one of his first smiles all day. "Go on and prove me wrong. If anyone can do that, it's you, Rosetti. If nothing else, have a good time and get a few decent meals out of the arrangement for me. If he starts pressuring you for more, all you have to say is no."

"When you put it like that, it sounds so simple."

"That's what I'm here for."

I told Jimmy to go home. Then I deftly ignored Melinda and Asha as I tried to slip out of the building. They'd caught wind of my evening plans with Gem earlier in the day, and I knew they weren't about to let me get off that easily. I was right.

"Where're you going?" Asha asked. "Home first or straight to meet Gem?"

Melinda stepped next to Asha. The two barricaded my way out the doors of the building. "What are you wearing?"

"Clothes," I said pointedly. "Now, if you'll excuse me, I'm running late."

"I expect an update," Melinda said. "At least, I'd very much like to know where you're going tonight. For safety reasons."

I gave her an eye roll. "For safety reasons."

"Hey, you're going out with a man," Melinda said. "It's good practice to let a friend know where you'll be."

"You're just nosy."

"That too," Asha agreed happily. "Might as well include me on that text chain because you know Melinda will just turn around and tell me anyway."

I sighed. "Fine. If I can let you know, I will. Otherwise, I'll see you in the morning. Call me if anything turns up with the case."

"Sure thing," Asha said, though her tone wasn't at all convincing.

I finally weaseled my way out from between my two friends and made my way home. Jane was over at her fiancé's place. She'd naturally been spending more and more time at Wes's house, and I was waiting for the day she packed the last of her things and left my place for good. Waiting anxiously, not because I wanted her to leave but because I'd grown used to her presence.

I hated to admit it, but I was somewhat worried about how I'd handle an always silent house once Jane officially made the move. I'd gotten used to making a big pot of coffee to share. I'd gotten used to the bright yellow of her pajamas in the mornings no matter how gloomy it was outside. I'd gotten used to coming home at all hours of the night to sometimes find her waiting up for me on the couch with a glass of wine.

Having her move in with me had been my worst nightmare. It was ironic how I was now dreading her move-out date. I even had an inkling that the only reason she popped back to my place at all was more for me than her. I suspected that if I was still dating Russo, she'd have been long gone already, but instead, my little sister was looking out for me.

I headed upstairs, conscious of the clock constantly counting down to the 6:00 p.m. deadline in which I'd find a billionaire waiting for me outside of my house. I headed into my closet to look for something that would be fitting enough to wear to dinner with a billionaire. *Billionaire.*

The word seemed to be thrumming in the back of my head no matter how hard I tried to separate the man from his money. It was just such a vast amount of money. Such a vast difference in lifestyle between us. My relationship with Russo had been on a much more even playing field. Russo understood me. He lived like me. He thought like me.

Gem didn't think like me. He was the opposite of me. Flashy, wealthy, playful. I was boring, average-incomed, and serious. I wasn't like the women he dated, the women he spent time with, the women he surrounded himself with. All it took was a look at his ex-fiancé or Lassie's blog to know that for a fact.

While this wasn't a date, I felt a jitteriness that could only be attributed to nerves—even if I wasn't sure why. How many times had I been in the same room as Gem? How many times had I interviewed him for a case? Asked him for a favor? I'd never been nervous before. He'd been nothing but easy to get along with. Maybe Jimmy was right, and the only reason there was so much pressure was because there was no such thing as a casual relationship with Alastair Gem.

I glanced at the clock and saw that I had fifteen minutes until go-time. I jumped in the shower for a lightning rinse and was out two minutes later. Thirteen minutes to go, and the doorbell rang.

I hurtled downstairs, one towel around my head, another wrapped around my body. I peeked out the peephole and found Alastair Gem standing on my front steps.

I pulled the door open a tiny amount and poked my head around the side. The only thing that was visible was the towel wrapped around my hair and a little bit of my forehead.

"You're early," I accused.

Gem's eyebrows inched up. "I see you took me at my word when I said informal. I'm glad to see you're comfortable with me."

"Ha ha," I said, pulling the door a little wider open and hitching my towel up higher. "Can you come back in a few minutes?"

"Oh, okay. Sure."

"Or you can come in and wait," I said. "But I'm sort of naked."

"You say that like it's a problem."

I stuck my forehead out farther so he could see my furrowed eyebrows.

Gem laughed. "I'll knock on your door at six o'clock on the dot. We'll try this again."

I closed the door and hustled back upstairs. I managed a quick blow-dry of my hair, then I pretty much closed my eyes and picked an outfit at random out of my sister's closet. I didn't have time to dillydally, and I knew nothing in my closet would work.

I was pleasantly surprised to find I'd selected some sort of black knit dress. I slid it over my head and found it was midi length but slim fitting. It had a high collar and long sleeves with cutouts on the shoulders. Elegant but casual, and altogether perfect for a wine tasting. I texted Jane a picture and asked if I could borrow it. Then I ran back downstairs without a response.

A double check of my makeup in the mirror told me my lipstick and mascara were presentable. I tucked extra tubes of both into my purse. I loaded and unloaded my gun about three times into the same purse. A knock sounded on the door. I took the gun out one final time and left it behind.

"You should know that I'm leaving my gun at home for you," I said as I opened the door. "I don't do that for just anyone."

Gem's eyebrows were up again. "Well, I am flattered, Detective."

"What about you?" I asked pointedly, remembering the gun he'd had stashed in his vehicle while we'd been chasing after the man who'd kidnapped my father. "Can you say the same thing for yourself?"

"How do you feel about roses?" From behind his back, Gem withdrew a single, beautiful, long-stemmed red rose. He handed it to me. "I thought a bouquet was too much. But this just says friendly and thoughtful. Right?"

He added the last bit as if truly unsure. I decided to let him off the hook and graciously accepted the flower. I excused myself to dash back to the kitchen and drop it into a little vase for later. Then I returned to the front and let Gem lead me outside.

"So where are we going?" I asked. "I hope you didn't do something ridiculous like rent out a restaurant or close one of your clubs down for the night or something."

"Oh, it's nothing dramatic like that."

"Good," I said. "So where are we going?"

Gem held open the door to his car, a shiny, black thing, and let me slide in first before walking around to the driver's side. He got in, started the car, and glanced over at me.

"Canada," he said simply.

"Oh, funny. Fine. I'll let it be a surprise."

Unfortunately, my hopes that Gem had been kidding started to evaporate the second we pulled onto land that I'd been on before. Specifically, an airfield. I recognized Gem's luxury private plane from the last time he'd taken me on it.

Except in that instance, he'd been doing the police force a favor. He'd taken Russo and me down to Texas to question a serial killer in prison. It'd been a business transaction.

While this wasn't a business transaction, I no longer knew exactly what to call it. I began having a funny feeling in my gut that I wouldn't be able to look into my partner's eyes tomorrow and tell him this evening hadn't been a date.

"Gem," I said warningly, "I hope you just set up some sandwiches on the airplane or something. I told you not to go all out."

"This isn't all out," Gem said. "If I wanted to go all out, you'd know."

I groaned. "You weren't kidding, were you? We're actually going to Canada."

"You'll have to see."

A short while later, we were situated comfortably on Gem's plane. The captain was finishing his preflight checklist, and a server appeared to offer us refreshments.

"A glass of ice wine?" the pretty young woman suggested, not really giving us an option as she handed us two small glasses filled with a champagne-colored beverage. "Please relax and enjoy the flight, and of course, let me know if there's anything I can do for you."

"Thank you, Jordan." Gem dismissed the flight attendant with a salute of his glass. Then he turned to face me. "A toast?"

"Okay." I hoped he couldn't hear the uncertainty in my voice.

"Relax, Detective."

"Relax? I am relaxed."

"You're more tense than I've ever seen you before, and I've seen you in the middle of hunting murderers."

"That's within my comfort zone. Private jets are not."

"I want to tell you to relax again, but I can see it's not working. Are you uncomfortable with my plans for tonight?"

Seeing as we were taxiing on the runway, I gave him a sardonic smile. "A little late for that, don't you think."

"It's my plane. We can turn around at any time."

"No, I'm not uncomfortable. I'm just not sure what this is."

"Which part?"

"This, Gem." I gestured around me. "You asked me out to dinner tonight, and now I find myself on a private jet leaving the country. Usually when someone asks if I want to grab a bite to eat, they're talking about a slice of pizza down the street. I didn't want you to go all out."

"That's what you have to understand, Detective. This isn't going all out." The look on Gem's face was a little quizzical, as if he didn't quite understand the problem. "This is my plane. Think of it like a taxi or an Uber."

I gave a hearty laugh. "Right. One that costs millions of dollars. This is not an Uber."

"It is when money's not an issue," Gem said. "There's a lovely little vineyard just across the border in Canada that makes the finest ice wine I've ever tasted. I know the owners, and they've prepared a little dinner for us. If we drove there, we wouldn't make it back in time for your work tomorrow. This is just more practical."

I could feel my heart pounding as I stared at Gem. "You don't get it, do you?"

"Get what?"

"This isn't normal." I stood and paced up and down in the cabin. "I'm not comfortable with this. Any of it."

"The flying?"

"The jet, Gem. The jet itself."

"I'm sorry?"

"I don't feel comfortable with your level of wealth," I blurted. "I'm sorry, but it's true. I don't get it. I don't understand it. I can't fathom it. I mean, my brain is broken trying to wrap my head around the idea that you asked me to dinner so casually, and yet here we are flying to a different country. People don't even do that for their weddings and honeymoons."

"There's nothing to 'get,' Kate," Gem said softly. "I have money. Would you like me to deny it? Pretend that's not my reality? Not use it?"

"I don't care what you do with your money. It's when I'm involved that things don't make sense."

"I've never gone out with a person who's had an issue with my money. Yet that seems like the one thing you can't get past." Gem stood and moved closer to me. He guided me onto the seat so we were both sitting as the plane took off. "I can no more give all my money away than you can suddenly turn yourself into a billionaire tomorrow."

"I don't think you should give all your money away. You've earned it. You donate to charity. You don't abuse it." I shrugged. "If anyone's going to have billions of dollars, it might as well be you. A lot of other people wouldn't be as scrupulous with their riches as you."

"I'm going to take that as a strange sort of compliment."

"You should," I confirmed grudgingly. "It doesn't mean I fit into your world."

"Can you, for one moment, Kate, stop thinking about money?"

"I don't think—"

"You're more obsessed with it than I am," Gem said. "And that's saying something."

"I'm not obsessed with money!"

"If you weren't obsessed with it, then it wouldn't bother you. You're bothered by it because you see it as a barrier in our friendship."

"Don't you?"

"No. And you shouldn't either. I'm happy to be patient, to bend to your comfort levels, Detective. But if this is a stumbling block in our relationship, I don't know how we're supposed to get past it."

"Patient for what, Gem?" I asked quietly. "What are you waiting for?"

He stared at me, silent.

"I told you, I'm not looking for anything romantic. I told you not to get any ideas."

"Isn't it obvious, Kate?" Gem asked finally, his voice quiet, articulate.

"No," I said, feeling the panic set in. "No, it's not obvious. I thought I was very clear."

"You are very clear. You're not ready for a relationship *now*. However, you've never once told me, 'Alastair Gem, I can never see myself with you.' You've always said you weren't ready for a relationship, and those are two very different statements."

"Is that the only reason why you're spending time with me?" I asked. "Because you're hoping it'll turn into something more?"

"No. If I can direct your attention back to a few months ago, I'll point out that I was engaged to another woman, and I still wanted to be your friend."

"Up until you told me we couldn't be friends."

"Yes, out of respect for her. That was because I loved Mindy. I would have been loyal to her. She wasn't a consolation prize; she was going to be my wife."

"I know."

"Yet I still wanted to enjoy your friendship. And if friendship is all you're willing to give me, I'm fine with it. Even if you were still with Russo, I would have liked to be your friend."

"If I was with Russo, I can guarantee you we wouldn't be going up to Canada in your private jet for a casual dinner."

"Also true. I would never have asked. I would never have put you in the position to have to say no, to feel conflicted about my intentions."

"But now?"

"Now? Kate, you're single. I'm single. I adore you as a friend. You're a beautiful woman. I like spending time with you." Gem threw his hands up in the air. "I enjoy good food, good wine. I enjoy having fun. That's all this is. Fun."

"Fun?"

"Yes. Would you like a dictionary definition?"

"Contrary to popular belief, I know how to have fun."

Gem gave a small smile. "I believe you. Hence the reason you're here with me tonight. I thought we could have a little fun. No, not in the way you're thinking."

"But—"

"You're forgetting that I just got out of a very serious relationship too," Gem pointed out. "You haven't asked me if I'm ready for a relationship."

"Are you?"

"No," Gem said, sounding sincere. "My heart was broken when my wedding fell through. It wasn't what I desired."

I nodded. Gem was opening up to me, and I could feel the pain in his words. The pain that he'd hidden behind fancy dinner dates and the company of his beautiful friends and parties.

"I'm sorry," I said. "I should have asked."

"I'm not looking for sympathy. I'm trying to illustrate a point. I'm not trying to rush into a relationship. Nor am I trying to use you as a rebound. You're simply a person I care about. A person I trust, a person I enjoy spending time with. I don't have many people in my life like that."

"You have Wes."

"He's much less beautiful than you." Gem winked. "And if you haven't noticed, he's quite taken with his new fiancée. He's supportive, but I'm afraid he's not at a place in his life where bachelor weekends in Vegas are on his radar anymore. I respect that. What he has is special, and I am happy he's found a woman who makes him so happy."

"Me too," I admitted. "I mean, the reverse, for my sister. They're really a good match."

"They are." There was a moment of silence. "In case you haven't gotten the picture yet, let me reiterate: tonight doesn't have to be something it's not. For me, taking the plane somewhere *is* the equivalent of someone else taking out their nice classic car or renting a limo. There's a nice restaurant I wanted to go to, and this was the fastest way to get there."

"It's just a little unrelatable to someone like me. Taking a cab and taking a private jet aren't even in the same playbook."

"Would you like me to take you home?"

I glanced out the window. We were definitely in the air. "No, that's not the point."

"Then what is the point?"

"I'm not comfortable in your world."

"I'm just me!" Gem flew to his feet, frustration in his voice. "I admit some aspects of my life aren't relatable anymore. But I don't know what to do about it. I'm still me, the same man who's been your friend for months. Nothing has changed, Kate, except the fact that we're both single. Is that what scares you?"

"I-I'm not scared."

"It sure sounds like it."

"It's not that I'm scared—"

"Are you scared that I was going to do this?"

Gem pulled me to my feet and placed his hands on either side of my face. He hovered there, his lips inches from mine, looking into my eyes. His breath came in raspy bursts, minty and fresh with a note of the ice wine we'd been served. We were closer than ever, a breath away from a kiss. A breath away from a moment that could change my life. I felt my own chest constrict.

Finally, Gem let me go and stepped back.

"I'm sorry," he said, breathing heavily. "I shouldn't have done that."

"No, it's fine," I said. "I'm not... I'm not upset."

"You can be. You warned me against getting too close."

"I knew what I was getting into tonight," I said. "As much as I pretended to be naïve, I'm not stupid, Gem."

"So you feel there's something between us?"

I shrugged. "I don't know what it is. I just know I'm not ready."

"Me neither." He rubbed a hand across his forehead. "Where do we go from here?"

"Let's just do what we came to do," I said finally. "Let's have dinner. I'll stop giving you a hard time about your jet."

He gave a playful grin. "You'd do that for me?"

"I still think it's preposterous. For the record."

"I didn't mean it to be."

"I know." I shook my head, unable to hide a smile. "That's the most preposterous part of all."

Gem laughed. "Money doesn't have to change a person."

"It so often does."

"Correct. But I hope in my case, it just changes how I do things. Sometimes I take a jet instead of a cab. I can afford to pay someone to help me do my shopping. I don't stress if something breaks; I just pay to fix it. That doesn't mean I've forgotten who I was before my life looked like this. I hope you can see that someday."

Gem and I sat next to one another on the plane. The space between us was comfortable, more relaxed after our little argument—or whatever it could be called.

"I know." I looked over at him. "I'm sorry. I knew who I said yes to when I agreed to go out tonight. Heck, I might have been disappointed if we'd gone through the drive-through at McDonald's instead of traipsing off to Canada."

Gem grinned. "For some reason, I doubt it. You're easy to please."

"Ouch."

"On the contrary, it's one of the things I love about you."

There was another moment of silence at Gem's awkward turn of phrase. But I was determined not to cause any more arguments tonight if I could help it. I let it pass, and Gem seemed relieved when I smiled at him.

"I know you're a good person," I murmured. "It's why I like you too. It's my own problem, the stuff I was saying before. I'm sorry."

"Forget it. Let's start over?"

I reached for my glass of ice wine. "To Canada."

"To Canada."

Chapter 8

The next morning, I made my way into the precinct wearing sunglasses. I made it in on time, but Jimmy was already there. He was looking a million times better than he'd looked the day before. At least, he appeared to be perspiring significantly less. I looked a million times worse than the day before, I was pretty sure.

My indoor sunglasses were not lost on Jimmy. He grinned at me.

"Where'd you go last night?"

"Canada," I muttered.

"Is that a new restaurant?" Jimmy asked. "What do they serve, poutine?"

I pushed the sunglasses on top of my head. "The actual country. Gem took me to Canada."

Jimmy spluttered into his coffee. "And you're going to try and argue it wasn't a date?"

I pushed my sunglasses back down and sat before my computer screen. One glance in the mirror after my shower, and I'd immediately known it would be impossible to conceal my bleary eyes. A part of me felt like I should be embarrassed, that I should regret my choices the previous evening, but the funny thing was that I didn't have any regrets.

After Gem and I had made up on the plane, we'd had an incredible time. It'd been a relaxed evening, a pure escape from reality that I'd desperately needed for far too long. We'd left conversations of love lives behind us. We hadn't spoken about money, and when Gem had casually paid a bill that had one too many zeros behind it, I'd deftly looked away.

When he'd dropped me off outside of my house, he'd walked me to the door but had refrained from any romantic overtures. He'd squeezed my hand and thanked me for the company. I found myself thanking him back for the experience and meaning it deeply.

The bleary eyes were merely a result of the late night, the ice-wine-tasting flight that we'd gotten seconds on, and the amount of laughter we'd shared. I remembered wiping tears from my eyes on more than one occasion during our conversation. I'd forgotten what it was like to have fun, and I only had Gem to thank for bringing a glimpse of it back into my life.

"What's on the docket for today?" I asked. "I assume I wasn't kept in the loop last night if there were any developments."

"Can you see your computer screen through those glasses?" Jimmy asked. "I sent you an email. We've got several confirmed interviews for today. Are you sure you're okay?"

"Better than you were doing yesterday. At least I can keep the contents of my stomach down."

"Hey, if the contents of my stomach were a thousand-dollar dinner, I'd work real hard at keeping them down too."

I couldn't help but laugh. "Touché."

"At least you're not trying to tell me it wasn't a date."

"Shut up."

"Uh-huh," Jimmy said. "Get your stuff. I'll drive. Need a latte?"

"No," I lied.

"Uh-huh," Jimmy repeated. "You're just scared to go into your mother's coffee shop because she'll ask you questions that you don't want to answer."

"What do I have to bribe you with to get me a coffee?"

"Lunch."

"Done," I said, looking up to see two of my friends waiting for me. "Go grab me a latte, and I'll meet you at the car."

Jimmy glanced at the door to the office and saw Melinda and Asha standing there, obviously waiting impatiently to question me about my evening.

"You've got ten minutes to grill her, ladies," he said as he slid past them. "She has stuff to do today."

I rose from my desk and made my way toward the two women waiting for me. I knew ditching them would be useless. They'd only hit me even harder later. As I approached, Melinda raised her eyebrows.

"Sunglasses indoors?" the medical examiner asked. "I take that as a sign of a very good night?"

"Very good," Asha echoed. "Very very good."

"It's not what you think." I pushed my sunglasses up and faced my friends. "I was just up late."

"Did you go home with him?" Melinda asked. "Did you even stop home this morning?"

"I didn't go home with him," I said. "It just so happened that the restaurant Gem chose for us was located in Canada."

"Little Canada?" Asha glanced at Melinda. "No offense to Little Canada, but I don't think of the Twin Cities suburbs as Gem territory."

"I think she means the country." Melinda looked carefully at me. "That's what you mean, isn't it? Gem whisked you away to another country?"

"Is Canada really another country?" I mused. "I mean, it's just a couple hours north of us."

"I believe it's safe to say Canada is officially another country," Asha said. "Wow. That's impressive."

"It wasn't anything fancy. I mean, okay, it was fancy," I admitted. "We took his plane up because there's this vineyard that makes ice wine that Gem loves. I guess he knows the owner. We had dinner there is all."

"Uh-huh." Asha didn't seem convinced. "Just dinner. After a private jet ride. At an exclusive vineyard where your date knows the owners."

"A very average first date," Melinda said dryly. "How'd it go?"

"You know, it went okay," I said, finding myself smiling a little bit. "More than okay. I had a lot of fun."

"Did you..." Asha waggled her eyebrows.

I glanced over my shoulder and saw Frankie Dunkirk staring at me. "Mind your own business, Dunkirk."

I pushed past Melinda and Asha until we reached Asha's desk where there was a little bit more privacy.

"No, there was none of that," I said. "I'm not ready and neither is he. We're on the same page."

"I find it hard to believe that Gem pulled out all the stops last night for a casual friendly dinner," Asha said. "I know the guy's a billionaire, but I just don't buy it."

"That's the thing. I don't think he thought it was a big deal. It's just who he is," I said. "Trust me, I made an issue about it. He was pretty clueless about the whole thing."

"He lives in a different realm," Asha said. "I can see that from a mile away."

Melinda seemed skeptical. "Are you and Gem entering into an official thing here?"

"Look, guys, he made me laugh." I shrugged. "After a month of wallowing, a week of being surrounded by couples in love, and a murder case, I just needed an escape. Gem gave me a night away—no strings attached, no pressure—and it was great."

"That's good, sweetie," Asha said. "I'm all for it. If anything, I say you could take advantage of the situation with a little more benefits, if you catch my drift."

"That's a bad idea," Melinda said. "Sleeping with Gem would make things very complicated when you're already in a fragile state."

"I'm not going there." I waved a hand. "It's not on my radar. We talked about it last night. He's still got a broken heart too. We're, uh, not interested in being one another's rebounds."

Asha and Melinda looked at one another. A glance passed between them that I couldn't quite decipher. I looked down at my watch.

"Now, if you'll excuse me, I'm headed back to the Luzzi estate. We've got another interview lined up with some guy named Anthony."

"Have fun," Asha said. "I hear he's a real hunk. And by hear, I mean I saw a picture, and he's a real hunk."

"I'm off hunks," I said.

"He's off-limits anyway," Asha said. "He's married with a kid. I'm just saying a girl can appreciate a guy who looks like Anthony looks. You'll see what I mean."

I said goodbye to my friends and promised to catch up with them later. Then I headed out to the car where Jimmy was waiting with two lattes. He passed me one as we got in the car and began our return to the outskirts of St. Paul.

This time, when we reached the impressive Luzzi estate, we had no trouble getting inside. Apparently, Carlos had been quite serious about keeping the little food poisoning incident on the down low so as not to hurt his wife's feelings. It was pretty cute, actually.

We followed the guard's directions past the main house where we'd stopped last time and made our way around back. Another few minutes of driving, and we came to a second house on the property. This one wasn't the ginormous, castle-like estate of Carlos Luzzi, but a much more modest farmhouse that looked like a real home.

Jimmy parked out front, and we climbed from the car. Unlike the main house, there were no armed guards wandering around that we could see. No butler waiting for our arrival at the front door. If I hadn't been aware of the last name attached to the property, it would have been possible to imagine this was a normal interview situation in a normal family home.

I knocked on the door and pulled off my sunglasses. A high-pitched screech sounded from inside. I barely had time to glance questioningly at Jimmy before the door was yanked open.

It was immediately apparent what Asha had meant about Anthony Luzzi being attractive. He was tall, broad shouldered, and well muscled. He wore jeans and a black T-shirt that seemed casual yet perfectly fitted to show off his physique. He had the dark hair and dark skin signifying his Latin heritage along with chocolatey brown eyes to match. When he gave a little smile, it drew everything together into one very attractive image.

But the best accessory of all was the little girl hanging over her daddy's shoulder. The source of the high-pitched screech was immediately apparent as Anthony raised his fingers and tickled the little girl on the belly. She shrieked with laughter.

"Hi," I said. "I'm Detective Rosetti, and this is my partner, Detective Jones. Is this a good time? I got a message saying you'd be expecting us."

"It's fine," Anthony said, "so long as you don't mind one troublemaking munchkin sticking around. Someone's mother fed this girl a doughnut for breakfast, then took off for a surprise day of work, and now I'm left to deal with the fallout of a sugar-riddled toddler."

I grinned. The Luzzi family was full of surprises. "That's fine by me. We'll try to keep things brief."

As Anthony led us into his home, I had a hard time picturing him as the murderer. Sure, I'd read his file and was well aware of the scary reputation he carried. He obviously hadn't gotten to be a trusted member of Carlos's inner circle without proving himself. But somehow, I couldn't see this playful father murdering a grown man and shoving him into the back of an ice cream truck just because Garrett Landers had been a little bit shady.

"Thank you so much for inviting us inside," I said. "We're here about the death of a man named Garrett Landers. It appears he worked for the family a few months prior to his death."

Anthony's eyes shot over to me as I used the word family. I could see that behind the glimmer of playfulness in his eyes, he was sizing me up. Calculations were flashing behind those careful eyes, and I had a moment of doubt that my initial observations about him had been wrong. In that moment, I understood just how dangerous he could be.

Then it passed, and he smiled again and swung his daughter onto the floor. The next time he looked at me, I doubted everything I'd seen. He crossed his arms over his chest and looked truly relaxed. Either I'd imagined that calculating look, or he was a master. I suspected the latter.

"Sure, he worked for the Luzzi estate. I manage a lot of the employees, though, and I can't say I'm as hands on as I used to be." He nodded at his little girl, who was buzzing around a Barbie car on the coffee table. "My priorities have shifted somewhat. I have taken on more of an administration role as of late. Plus, my wife works as well, so I do some child-care duties when I can steal Bella from her grandmother."

I remembered Nora and the sparkly syrup she'd purchased for her great-granddaughter. All three hundred bottles of it. "Could you tell me about your relationship with Garrett Landers?"

"I wouldn't say what we had was a relationship," Anthony said. "At best, you could call it a working relationship."

"You were his boss?"

"I guess you could say that."

"Is there someone he worked more closely with?"

Anthony watched me carefully. After a long minute of silence, I realized that was his way of saying he wasn't going to answer the question.

"We've learned that he was fired from the company. Was that your doing?"

"I suppose."

"That's interesting," I said, "because both Carlos and Nora have also claimed to be responsible for firing Garrett. Who really was responsible for his leaving?"

Anthony gave me a wry smile. "I guess it was a family affair."

I gave a sigh and looked directly at him. "I understand that you are protecting your family. I also don't believe that you or Carlos are responsible for Garrett's death, but when you lie, it makes you look guilty."

"I'm not lying. As Garrett's supervisor, I was technically responsible for his firing."

"Yes, but three people didn't fire him. Was it your choice? Was it Nora's, and you just backed her up? Carlos's? Help me out a little bit, and we'll leave you alone."

"I don't owe you anything." Anthony's voice wasn't mean; it wasn't resentful. It was calm, cool, collected. Very businesslike, simply stating facts. "I didn't kill Garrett, so you'll never find any evidence against me. I'm cooperating because I was asked to do so."

"Not giving me answers isn't really cooperating," I pointed out. "I'm just trying to figure out who stuffed a man into the back of an ice cream truck. Seems like a lot of people didn't like him. Seems like a lot of people wanted him dead. I was hoping you might know who wanted him dead more than most."

Anthony glanced toward where his daughter was playing happily with her doll. He rubbed at his forehead, obviously somewhat uncomfortable with the idea of cooperating with the police. I didn't take it personally. For people like Anthony, a distrust of the law ran deep in their blood. In a funny way, I appreciated that he was trying.

"He was fired, I guess you could say mutually, by Carlos, Nora, and myself," Anthony said. "It wasn't a lie that it was a group effort."

"He was caught stealing?"

"A bunch of Nora's best china," Anthony said. "She fired him, but he tried to deny doing it. Carlos swept in seeing red, on the verge of, well..."

"Got it," I said quickly. "Then you came in to handle the situation more diplomatically?"

"I like that." Anthony nodded. "Diplomatically. I escorted him off the property and let him know if he showed his face around here again, it wouldn't be beneficial for his face."

"Right. Did you ever see him again?"

"No."

"What about the people he poached from you and Carlos? The employees?"

A twinge of surprise appeared in Anthony's eyes, and his head jerked up ever so slightly as he glanced in my direction.

"You're good at your job," I said, "and I'm good at mine."

He smiled, a genuine smile. "I respect that. Yes, he took two guys from us. But I didn't kill him because of it. If he could get those guys to leave, then good riddance to them. We've got no place in this family for anyone who is less than a hundred percent invested. One hundred percent loyal. We don't deal in half-hearted anything around here."

"I'm beginning to see that it's sort of an all-in situation."

"It's a family," Anthony stated again. "Either you're in or you're not."

"That had to make you upset. Both about the two employees leaving, and about Garrett stealing them away. He was obviously doing it to get revenge."

"I wasn't happy about it. I wouldn't have killed anyone over it. If anything, I was disappointed in myself for not seeing it sooner." Anthony gave a shake of his head. "None of those three men should've been hired in the first place, and that's the part that irked me the most."

"I imagine it's hard to do a proper background check when you're hiring people with suspect histories for a suspect position."

Anthony's lips tightened. "Any other questions, Detective?"

I glanced down at my hands, gathering my thoughts. "What do you know about Garrett's personal life? Do you know what sort of work he was doing once he left here? Do you know why he'd need two additional guys to complete the job? What about girlfriends?"

"I don't know anything about girlfriends."

"What about the job?"

"It's not as if he told me anything."

The dodginess of Anthony's answers made me press deeper. "But a guy like you hears things."

He sighed. "It's just about nap time."

"Give me a direction, and we'll let you get back to your Barbies. I know the guys were called Jelly and Pound. Can I get some real names?"

"Ricky Navarro and Henry Dunwoody," Anthony said. "They'd both been with us less than a year. All three were the newest guys on staff, and I think that's why they were a little closer together than the rest of us. They were the outsiders. Everyone else has been here much longer."

"That makes some sense. What are their backgrounds?"

"Like you said, we don't do traditional background checks here."

"No, but you hired them for a purpose."

"Ricky Navarro—Jelly—is the mean muscle. He follows orders."

I nodded along. "And Henry Dunwoody?"

"He and Jelly came as a pair. They'd worked together before and claimed they made a good team. Henry's the brains. He can pick locks and disarm security systems. He's a good shot. I mean, a really, really good shot. He's someone you want on your side if you're doing a job."

"And Garrett Landers?"

"He's the one with the big ideas. The linchpin, if you will. Brings the others together."

"Do you know who Garrett might be working for?" I asked. "I was under the impression that this wasn't a job Garrett specifically planned himself. It sounded like he was promising these guys a big payoff for something above his pay grade."

"I could only guess. I don't run in those circles anymore."

"A guess is better than nothing."

"I've heard rumors the Mathematician is back in town."

"A mathematician?"

"*The* Mathematician," Anthony corrected. "I don't know his identity. I do know that we won't even know he's here until he's gone."

"I'm not familiar."

"You work homicide. The Mathematician isn't a killer, so I don't see why you'd have heard of him."

"What's he known for?"

"High-stakes robbery. Big-ticket items. It would line up with the crew he was gathering. Garrett would be the local honcho, the manager—if you will—who gathers the others, stakes out the targets, reports to the Mathematician. The other two would be support. Jelly would do any of the physical intimidation necessary. Pound might assist with the alarm systems or as backup with a long-range rifle."

"And the actual Mathematician?" I asked. "If he's so infamous, why have I never heard of him?"

"First, he rotates locations. Like I said, you won't know he's hit a target until he's a thousand miles away. Aside from that, the name is self-explanatory. The Mathematician is exacting, precise... perfect."

"No criminal is perfect."

"Maybe not, but this one comes close. There's never been a sighting. No DNA. No eyewitnesses. Even the people he chooses to steal from don't report their stuff missing half the time."

"There aren't too many reasons I can think of for a person to not report their stuff as missing, unless it wasn't their stuff to begin with."

Anthony acquiesced my point with a slight nod. "That would be one reason. Another reason is because the cost of involving the police isn't worth the value of whatever they might recover with law enforcement's help. Then there's the little fact that most people of a certain caliber have their own team to deal with these sorts of things."

"Like you do for Carlos," I said. "If he had something stolen, he probably wouldn't call the chief and report it missing."

"We like to handle things within the family when possible. You understand."

"I know this is a long shot, but I'm wondering if you might have any idea who the Mathematician's next target could be?"

"I have no possible way of knowing that."

"The circle must be small," I pressed. "You found out that he's in this city somehow. You're sure you haven't heard any rumors circling about who might be the target?"

Anthony pursed his lips.

"It wouldn't be the Luzzi family, would it?" I asked. "We'd be happy to help offer protection in exchange for your cooperation. Who knows? Maybe together, we could catch the Mathematician."

"It's not us."

"You sound very sure," I observed. "How can you be so sure?"

"Because I'm in charge of the Luzzi family security team, and I can tell you that even the Mathematician wouldn't try to rob Carlos Luzzi under my watch."

"I see. But didn't we just confirm that someone, Garrett Landers specifically, tried to steal from you?"

"He was an idiot." Anthony gave a cough. "Sorry to speak ill of the dead. My point is only that the Mathematician is not an idiot."

"Ah."

"Not to mention he went after some of Nora's china. He wasn't fired because he stole something of value. It was the principle of it. In order to steal anything of value from Carlos, the Mathematician would need a much larger team of people to be successful. Two guys named Pound and Jelly aren't going to cut it."

"You do have to admit that all three would have insider knowledge," I said. "They worked on the premises, knew the family, protocols, et cetera."

"They had the lowest clearance possible. The only person who could steal successfully from Carlos would be me."

"If all you've said is true so far, and I'm going to assume it is, then it still isn't getting at the issue of Garrett's death. Are you insinuating that the Mathematician killed Garrett?"

"I'm just telling you what I know. It's up to you to do the insinuating part."

"Humor me. What do you think?"

Anthony considered for a moment. "Where'd you find his body?"

"He was stuffed in the back of an ice cream truck."

"The Mathematician didn't do it," Anthony assured me. "He might've given the orders, but he didn't kill him. This guy doesn't deal in situations where there could be a mistake, and dumping a body in a place like an ice cream truck isn't his style. Too messy, too risky."

"But it could've been related?"

"Sure. Garrett didn't have the best track record. Just look at his employment here. If he tried to steal from Carlos Luzzi, it is possible he tried to steal from the Mathematician. Or worse. In that case, he would've been disposed of. It's very possible the Mathematician gave the orders for the kill, and the person doing the actual job botched it, leading to a messy stash of the body."

"Why in that location?" I asked. "Why behind the bar of someone who's part of the Luzzi family?"

Anthony cringed. "Meg's not a blood relative."

"With all due respect, neither are you."

Anthony looked even more annoyed at the comparison. "I don't have an answer to your question. I know Garrett hung out around the bar. A couple of the employees do. I'm sure Jelly and Pound have been there on occasion. Meg offers big discounts to the guys who work at the Luzzi estate. She's not shy in trying to drum up business for her bar."

"She doesn't seem shy, period."

Anthony snorted. "You've had the pleasure of meeting her."

"I don't know if I met her so much as listened to her talk to me without my getting much of a word in edgewise."

Anthony and I shared a smile. It was a small, friendly bonding moment. Then it was gone as quickly as it had happened.

"Is there anything else?" he asked. "I should grab Bella a snack, or she's going to start losing it. She inherits her appetite from her mother."

"No, that's all for now." I stood. "Thanks for your insights. If you do hear anything more about the Mathematician, specifically his intended target, please let us know. Same goes for word on Garrett's murder."

"Will do."

I noted that Anthony didn't ask for my card. I hadn't offered it as a test. But I wasn't completely sure if the reason he hadn't asked was because he was confident in his abilities to find me if needed, or if he had no intention of ever speaking to me again.

"There's actually one more thing," I said as Anthony walked us toward the door. "Is there any reason that you wouldn't like us looking into the identity of the Mathematician?"

Anthony looked genuinely surprised for the first time. "I told you, I'm not involved in those circles anymore."

I nodded. "Just wanted to check."

"You wanted to warn me."

"I like you and your family," I said. "I just wanted to make sure I wasn't stepping on any toes here."

"Consider my toes well protected." Anthony smiled. "It was a pleasure to meet you, Detectives. Let me know if there's anything else I can do for you."

Though the promise felt a little empty, I was quite pleased with the interview in and of itself. I'd satisfied my curiosity about the Luzzi family. While they were wrapped up in this mess in a peripheral sort of way, I had strong doubts that they'd initiated Garrett's killing. We'd also learned a valuable tidbit about this Mathematician person. I was anxious to get back to the precinct and hand over the information to Asha and see what she could turn up on him. It was quite possibly the first lead that made a lot of sense in our twisted, twisted case.

Chapter 9

"What do you think?" Jimmy asked as we drove away from the Luzzi estate. "Guilty or not?"

"I sincerely doubt the Luzzi family had anything to do with the ice cream truck murder," I said. "It's that whole weird logic thing, but I don't think they would've risked prison time for killing Garrett Landers. They'd save that risk for something more important, in their minds."

"Now you're thinking like a criminal."

"Everything I've heard on the street makes it seem like Carlos has retired from the business, at least mostly. I don't know how to read Anthony as well, but he seems to care for that little girl of his, and I don't think he'd risk losing time with her over Garrett."

"Agreed. And this Mathematician person?"

"I'm tempted to think there might be some truth to that. I texted the details to Asha, and she's going to look into it and get back to us. In the meantime, are you ready to stop back by Dominique's place?"

Jimmy's phone beeped, and he read the message on top. "Yes, with one change of plans."

"What's that?"

"Asha just texted me that Dominique's holding an open house not too far away from us. Feel like seeing if she serves cookies at her open houses?"

As it turned out, Dominique didn't serve cookies at her open houses, but she did serve fancy little bottles of Fiji water. I helped myself to one as Jimmy and I entered the new

McMansion on the outskirts of St. Paul that Dominique was in charge of selling.

"How much do you think she gets from making a sale?" Jimmy asked, glancing around the place. "I'm starting to think I'm in the wrong profession."

"Well, you can always have a second career during your retirement years."

"I was thinking competitive eating. Maybe gaming."

"You've never played a video game in your life."

"Nah, but I could learn." Jimmy shrugged. "This place is hopping with people. Does anyone really need six thousand square feet to live?"

I was spared answering as Dominique came into view. She stood in the kitchen in a black power suit and gold jewelry. Her stilettos added a few inches to her height that she hadn't had when we'd interviewed her the previous time. She had a brilliant smile on her face that faded the instant she recognized us.

"You," she said, her voice a low hiss. "What are you two doing here? This is a professional setting. I was kind enough to volunteer answers when you visited me at my home, but this is too much."

A young couple strolled into the kitchen. I glanced at them, then at Jimmy, then back to Dominique.

"One problem with our last visit," I said loudly. "You lied to us. Lying to detectives during a murder investigation doesn't look very good, Dominique."

Dominique paled as she glanced at the young couple as they quickly turned on a heel and began retreating from the kitchen. "Look what you did!"

"I could probably talk a little bit quieter if you felt like cooperating," I said. "Otherwise, we could just cancel this open house and bring you down to the precinct for questioning. The chief doesn't look kindly on folks who impede murder investigations."

"Fine, I'll answer your questions. Just come onto the porch and pretend you're looking at the property." Dominique stormed toward the center island and grabbed a sheet of paper off the top. "There's a Jacuzzi out back," she said louder, "and we've already had two offers. I'm afraid you'll really need to move on this place quickly if you're interested."

Once we were on the porch, Dominique shut the door behind us.

"Are there really two offers on this place?" I asked. "Or were you lying about that too? I admit you're a good liar. I can see how you sell houses."

Dominique glowered at me, and I took that to mean I'd caught her in another fib.

She crossed her arms. "What do you want?"

"You knew about Garrett's other girlfriends."

"What are you talking about?" Her gaze shifted between Jimmy and me. "His other girlfriends?"

"There's no use lying about it," I said. "We know you had lunch with Ellen just last week. We know you're familiar with Marissa. Apparently, there's a new girl named Jessica you've been stalking. I'm not sure what the deal is there just yet, but we'll figure it out."

"I haven't been stalking her," she blurted, then stopped herself quickly. "And I wasn't lying."

"You told us you were certain Garrett was exclusive to you." I studied her, wondering how she could continue to lie so easily when we'd clearly caught her in a web of fabrications. "You'll have to excuse our confusion when we heard that you were having lunch with the woman who's pregnant with Garrett's baby. Not to mention hanging around the place where Garrett was quite possibly picking up a fourth girlfriend."

"You've got it all wrong." Dominique's eyes flashed. "They weren't his girlfriends. They were nothing to him."

"Ellen was having his child."

"She tricked him," Dominique said. "It wasn't his fault. Plus, she didn't want anything from him. When I told her she had to break things off with Garrett because I was going to marry him, she agreed."

"She did?"

"Yes. She shrugged and said fine," Dominique said. "That was why we were having lunch last week. I was just trying to clear up Garrett's little messes before I printed our engagement announcements."

"Little messes?" I stared at her. "You mean, the baby?"

"Ellen can have the baby, just so long as she leaves my man out of it," Dominique said. Then she corrected. "Left him out of it. I guess it's a moot point now."

I cleared my throat. "Marissa?"

"Marissa's a crook, but she wasn't seeing Garrett romantically. At least, not anymore."

"Did you confront her?"

"I went into her stupid PI business under the guise of trying to hire her. Then I decided to just confront her. She told me that she was just working with Garrett. That was all. Nothing else."

"You believed her?"

"She wasn't Garrett's type. She was way too boring to keep him interested."

"What about this Jessica girl?"

"Garrett is a good-looking man. Sometimes women show an interest in him," Dominique said. "I guess that should be past tense. You get the idea. I just stopped by the bar this Jessica worked at a few times to feel her out."

"What'd you feel?"

"I just asked her nicely to leave my man alone."

"When did you do that?"

"A couple of days ago. Sometime after my lunch with Ellen. I told you, I was just trying to clean up loose ends. The invites were going to the printer this week and—" Dominique paused to curse. "I have to cancel that. I forgot to cancel the invites. Crap. I'm not getting my deposit back."

"I guess that's why most people wait for the engagement ring before they start booking invites and venues."

Dominique didn't look bothered by my jab. "I'm not most people. I go after what I want until I get it."

"What if you weren't getting what you wanted?" I mused. "You've already lied through your teeth to us. Your story doesn't match with the other women's stories. Do you want to know what I'm thinking?"

When Dominique didn't respond, I continued, unprompted.

"I think that maybe you tried to get Garrett in gear to get married, but he wasn't having any of it. Maybe you found out he'd just hooked up with another girlfriend, this Jessica girl. Maybe you found out that he was still seeing Ellen. Maybe you found out that Marissa had actually made out with your man a couple of times. Maybe you just found out that Garrett didn't want to get married. So you killed him."

"I didn't kill him."

"Honestly, you're looking like the best suspect we have. You've got plenty of motive to do it. You would've had the opportunity to kill Garrett and dump the body behind the bar where he was hanging out with his new girlfriend. You've already confirmed that you were at that bar checking out Jessica, and I'm sure she'll confirm that for me. Dominique, where were you last Friday night?"

"I don't remember," she said. "I'll have to check my calendar. I was probably at home. I work from home unless I'm at a showing, and I didn't have any social plans until Saturday."

"Alone. Convenient." I glanced at Jimmy. "I think we're done for now. Don't leave town until we get this case wrapped up. Got it?"

"I don't appreciate being spoken to like that," Dominique said. "I didn't kill anyone. Why would I have killed Garrett?"

"You have plenty of motive," I said, shocked she couldn't figure out why I might think she was guilty. "The man you were wanting to marry was seeing several other women. One of them was having his child. Love, jealousy, that whole thing is one of the primary motivations we see in murder cases."

"You're missing the point." Dominique looked to Jimmy for help. When he appeared just as confused as me, she continued. "If I killed Garrett, I wouldn't be able to marry him, would I?"

"I think we're done here," I said to Jimmy. "Let's go see what Jessica has to say."

"She's crazy," Dominique said. "She probably killed him when he broke things off with her. He wouldn't have married her. She's got a nose ring."

We left Dominique stewing on the porch as we made our way outside.

"That woman is a piece of work," Jimmy said. "But I almost believe her."

"Really?"

"I don't know. Either I'm losing my edge and she's a very good liar, or that woman really believed everything she was saying."

"She might have believed it," I said, "but she's already proven she's a very skilled liar. She could've been telling the truth up until the part about her killing him. Who knows? Maybe it will turn out to be an accident. Blunt force trauma to the head... She could've gotten mad and smacked him with the nearest object, not planning to kill him, and then had to clean up her accidental mess."

"It's possible." Jimmy led the way back to the car. "What do you say we go find out what Girlfriend Number Four has to say about it?"

Chapter 10

"I wasn't his girlfriend."

I slid onto a stool at the bar where the victim's body had been found. Jimmy sat next to me. Jessica stood across the counter from us, systematically drying glasses and putting them back on a rack. My eyes were drawn to the nose ring that Dominique had found offensive.

I wasn't completely sure Garrett had a type, contrary to what Dominique thought. Ellen, Marissa, Dominique, and Jessica were completely different sorts of women. The only thing they all seemed to have in common was the ability to lie.

"But you knew him?"

"I mean, yeah, he was a regular here," Jessica said. "He used to work at the Luzzi estate. A couple of the guys come here regularly. It's Meg's family, so she gives them discounts sometimes."

"So you're not going to admit to having any sort of relationship with Garrett beyond you serving him food and drinks?"

She rolled her eyes. "That crazy woman got to you, didn't she?"

"Crazy woman?"

"Dominique."

"We did speak to Dominique," I said cautiously. "Why? Did you have an issue with her?"

"She's a creep. She started coming here over the last few weeks. Once in a while she'd come here while Garrett was around and would sit way on the other side of the room in some stupid disguise. Huge sunglasses, a wig, that sort of thing. Eventually she stopped coming when he was around and made her appearances when it was just me. I think she was trying to get up the guts to confront me."

"Did she?"

"Confront me? No. She's a creepy stalker. She never said a word to me. I had to confront her."

Already, Jessica's story was different from Dominique's. I wasn't totally sure who was lying, but my money was on Dominique.

"How did that go?"

"I just walked up to her and told her if she had a problem with me to say it to my face."

"Did she say anything?"

"She told me that she was going to marry Garrett and to stay away from her man."

"Why would she think you had any interest in Garrett beyond a strictly professional setting?"

"I mean, fine, we hooked up a couple times. Then I found out he was dating other people, and I broke things off with him."

"Was he upset when you broke up?"

"Sure." She shrugged. "I was his newest shiny thing. Garrett didn't like being dumped. He liked to date people he could control in some way. I'm not his type."

That was one thing Dominique and Jessica agreed on. "Did you ever mention Dominique's actions to Garrett?"

"Yeah, I talked to him about it. That's how I found out he was dating other people. Her sitting there staring at me like she wanted to eat me for dinner. I asked him what the deal was, and he told me she was nuts."

"Garrett told you Dominique was nuts?"

"It was the truth. It *is* the truth."

"Okay, but if he thought she was nuts, then why did he keep seeing her?"

"Dude. Why do you think? She bankrolled him."

"You knew about the money?"

"Garrett was an idiot. He didn't know how to lie correctly. I could see right through him. Plus, he didn't ever know when to stop running his mouth. He told me half these things himself, and the other half I figured out on my own by reading between the lines."

"You must have been pretty upset to find out that a guy you liked was seeing other women. Not only one other woman, but several."

"It was more of an annoyance than anger." Jessica refilled the garnish tray, plunking olives and cherries into their rightful places. "We'd only been hanging out for a few weeks."

"Obviously you thought things were exclusive," I ventured. "Otherwise you wouldn't have cared if he was seeing other people."

"The dude was more trouble than he was worth. He had a psycho lady following him around printing out wedding invitations. Garrett was never going to marry her. He was just using her for her money."

"This guy sounds like a real gem," Jimmy said. "And he was having a baby with another woman."

Jessica froze. "I didn't know that part, I swear."

"It's true," I confirmed.

"It's not like it matters to me. It's in the past," Jessica said. "Finding out about Dominique was enough to spook me. Guys like Garrett aren't worth the effort. Heck, I was more afraid of Dominique than of Garrett."

"Understandable," Jimmy muttered.

Jessica gave a small smile. "So am I good to go?"

"Can you tell me where you were last Friday night?"

"I think I was working that evening. You'll be able to check the schedule." She glanced between us. "But I'm not stupid enough to think that counts for an airtight alibi. No, I don't think my time here could be accounted for every second of the night. I had to use the restroom I'm sure, and I'm allowed breaks. I know y'all are thinking I could've killed Garrett and dumped him out back and nobody would have noticed."

"Did you?" I asked.

"No," she said. "Good luck trying to prove it. You'll just be wasting your time. If you ask me, Dominique finally got sick of her man mooching off her money and offed him. She was here all the time. She could've ducked out back even easier than me."

"Thanks for your time." I started to stand. "We'll be in touch if we have any additional questions."

"Going so soon?" Meg appeared from behind the bar out of nowhere. "Cops are some of my favorite types of people. Sit yourselves back down and have a drink. Kamikaze? Jell-O shots? Purple Nurple?"

"No, thanks," I said, waving her off. "We're on the clock."

Jimmy looked intrigued by several of the options, but a swift pat on the shoulder shook him back to attention.

"My partner here is just recovering from an illness, so he's not feeling up to alcohol either."

"Aw, nuts," Meg said. "Come back when you're ready for a night of debauchery, yeah? You uptight cops know how to let loose. Know how I know?"

"Nope," I said. "I don't."

"I used to be a cop," she said. "Then someone called me fat, and I sort of overreacted and got myself fired."

I let out a low whistle. "Wow."

"I know, it's a cryin' shame. The police force can always use a good woman like me, but alas, I make more money at this place, and the rules aren't as strict when it comes to flashing my weapon around."

"Uh—"

"You guys should probably go before you have to arrest someone and fill out lots of paperwork," Jessica said. "Your drinks are on me."

I glanced down at the waters that sat untouched and frowned. "Thanks for the generosity. We'll be in touch."

We made our way out to the car and climbed inside. Jimmy looked like he wanted to say something but couldn't quite find the right words. Somehow, I knew exactly what he was thinking.

"It's like everyone on this case has had a sip from some crazy Kool-Aid," Jimmy said, scratching at his head. "I've never been more turned around on motive."

"Trust me," I said. "I feel the exact same way. Let's get back to the precinct and hope Asha has some information on the Mathematician that can point us in the right direction."

"Am I nuts for hoping this Mathematician is a real person?" Jimmy asked. "Somehow it seems more straightforward to deal with a logical killer slash thief than it does to deal with Garrett and his harem."

"My vote's on the Mathematician too," I confirmed. "Speaking of, maybe Asha's got some information on the guys Garrett was supposed to be working with. If anyone has connections to the Mathematician, it would likely be them."

Chapter 11

Once back at the precinct, Asha, Jimmy, and I gathered around a table in the conference room. Asha dialed in our remote employee via the phone in the center of the table and put it on speaker.

"Hi, guys," Chloe chirped from her new place in Washington, D.C. "How's everything going?"

"Pretty good," Jimmy said, "if you don't count the fact that everyone we interview for this case is nuts. And I got poisoned by a mobster's waffles yesterday."

"Do I want to know the details?" Chloe asked. "Because I have to admit my curiosity is piqued."

"You don't want details," I said. "How's the living situation in DC? Are you and Agent Brody getting on one another's nerves yet?"

Chloe let out a high-pitched giggle. "Are you kidding? We can't keep our hands off each other. It's amazing. I've never lived with a guy before, but dang, I didn't know what I was missing."

"Trust me, it's not always like that," Asha muttered. "It's only like that when you've got one of the good ones. Otherwise, it's the most miserable thing ever."

"Let me tell you," Chloe drawled playfully, "he is definitely a *very* good one."

Chloe Marks, my former trainee, had moved out to Washington, D.C., after a whirlwind romance with an FBI agent she'd met on a case here in the Twin Cities. Coincidentally, the only reason Agent Brody had been in town in the first place was because my boyfriend at the time had invited him. We'd since traded spots—Chloe was now happily planning her wedding to a federal agent, while I was spending my holidays in Hawaii with my parents.

Hearing Chloe's happiness had a twofold effect on me. I was beyond pleased for her. She and Agent Maxwell Brody seemed made for one another. There'd been hardly a doubt in Chloe's mind about dropping her life, her career, everything to move across the country. It had been eye opening for me, and in a way, the beginning of the end of my relationship with Russo.

Even though he'd technically been the one to call things off, I hadn't made any huge gestures to try and win him back. I could've done as Chloe had and dropped my career, left behind my family, my home, and everything familiar to me to move across the country and join Jack in Washington, D.C. But I hadn't been able to pull the trigger. Was it because I hadn't loved Jack enough? Or was it because something was wrong with me?

I didn't think it was the former. I knew I had loved Jack Russo fully. I wanted a relationship with him to work. I just couldn't seem to get the logistical part of Kate Rosetti to cooperate with the part that loved Jack. In the end, it'd been too much weight for our relationship to bear, and we'd cracked and broken.

I swallowed, realizing Asha and Jimmy were both staring at me as if waiting for a response. "Sorry, what?"

"Chloe asked how you're doing," Asha said quietly.

"Sorry," I muttered. "I was thinking about the case."

The lie was a half-hearted one that I doubted anyone believed. But I took the opportunity to segue the conversation back to the case anyway.

"What have you guys turned up on the Mathematician?" I asked. "Or Garrett's girlfriends?"

"I'll start," Chloe said. "I've been following up on this girlfriend business, and I admit it's a little confusing. Let's start with Dominique. The woman wasn't lying about the engagement invitations. I hacked into her computer and found the proof copy that she approved last week for the printers. If she doesn't cancel them before tomorrow, she'll be spending a pretty penny on a wedding that's not happening. If it makes any difference, this is the third iteration of invites. The other two dates have already passed."

"Third time's a charm?" Jimmy mused.

"Or it wasn't, and she killed him," Chloe said. "No offense to this woman—I do like a go-getter after all—but this screams desperation. If she sensed that she was losing Garrett for good, her desperation may have grown."

"How'd a woman the size of Dominique get Garrett Landers shoved into the back of an ice cream truck?" Jimmy asked. "Determined or not, there are limits to what a five-foot-two woman can do. Not to mention the fact that Garrett was literally dead weight."

"Still working out the kinks," Chloe said, "but maybe she had help. One of the other girlfriends?"

"It's possible," I said. "Maybe she and Jessica are both telling us lies. Maybe they didn't dislike each other at all and were working together."

"Or maybe they did dislike each other," Chloe suggested. "They just disliked Garrett even more. A hate-fueled partnership sounds very deadly."

"It's a good theory," Asha said. "Now tell them about the money."

"Oh right," Chloe said. "In case you needed more motive from the Dominique angle, I calculated that over the course of her relationship with Garrett, she bankrolled almost fifty thousand dollars for Garrett's business enterprises. And those are only the funds that went to his business ideas. I'm not counting whatever she might've paid for regular expenses. You know, meals, rent, cash, whatever."

"Yikes," Jimmy said again. "That's a lot of motive. Maybe a five-foot-two woman could hoist Garrett into the back of a truck with fifty thousand dollars' worth of motive."

Asha agreed. "I had the same thought. Then there's Ellen, who's in debt."

"Ellen's in debt?" I asked. "With the tattoo parlor? She didn't say anything about that. She made it sound like her business was successful."

Asha nodded. "Chloe picked up on that. Ellen recently re-mortgaged her house and still isn't making ends meet."

"She made everything sound kosher," I said. "She gave us this whole spiel about how she could take care of herself."

"Mark my words, she would've gone after Garrett for child support," Asha said. "Even if she swore up and down she wouldn't, I don't believe it. Chloe found her selling her grandmother's china on some sketchy auction site. Don't ask me if the china was stolen or gifted. Nobody sells their grandmother's heirlooms unless they're desperate."

"If Ellen found out that Garrett wasn't intending to pay anything in terms of child support," I theorized, "that could be motive."

"Let's talk about Marissa," Asha said. "She was going into business with this guy, right?"

"So she said."

"She hasn't applied for a PI license anywhere," Asha said. "She hasn't signed up for any classes, hasn't been Googling about business permits, nothing. If she was planning to legally start a company, I can't find any trace of it."

"It's possible she hadn't gotten started yet," I said. "Or it's possible she's a scammer and was just trying to weasel five grand out of Garrett. A con woman of sorts."

"I think it's very possible," Asha said. "And Garrett was just the sort of sucker to do it."

"Why would Marissa kill Garrett if she was still hoping to get money out of him?" I asked. "She told us the money wasn't due until next week. Unless that was a lie."

"She could've lied about that, or it's possible Garrett found out the truth about the business and called her bluff," Asha said. "It would make me mad to find out I was getting scammed by a potential business partner. Maybe he threatened to tell someone or turn her in, and she killed him to keep him quiet."

"Maybe," I said. "But why would she dump him behind the bar? Does she have any real connection to the place? I think we're missing a piece with Marissa."

"I'll keep digging," Chloe said. "I'll let you know what else I turn up."

"It's a great start," I said. "They all have motive. It's just fitting together the logistics of it all. Then again, I'm not even sure the girlfriends are part of the puzzle. Have you gotten any word on the Mathematician?"

"I've confirmed he exists," Asha said. "Which was a task to complete in and of itself. I had to get clearance through two federal agencies before anyone would talk to me. I even called in a favor from Agent—" Asha stopped and glanced at me, then cleared her throat. "I called in a federal favor to get things moving."

"You can say Russo's name," I said. "We're fine. There's no bad blood between us."

"The feds have had people tracking this guy for three years now. It doesn't seem like that long, but he sort of came onto the scene and made a splash. Big-time theft. He had well-targeted victims—at least, the ones that are documented. That's the beauty of this guy's game. He's so discreet most of his crimes go unnoticed because he chooses victims that rarely want to report their goodies stolen."

"Have you found any patterns to the type of people he targets?" I asked. "Locations, professions, that sort of thing."

"The targets are often rich people who you've never heard of." Asha glanced down at her notes. "I've got files here on all the targets the feds have recorded as being attributed to the Mathematician. None of them are celebrities. All of them have a net worth over ten million dollars. Most of them have their money in odd areas. For example, one of his targets had a very expensive collection of coins that was stolen. Other examples are people with art or jewelry worth tens of thousands of dollars. He once stole a classic car that would've been auctioned off for over a million bucks."

"How does this guy fence items like this?" I asked. "If they're so unique, I'd think that would be more dangerous to unload in the long run."

"That's the thing. Nobody knows," Asha said. "The feds have been scratching their heads about it for years. They haven't recovered a single item from the Mathematician's collection of stolen goods. Pretty impressive, if you ask me."

Jimmy scratched his head. "Are you telling me this guy steals for the fun of it, then stashes all his goodies in some huge barn on some remote piece of property? Where's the reward in that if he's not able to use any of the cash?"

"There are a few options," Asha said. "The FBI has had three different profilers work on the case at various points, and their opinions all differ. Some think this person could be independently wealthy and a genius. Someone who enjoys the thrill of the hunt more than the actual reward."

"Seems like a dumb way to get your rocks off when you could just go skydiving," Jimmy said. "Then again, I guess skydiving doesn't come with the added risk of a lifetime in jail."

"Another way to look at it might just be that this guy has incredible patience and discipline," Asha said. "Even the biggest heists cool off after some time. He's only three years in, which means this guy could just be getting started. If he's young enough, say twenties or thirties, he could be biding his time to unload his stash later."

"That's some patience," Jimmy muttered.

"The one thing all the profilers agree on is that this guy is exacting and calculating. It's the reason he's never been caught, glimpsed, fingerprinted, whatever. That all takes patience. Not to mention, he's well on his way to hitting the five-year mark on some of his first stolen goods. Say he wanted to wait five years, even ten before unloading, he'll be there soon enough. He can start selling things off and immediately be retired for a lifetime. A five-year career that's lucrative enough to live off for the rest of his life?" Asha shrugged. "Not bad. Even I could be patient for that."

"Is there any reason to believe the Mathematician has made his or her way to the Twin Cities?" I asked. "Are there any potential targets the feds were able to list in our area?"

"There's never been a strike here," Asha said. "The last few were scattered far and wide—South Carolina, Arizona, and Washington State. It appears to be completely random, save for the fact he's never struck the same state twice that we know of."

"The targets?"

"The feds are putting together a list of potential targets," Asha said. "Keep in mind, they've never successfully predicted an attack, so I wouldn't hold your breath."

"Are the feds, uh, sending anyone out?" I asked, glancing away from the gazes swiveling in my direction. "You know the FBI. They catch a whiff of a case within their jurisdiction and the game's over for the local law enforcement."

Asha gave me a sympathetic smile. "I'm not sure, sweetie. But Russo's not on the case. He just directed me to the person in charge of it."

"I didn't mean—"

"I think the best thing to do is what we've been doing," Jimmy interrupted, sparing me from having to stumble through an awkward explanation. "We've got Jelly and Pound to interview. They might be our only links to the Mathematician."

"That's if the Mathematician has stuck around," Asha said. "I have a feeling this guy has abandoned more heists than he's completed. It's probably why he's so successful. The second things start to go off the rails, he might ditch town. Garrett's death could point to a botched heist that has the Mathematician scrambling."

"If he's blown town, that doesn't bode well for closing this case," Jimmy said.

"We've still got the issue of four girlfriends," I said. "Even if the Mathematician happens to be in town, Garrett's murder could be unrelated. It doesn't seem like it's his style if he's so careful. Have there been any other deaths associated with the Mathematician's thefts?"

Asha shook her head. "Nothing confirmed. The feds say they've got one or two open murder cases that have the Mathematician's fingerprints all over it in theory. But they were in areas the Mathematician never ended up striking a target."

"You think something went belly up, he killed someone, and got out of Dodge?"

"That's exactly what I'm saying." Asha nodded. "It's possible that's what this is here too. I think we might have to stomach the possibility that this murder will be turned over to the feds if there's enough to tie it to the Mathematician."

"There's not enough to tie it to him," I said. "We're just finding out he exists. A rumor from a mobster isn't exactly evidence."

"We'll keep looking," Jimmy reassured me. "We'll run any and all leads into the ground. We'll deal with anything else as it comes up."

"Fair enough," I said. "Jimmy, you ready to hit the road?"

Jimmy groaned. "Two more interviews, then I'm calling it a night. My head hurts with all these lies. And I wasn't even out late sipping expensive ice wine last night."

I deftly ignored Jimmy and stood. I glanced at Asha. "Let me know if you hear anything else from the FBI. If they have a good list of targets, it might be worth it to add a little surveillance if we can get some extra bodies."

"You got it," Asha said. "So was it worth it?"

"Worth what?"

"The headache?" Asha winked. "From the ice wine."

"I'm confused about this ice wine," Chloe piped up from the phone. "Who was drinking ice wine?"

"Forget it," I said. "It's not important."

"Well, while you're all on the line," Chloe said, "I might as well throw this out. All that talk about Dominique and her wedding dates has me too excited to keep it a secret anymore. Maxwell and I have set a wedding date, and you're all invited."

A little cheer of congratulations went up from around the conference room.

"When's the big day?" Asha finally asked. "I've got to block it off on my social calendar sooner rather than later. Plus, I've gotta find a date."

"Your Save the Dates are in the mail or will be soon. I'm not going to spoil the surprise," Chloe said coyly. "Let me just say you shouldn't make too many plans for spring."

"Spring," I echoed. "That's a little broad."

"Like you have any plans besides work," Jimmy said. "Then again, I suppose we'll have to plan it out a little in advance seeing as half the crime-solving unit in the Twin Cities will be gone at once."

"Surprise! It's going to be a destination wedding. To the Twin Cities," Chloe said. "All my family is there, plus you guys, plus my friends. I figure it's the least Maxwell can do for me if I'm giving up my life to live in DC with him forever. His family and friends can travel and experience spring in the cities. By the way, you all get plus ones. Detective Rosetti, will you be bringing someone?"

I cleared my throat pointedly. "I find it a little bit preemptive to be worrying about a date when I haven't received an official invite."

"Well, you're welcome to bring a date," Chloe said. "I'm really excited to see you all again."

"We see you three times a week via video," I said. "We're not exactly strangers."

"It's not the same. You guys are required to give me hugs since I'm the bride and it's my day."

"Let me know if you need help planning the bachelorette party," Asha said. "That's sort of my area of expertise."

"That would be lovely," Chloe said. "I was thinking maybe Vegas—"

"Leave it to me," Asha said. "Okay, everyone got what they need for next steps?"

"Got it," I said, pushing back my chair to stand. "Keep us posted when you turn up something else."

Asha hung up the phone, then let Jimmy leave the room first. She grabbed my arm and held me back a moment until we were alone in the conference room.

"How are you feeling?" she asked me.

"Fine," I said. "I wasn't hungover. Just tired."

"I'm not talking about your date last night," Asha said. "I'm talking about the wedding invites."

"Why would I be bothered by that?"

"A wedding in which your ex-boyfriend's best friend is getting married?" Asha stared at me until it clicked. "You know Russo's going to be there. Are you ready to see him again?"

"Sure." I shrugged. "We're not together. We still have mutual friends. It's no big deal."

"Are you prepared for the fact that he might be the best man? And he might be bringing a plus one?"

"Like I said, we're not together. I have no control over what he does or doesn't do. I wouldn't be surprised if he were dating again."

Even as the words left my mouth, I knew deep down that wasn't entirely true. It had never actually crossed my mind that Jack might've resumed dating. Dating hadn't been on my mind at all, at least not until my odd extravaganza with Gem last night. Now the thought hit me like a sack of bricks. Imagining Russo with his arm around another woman—or worse—set my stomach to plummeting.

"Right," Asha said, watching my expression. "You didn't even think about it."

"I'm just focused on Chloe," I lied. "I'm happy that she's happy. I wouldn't dream of raining on her parade with drama around Jack. Not to mention, there's no reason for drama. We're both mature adults. We can handle ourselves around one another."

"I'm not talking about drama." Asha reached out and squeezed my shoulder. "I just asked if you were feeling okay about seeing him again."

I wrinkled my nose. "I've got some time to think about it. In the meantime, I've got two guys named Jelly and Pound waiting for me."

She wrinkled her nose back. "Enjoy."

Chapter 12

"Are we starting with brains or brawn?" I asked Jimmy as we made our way to the car. "And are you driving, or am I?"

"You drive, and let's start with the muscle. Hopefully he won't know any better and will give us some ammunition to use in our visit with Henry Dunwoody."

"Works for me," I said, beeping my car open. "I can't believe Chloe's getting married this spring. That'll mean she and Agent Brody won't have known each other for a full year before tying the knot."

"When you know, you know," Jimmy said, sliding into his seat. "At least, that's what they say."

"What about you?" I asked. "Did you know?"

"I think so. But in the dumb way guys know. Not in the way girls know."

"What do you mean?"

"My wife and I were friends first. It took me a long time to realize I actually liked her. Then as soon as she started dating someone else, I realized I was in love with her. Like I said, I was stupid."

"So did you wait for your wife to break up with this guy or what?"

Jimmy glanced out the window as we cruised down the street. "I told her how I felt when she started dating him. Nothing happened, I just figured I wanted to let her know how I felt before she took any serious steps. I wanted her to have all the information."

"How'd she react?"

"She slapped me." Jimmy glanced at my shocked expression. "She told me I was dumb. She said she'd been waiting two years for me to ask her out, and she was annoyed it took me until she went on a date with someone else."

"Sounds fair to me."

"Hey, I agreed," Jimmy said. "Especially knowing how it all ended."

"Well? How did it end?"

"She dated the other guy for six months," Jimmy said. "I didn't say another word to her about my feelings during that time. The day they broke up, I proposed."

"No, you didn't."

"I wasn't going to let her get away again. She said yes. It was like we'd both known the whole time. It just took us a while to realize it."

"That gives me an odd sense of hope," I said. "Seeing as I can't see myself falling in love at first sight. I just don't think I'm someone who works like that. The thought of moving across the country for someone I've known for just a few months gives me hives. I won't tell you how I feel about the thought of getting married."

"You loved Russo."

I gave Jimmy the side-eye. "You didn't ask that like a question, so I'm going to assume you know the answer is yes."

"I'm just stating the obvious," Jimmy said. "I also told you my story to give you hope. I'm glad you figured that much out."

"How is that hope?" I asked. "My story's different than yours. Russo and I already tried and failed. You and your wife just took a little longer to figure out you liked each other. I *know* I like Russo. I just don't know how to work out the rest of it."

"Sometimes it takes something big to shock you into understanding what you really want. For me, it was the other guy stealing the woman I'd just realized I loved. For you, maybe it's something else. Maybe it hasn't happened yet."

"That's the thing, Jimmy," I said, trying not to sound annoyed, "I know I like him. I don't need to see Russo dating another woman to know that. It doesn't solve anything."

"You'd be surprised," Jimmy said faintly. "I'm not saying you need to do anything. I don't want you to have to go through what I was going through, watching the woman I wanted to marry date someone else. It was the worst time in my life. I thought I'd missed my true chance at happiness. I'm just giving you my two cents."

"Two cents taken. Thank you," I added grudgingly. "For what it's worth, I'm glad you and your wife were able to make things happen. Obviously it was the right choice, seeing as the two of you are still happily married."

"It wasn't a choice," Jimmy said. "It was just a thing I knew I had to do. A feeling. Fate, if you believe in that."

"I don't know that I believe in fate."

"You just might someday."

"This is getting a little too philosophical for my taste. I do better with hard facts. You forget, I'm a cold-hearted detective, Jones."

Jimmy winked. "You make it hard to forget."

I laughed and pulled the car over as we reached the address Asha had given me. I double-checked we were in the right spot. Then I parked in the parking lot.

"He lives in a motel?" Jimmy asked. "Interesting."

"According to Asha's notes, it's a new move," I said. "He's been here a couple of weeks."

"Coincidence this lifestyle change happened around the same time he gave up his job for the Luzzi family?"

"I'm guessing not." I made my way around the car. "Keep your guard up. He might be armed, and he might not have much to lose. If he's not expecting a visit from us, we could spook him."

"I'm not running anywhere, I'll tell you that much. If he decides to shoot at me, I'm a goner."

"Just pay attention," I said dryly, "and I'll do the rest."

"You got it, partner."

I knocked on a door that had a rusted number 8 hanging on the outside. The curtains were drawn. Only one or two other cars were in the grimy parking lot. The motel sign flickered on and off, announcing room rates for five dollars a night, which I was pretty sure was a typo. A few of the neon lights looked to be burned out.

The door opened to reveal a man wearing an oversized bathrobe and a pair of boxers with little Valentine's Day hearts on them. He scratched at a hairy chest, his knuckles bumping into a thick gold chain that hung around his neck.

"What's up?" he said gruffly.

"Are you Ricky Navarro?" I asked.

"Who's asking? You or the dude?" Ricky gave me a little smile. "Because I'll invite you in if you agree to take off a few layers."

"Funny," I said. "I'm Detective Kate Rosetti, and this is my partner, Detective Jones. We're here investigating a murder."

"Rats," Ricky said, continuing to give me that leering sort of smile. "I was hoping you was just dressed up like a cop. I was hoping maybe you was an exotic dancer or something. My birthday was last week, you know."

"I'm not dressed like a cop," I said, glancing down at my slacks and shirt. "I'm in regular clothes."

"She looks like a cop," Ricky said to Jimmy. "I hope you don't try to send that one undercover. Anyone who's ever been in trouble with the law would smell her coming from a mile away."

"You do have a little bit of a cop vibe," Jimmy agreed reluctantly. "Sorry, Rosetti."

"I think it's the smile," Ricky said. "Or lack of one. All business and no play makes Cop Barbie a very dull lady."

"I'm not all business," I said, "and I'm not a Barbie Cop. We're here about a known associate of yours. A guy by the name of Garrett Landers."

"He did it," Ricky said. "I don't know what it is, but he did it. Thanks for swinging by. If you want to use me as an eyewitness, I'd be happy to. Just tell me what I saw and when I saw it. Free of charge on account of you're a really pretty cop."

I groaned. "Can we come in for a minute?"

"Sure," he said. "But I want a lawyer."

"You really don't," I coaxed. "We don't even think you did anything wrong."

"I told Pound that we should never have left our jobs." Ricky stepped back from the door to let us into the motel. He plopped on the bed and watched us come in. "We were onto something real nice at the Luzzi estate. Then Garrett screwed us over. Put him away for life if you can."

"You were onto a good thing?" I asked. "What do you mean?"

"Talk about a cushy job," Ricky said. "The Luzzi family paid well. We mostly walked around their expensive property and sometimes got sent home with leftovers from Mrs. Luzzi's cooking. You could actually eat the leftovers about half the time."

"Why'd you give it up?"

"Garrett promised me and Pound that we'd be able to retire off the funds we'd get from his next job. I mean, how good of an offer is that?"

"One that sounded too good to pass up," Jimmy said soothingly, easing into the role of buddy-buddy cop. "Heck, I'd give up my job for a gig that paid like that."

"Right?" Ricky seemed oblivious to the fact that Jimmy was just telling him what he wanted to hear. "I'd have been an idiot to say no."

"A lot of times, things that sound too good to be true really are," I said. "Did that cross your mind?"

"Don't talk to me like I'm stupid, lady," Ricky said. "I'm not. I did my research. My homework. So did Pound, and he doesn't make any stupid decisions."

I kept to myself the fact that Henry Dunwoody had also quit a cushy job at the Luzzi estate for the promise of something that hadn't paid off. Possibly a very stupid decision that had resulted in a friend of his getting murdered.

"What sort of job was it?" I pressed. "It obviously fell through."

"You think?" Ricky snorted. "Look at me. I had to give up the nice apartment I was leasing behind the trailer park because I couldn't afford it. Now I live in this dump because I'm unemployed and got no money. I was promised ten grand up front and fifty when the job was done."

"That's a lot of money," I agreed. I personally wouldn't have said it was enough to retire with, but then again, maybe my standard of living was too high what with my free lattes from my mother's shop and the TJ Maxx outfits I'd had since high school. "Did you see any of it?"

"I just told you, I wouldn't be here if I'd seen any of the money. Garrett disappeared first. I think he wanted all the cash for himself."

"Why'd he hire you on?" I asked. "I mean, what was the job description?"

"I didn't know yet."

"I thought you just said you did your homework."

"I did do my homework," he said. "Garrett took us out to this place to show us some goodies."

"Goodies?"

"Apparently the person we were going to be working for was a real professional. This dude had a barn full of stuff he'd stolen. Garrett took us there to prove they were legitimate."

"A legitimate thief, you mean."

"Lady, you don't get paid fifty grand for an honest day's work. And I can tell you that with a clear conscience now because I didn't do any of the work nor did I take any money, so you don't got any proof I was even gonna do it."

My head was spinning with Ricky's faulty logic, but I was more than a little intrigued by the promise of nearby goodies. If that were true, and if these goodies belonged to the Mathematician, this could be the first real break in the case we had linking the notorious thief to our dead body.

"We're going to need the location of these goodies," I said. "You understand."

"I hear you loud and clear, but that ain't happening."

"Then you won't mind getting charged with obstruction of justice."

Ricky rolled his eyes. "I mean, I *can't* tell you where it is. I wasn't conscious during the drive there. Or back."

"What'd they do to you?" I asked. "Were you blindfolded?"

"On the way there, they just got me drunker than a skunk. I passed out. When I woke up, I was locked in a truck. A little while later, the trunk opened, and we were standing before a literal treasure chest full of expensive stuff."

"And on the way back?"

Ricky reached up and rubbed the back of his head. "They clocked me over the head to knock me out."

"Nice friends."

"I wasn't even mad," Ricky said. "Not after the stuff I saw."

"What did you see?"

"I can't even remember it all. A couple of vintage cars that Pound told me were worth a couple of hundred grand each. Some crappy old art that I guess would sell for a pretty penny to the fancy folks. Lots of shiny jewelry. Some actual blocks of gold. Can you believe it? Gold blocks. Felt like I was on the set of *The Italian Job* or something. All I needed were some Venice canals and a sexy sidekick."

Ricky eyed me as if I might be interested in the sidekick gig. I shook my head. He sighed.

"Then what?"

"I woke up outside of my apartment with a headache. You can still feel the bump if you want. You wanna?"

It looked like Ricky hadn't showered in a few days, and I had no interest in touching his greasy hair. I shook my head again. Ricky sighed again.

"Then I never heard from Garrett again. The idiot left town. I don't know if he got spooked or if he was trying to screw us over, but I wasn't standing for it."

"Of course not," Jimmy said, jumping back into the conversation to sooth Ricky once more. "You would've wanted to confront him. After all, you'd given up your livelihood for this guy."

"Exactly! So I went to his house. Nobody there. Called his phone. Nothin'. I asked Pound about it, and he told me to just back off and cut my losses."

"That couldn't have made you happy," I said. "Do you think Pound knows what happened to him?"

Ricky shrugged. "Pound's a good guy. I trust him. If he says the jig's up, then I believe him. I didn't ask why. Doesn't really matter to me in the end since it doesn't change the outcome. Doesn't change the fact I'm gonna strangle that idiot when I see him next."

I glanced at Jimmy. "Garrett Landers is dead."

Ricky blinked at me. "Huh?"

"We're here investigating Garrett's death," I said. "His body was found in the back of an ice cream truck."

Ricky leaned back and burst into laughter. He laughed and laughed until tears leaked from his eyes. His cheeks turned a vibrant shade of red that didn't do his oily complexion any favors.

"And now you're trying to find out who killed him?" Ricky pointed between me and Jimmy. When I nodded, he grinned again. "Do me a favor and send them a thank-you card before you send 'em off to prison. In fact, you should probably write this one off as a Good Samaritan act. Garrett Landers was a fool and a thief and an all-around slimy dude. Whoever offed him did the world a favor."

"You really disliked him."

"I guess I'm just lucky someone beat me to the punch," Ricky said. "Now I don't have to risk the jail time for strangling the guy."

"Can you think of anyone else who might want him dead?"

"I think the list would be shorter to name who didn't want him dead," Ricky said. "I don't know any specifics. I'm just saying that the guy couldn't walk down the street without making an enemy. Just the sort of guy he was. He could come off decent at the start, but it never lasted long. I doubt anyone that really knew him would be sad about his death."

"What about his personal life? Girlfriend?"

"I don't think he was crazy about anyone, but what do I know?" Ricky mused. "I know he was seeing a few girls. I don't think it was anything serious."

I considered an impending wedding engagement with one woman and a baby due with another to be very serious things, but then again, most of the logic in this case wasn't making a ton of sense to me.

"What about Henry Dunwoody?" I asked. "Could he have killed him?"

"Could he? Sure. He could kill just about anyone. Guy's a great shot. He's cool as a cucumber under pressure."

"Do you think he did?" I asked. "Would he have been mad enough over the loss of income to murder him?"

"You ask me that like I'd tell you. I like Pound. I'm not snitching on him."

"Obstruction of justice," I reminded him. "I'd hate to have to take you to the station. I'm sure we could find some outstanding charges to hold you on."

Ricky heaved a sigh. "You said he was shoved in the back of an ice cream truck?"

I nodded.

"Then Pound didn't kill him," Ricky said with certainty. "If Henry Dunwoody killed Garrett, it would've been, like, a fancy sort of death. You know, a bullet to the head from a mile away. He wouldn't have gotten his hands messy dumping a body anywhere."

"Okay," I said. "Well, thanks for your help. What about the person you were supposed to be working for? Might they have killed Garrett?"

"Sure. Possibly. Maybe even probably," Ricky said. "But I've got no idea who that person is. I never got a name, never saw any money, never spoke to them—nothing."

"Before we finish up, we'll need a few more details about the items you saw during your little field trip and the location where you saw them."

Ricky spent the next ten minutes regaling me with tales of the treasure he'd found. I jotted down the color, make, and model of several vehicles. His attempts to remember the artwork were lukewarm at best. His descriptions of jewelry were a little more accurate.

"The location?" I asked. "Was it hot or cold inside?"

"It's Minnesota in January," Ricky said. "It was chilly. It honestly looked like a huge barn. A showroom. I do think there was some temperature control, but there was definitely a draftiness to the place."

"Do you have any idea how long you traveled to get there? Did you see outside?"

"Nope. We drove straight into the barn; they unloaded me from the trunk, gave me a peek, and then conked me over the head. No clue about the rest of it. Still got that bump if you're hankering to cop a feel."

"I'll trust you on it," I said. "What's next for you?"

"Honestly?" He gave me a sly glance. "I'm sort of fancying myself a treasure hunter right now."

"Is that right?"

"Darn right. I figure there's over a million dollars in loot easy in that barn," Ricky said. "If I can find it again and make it mine, I'll be set for life."

"Your big plan is to steal from a master thief?" I looked at him skeptically.

"Yep." He puffed out his chest a bit. "The guy's never gonna see it coming. Plus, it's not illegal seeing as I'm pretty sure he stole it all himself."

"It is still illegal."

"Dude, you need to refresh yourself on the law," Ricky chastised me. "That just ain't true."

"Okay, well, as a token of my appreciation for your co-operation, I'm going to forget you told me that for now." I stood. "If you think of anything else, give us a call, will you?"

"Does that mean you're going to finally give me your number?" Ricky waggled his eyebrows. "I see the way you've been looking at me. It's all right, sweetheart. I can play this song and dance all day long."

"Jimmy, give him your card," I said with a nod of my head in his direction. "Give us a call. We're partners."

Ricky looked annoyed. "Playing hard to get. Fine. I didn't like you much anyway. Hey, do me a favor though."

"What's that?" I asked, more nervous than I wanted to admit about this incoming request from a guy called Jelly.

"I wasn't joking about the thank-you card," Ricky said with another grin. "I mean it. You give the son of a gun who killed Garrett Landers a pat on the back for me."

Chapter 13

"I slipped Ricky Navarro your card," Jimmy said as we returned to my car. "I hope you don't mind. I figured he had the hots for you. With Chloe's wedding coming up and all, I thought you might be hankering for a date."

"You didn't!" I whirled on Jimmy. "Tell me you're joking. The only thing worse than showing up single at Chloe's wedding would be to show up with a guy named Jelly."

Jimmy was grinning ear to ear by the time I calmed down.

"Yeah, I'm kidding," he said. "The guy's a piece of work. In a way, I have a feeling we're not going to get much out of Henry Dunwoody. If Henry's half as smart as these guys are saying he is."

"Fair enough." I glanced at the address for Henry Dunwoody's place and set my GPS. As I started driving, I looked over at Jimmy. "Do you think he was telling the truth about the treasure?"

"I don't think Jelly's got a creative bone in his body. I think he was telling us exactly how things went down."

"Agreed. If that's true, then he seemed genuinely surprised that Garrett Landers was dead."

"I take that to mean one of two things," Jimmy mused. "Either Garrett's death had nothing to do with the Mathematician, and one of the girlfriends got jealous and put an end to Garrett's philandering ways, or someone further down the line in the Mathematician's chain took out Garrett and didn't bother to tell Ricky,"

"It could've been Henry Dunwoody or the Mathematician himself," I said.

"Seems like Henry and Ricky were sort of partners though, in a way," Jimmy said. "I'd think they would talk. Especially if they were part of a business deal together going bad."

"While I agree that's likely true, I think we need to entertain the idea that Henry might actually be more intelligent than Garrett and Ricky. If that's the case, he'd be smart enough to *not* admit to murdering a guy to Ricky Navarro. I mean, partners don't tell each other every single thing, right? I'm sure there are a few things it's better that your wife doesn't know."

"Not true at all," Jimmy said with an exaggerated cough. "I'm always honest with my wife."

"Then why do you make us take my car whenever you have a hankering for fried chicken?" I raised my eyebrows at him. "It couldn't be because she can smell it on your upholstery and gets upset with you for disobeying the doc's orders?"

"I'd like a lawyer," Jimmy muttered.

We drove the rest of the way to Henry Dunwoody's place in easy silence. I parked on the street, noting this place was vastly different than the dump of a motel where Ricky was currently shacking up.

"I guess Henry's a little better at investing his money," Jimmy said with a low whistle. "This place is nice."

"The guy was employed by the Luzzi family and was almost hired for a job with the Mathematician," I said. "I guess he's doing okay for himself. And somehow, I doubt he's paid half as much in taxes as I have."

Jimmy gave a snort of agreement. We headed up the front lawn of a newer house on one of St. Paul's pretty, tree-lined streets. Most of the homes in this area were older, full of character and creaking front porches. Henry's was the exception to the rule.

His house looked to be a perfectly shaped box. Large front windows were covered by breezy curtains. The front lawn was minimally landscaped but neat and orderly. Porch chairs were stacked neatly in one corner to avoid the snow. There was nothing in the way of outward decoration lingering from the holidays.

I knocked. It took a second attempt before the morbidly oversized front door eased open. A neatly groomed man stood in the entrance. Behind him, a highly modern and highly minimal home was visible. I suspected even the forensics team would have a hard time finding so much as a hair on the pristine furniture.

"Hello," the man said in a soft-spoken voice. "May I help you?"

"Henry Dunwoody?" I asked. "Also known as Pound?"

He gave a thin smile. The man looked like Captain America with his tall stature, neatly combed hair, perfectly fitting jeans, and long-sleeved Henley shirt. "Please, it's Henry."

I was finding it difficult to believe that a man like Henry kept company with a man like Ricky Navarro. I found it even more difficult to believe they worked together. This case was full of surprises.

I introduced myself and Jimmy as detectives investigating a homicide. Before I could ask, Henry invited us inside.

"Can I get you something to drink?" he asked. "I've got a Nespresso machine warmed up. Cold water in the fridge. A craft beer, if that's your thing."

"No, thank you," I said. "We're fine. We appreciate the hospitality, but we won't take up much of your time. We're just here to ask a few questions."

Henry showed us into the living room. There were two white couches sitting across from one another with a black coffee table in between. On the table were two extremely tall, thin taper candles in twisted black holders. An untouched book on architecture in the Twin Cities sat next to it. There was no sign of a television anywhere in the room. The only personal effect at all seemed to be the grand piano perched before the front windows.

"Thanks again for seeing us today." I started off the conversation with a look at Henry. "We're investigating the murder of Garrett Landers."

Henry just nodded.

"We've recently learned that you were colleagues with him at the Luzzi estate."

Henry watched me carefully.

"Is that true?" I prompted.

"Yes, it is."

"Did you know him well?"

"No. As you said, he was a colleague. A newer one at that. We'd only been working together a year or so when he left the company."

"You left the company as well, no?"

"Shortly after he did."

"Was it related?"

"Not particularly."

"We know you also left at the same time as your buddy who calls himself Jelly," I said. "Are you telling me that the three of you leaving at the same time was a coincidence?"

"Things happen in waves of three," Henry said cryptically. "Often when one person is unhappy at a job, it's for a reason, and other people feel it too."

"Look, I'm going to be honest with you," I said. "I don't see how you and a guy like Jelly get along, but I've got it from multiple sources that you do, so I'm just going to run with it. My partner and I just came from a nice little chat with Ricky Navarro. He was plenty upset with Garrett Landers. So upset, in fact, that he didn't mind sharing some of the details with us. Including the fact that Garrett had poached you away from the Luzzi company with the promise of a job that was too good to be true."

"Things that are too good to be true often are."

"I agree. Which is why I'm surprised Garrett's promise worked on you. You seem like an intelligent, organized, successful man. Why would a man like you give up a cushy job to work with two goons like Garrett and Ricky?"

Henry didn't say a word.

"That makes me think you did your own homework," I said, using Ricky's exact words. "And something Garrett said proved to you that this job wasn't just a promise full of hot air."

"Interesting theory."

"Even more interesting since Ricky told us exactly what the Mathematician showed to you, Garrett, and him as proof. As Ricky called it, the stolen treasure."

I watched Henry for a reaction, but he didn't give us one. Zero. The guy was harder to read than a brick wall.

"The way I figure is maybe things went south, and you got upset with Garrett and killed him. Smartly, you didn't tell your buddy Jelly."

"I imagine if you had any evidence, you would've come bearing handcuffs."

"I'm just asking for a little cooperation," I said. "The feds have been looking into the Mathematician for years. I know people there. I can get them to cut you a deal. They'll go easy on you if you can provide some information that helps them catch the bigger fish."

"If that's all," Henry said, standing, "then I'd like my lawyer. Have a lovely day, Detectives. Can I walk you out?"

It was the most clinical dismissal I'd ever gotten from a suspect before. I'd say it was cold, but that would imply there was actual emotion, actual feeling behind it. There was something in the way that Henry spoke, very matter of fact, that was even more chilling than outward malice.

"It's not necessary for you to have a lawyer here yet," I said. "We're not accusing you of anything. We're just trying to talk."

"Then you may speak with my lawyer." Henry smiled. "I'll look forward to speaking with you again once my attorney is present."

Jimmy cursed under his breath once we were let out of Henry's house.

"That was the politest and also harshest dismissal I've ever had," Jimmy said, echoing the same thought I'd had minutes before. "That guy is—how did Ricky put it—cool as a cucumber."

"Tell me about it." I unlocked the car and we hopped in. I glanced over through Jimmy's window and caught a glimpse of the front curtain twitching closed as if Henry had been watching to make sure we actually left. "He gives me the creeps."

"His house is almost clinically clean," Jimmy said. "It's weird. The dude's not married, so it's supposed to be more of a bachelor pad. I don't think there's a fingerprint we could lift from a single surface in there."

"That's exactly what I thought," I said, pulling away from the curb. As I drove, I tapped my fingernails against the steering wheel in thought. "Do you think Henry could be it?"

"It?"

"The Mathematician," I said. "If we put the profiles together that those three feds prepared, the overlap in the Venn diagram seems to match with Henry."

"You mean the fact that he seems to be cold and calculating and meticulous? Yeah, I'd agree just based on the fact that he's a single guy with white couches that don't have a single stain on them. No TV anywhere in the place. I'm already convinced he's a psychopath. What sort of guy doesn't kick their feet up once in a while to watch a game with some hot wings? You can't eat hot wings on a white couch."

I gave a good-natured eye roll, but I agreed with Jimmy's overarching point. "It's possible he doesn't spend much of his time in this place. It could just be a base of operations for him. It would explain why it looks like he's living in a staged house if he's just passing through town."

"It's an expensive property for someone who doesn't live here full time."

"We're talking about a thief who steals millions of dollars."

"He's only been doing it a few years," Jimmy countered, "and there haven't been reports of him fencing off the items he's stolen."

"Nothing that's been reported. It's entirely possible he's been grabbing stacks of cash, gold, you name it on his heists that were never reported. According to the reports, he targets people who don't always mention their items missing. If that's the case, we might not have even uncovered the tip of the iceberg for how much this guy's stashed away."

Jimmy nodded his head in agreement. "So, what? This guy's got a couple of houses across the United States?"

"I wouldn't put it past him. It's also possible that this is simply his main home base for the moment, and he rents out hotels or Airbnbs or whatever when he travels. I'm sure he's got a stack of aliases as long as my arm. He's never been sighted, never identified. The feds don't have a single working alias for this guy. It's why they call him the Mathematician. They don't know what else to call him."

"That could line up with what Ricky Navarro told us," Jimmy said. "He might want a more permanent home base in the same state where he stashes his loot. If Ricky's report on what he saw is true, that means at least some of the Mathematician's treasure is somewhat local. He'd want to keep an eye on it, I'd imagine."

I tapped my fingers against the steering wheel again. I thought some more. Then I dialed Asha and explained our theory to her.

"The main issue I can think of is his history," I said when I wrapped up telling her about our interview with Henry and my feelings on him potentially being the Mathematician. "By history, I just mean that he seems to have one. If Henry were really an alias, would he have this much backstory in the Twin Cities?"

"How do you mean?" Asha asked.

"I just mean that we've heard it from a few sources that he's worked with Ricky Navarro a few times. Ricky mentioned it too. Sort of insinuated they were friends. Or at least a little more than any old acquaintances or colleagues."

"I see," she said. "Maybe Henry Dunwoody is his real name, and you've stumbled across his real identity?"

"It's possible. I just had my doubts that someone as careful as the Mathematician would ever voluntarily be exposing their real identity if they could at all help it."

"I admit I haven't looked into Dunwoody in depth yet, but I'm on it."

"Why would he go around getting hired for odd jobs if he was actually the Mathematician?" I continued. "We're talking about a guy who's supposedly got loads already stolen and could probably just steal more if he needed. Why work at all?"

"Why does anyone work?" Asha asked. "Any rich guys, I mean. Because they like it? They're bored? They need the human interaction?"

"That's why he'd be doing his big jobs. These little jobs don't make sense."

"He could be feeling out prospective targets," Jimmy said, raising a finger as if a light bulb had clicked on in his head. "Think about it. The types of jobs that Ricky Navarro's working aren't exactly boring accountant jobs. He's working security for sketchy types. The very sorts of people that probably have lots of cash."

"And the very sorts of people who wouldn't be likely to report it missing," I said. "The chances of Carlos Luzzi going to the cops if something went missing are slim to none. We've already established that."

"I know that Anthony Luzzi said the only person who would be able to successfully steal from Carlos was himself, but I'm starting to wonder if that might not be true," Jimmy said. "This Mathematician is untouchable so far. I don't know if the Luzzis have ever been challenged by someone so intelligent. They're dealing with mobster types and thugs. Not high-end art thieves."

"It's possible," I said. "Or it's possible that Henry took the job at the Luzzi estate to feel out the potential haul that could be garnered from a hit on the family. Maybe he weighed all the risks and calculated it was too dangerous."

"So when Garrett proposed a new gig, it made sense for Henry to throw in the towel at the Luzzi estate and cut his losses," Jimmy continued. "That way, he'd have been spared having to come up with a real excuse to quit. It covers his tracks. He can blame it on Garrett Landers if asked."

"Like I said, I'll look into his history," Asha said. "If we assume for a minute that Henry's our mastermind, that means you two have either stumbled across his real identity, or Henry Dunwoody is a carefully crafted alias that comes with more history than a simple fake passport."

"Let us know what you find," I said. "I'm going to get some surveillance set up on Henry in case we've spooked him."

"A guy like Henry doesn't spook," Jimmy said. "I think he proved that today."

"That's why we need surveillance. I'm not sure what his next move would be, but I think he might consider heading for the hills by dark."

I hung up with Asha, then made a quick call requesting surveillance at Henry's address. A squad car was sent over and would be reporting any of Henry's movements to me throughout the night.

"Speaking of overnight," Jimmy said, "let's call it a day."

"I agree," I said. "I don't think we're getting anywhere else tonight. If Henry's the Mathematician, we've got people watching his every move."

"And if it turns out one of the girlfriends murdered him, then there's less of a rush," Jimmy said. "I don't think they're going to run around killing other people. We can pick it up in the morning and go from there. I'm exhausted trying to keep up with all these liars."

I dropped Jimmy back at the precinct and bid him goodbye. Then I headed for home where I hopped in the shower and changed straight into pajamas. I helped myself to some leftover curly fries.

Sometime around midnight, I woke up on the couch with a french fry still clutched loosely in my hand. I'd been so tired from my night of little sleep the day before that I'd passed out mid-dinner. It took me a few disoriented seconds to realize that the reason I'd woken up at all was because my sister had arrived home.

"There you are," Jane said, then she paused as she entered the room. "Did I interrupt something?"

"Sleep sort of interrupted my dinner." I stretched. "Long day."

"Long night, you mean. How'd it go with Gem?"

"Fine. We're just friends."

Jane raised her eyebrows. "I didn't ask."

"No, but you have that nosy look in your eyes, so I thought I'd ward off the questions before they got started."

She raised both her hands. "Okay, then. It's a sensitive subject. I get it."

"It's not sensitive. I've just been quizzed already about four times today, and I have run out of explanations. Sorry."

"No need to apologize. You should get to bed. You look like you're ready to pass out before you can finish that fry."

"I think I will."

"Before you go, you should know that we need to get started wedding planning soon," Jane said. "I want to get a dress by spring. Autumn is coming fast, you know."

"So many weddings," I grumbled. When Jane gave me a confused look, I explained about Chloe. "Her wedding's going to be local here."

"That's good?" She watched me carefully. Then it hit her, and she gave a knowing nod. "Jack's going to be there."

"It's coming soon. This spring. Not even a full year after they met."

"Are you nervous to see Jack?"

"I don't know," I admitted. "I didn't think so. I *don't* think so. But maybe. What if he brings someone?"

"Kate, I'm so sorry, sweetie, but you do have to accept that might be a possibility." Jane came over and slid onto the couch next to me. "That's what happens when people break up. They move on and date other people. I know it'll be hard if that happens, but you broke up with Jack for a reason."

"Did I?" I asked. "I think he broke up with me technical-ly."

"Technically."

"What's that supposed to mean?"

Jane squeezed my leg. "You don't think you could've stopped it if you really wanted to? You didn't ask him to stay, did you? You didn't offer to consider moving in with him?"

"I wasn't thinking about moving anywhere. I mean, I thought about it, but I decided against it. For the time being, at least."

"I'm just saying, it was sort of a mutual thing. On the flip side, I bet Jack's even more nervous to see you."

"Jack Russo? No way."

"Honey, he cared about you a lot. I mean *a lot*. That doesn't just go away overnight, especially since nothing was particularly wrong with your relationship except for distance and some fear of commitment."

"If Jack still cared about me that much, he'd have tried to reach out," I said. "I think our breakup was for the best. It just stings, and it'll sting worse to see him, especially if he's with another woman, but that's to be expected."

"That's how you know it was a good one. If it wasn't a good relationship, it wouldn't hurt so much."

I sighed. "I wish that made it better. I'm going to bed."

"You could ask someone to go with you."

"Huh?" I turned around at the doorway and glanced at Jane, who was still sitting on the couch. "Go where?"

"As a plus one to the wedding."

"I don't have anyone to ask."

She raised her eyebrows.

"I told you, Gem's just a friend. I made that clear to him. Neither of us are ready for a relationship."

"Did the invitation say your plus one had to be your be-trothed?" Jane flashed a sardonic smile. "No? Then it would be safe to ask Gem as a friend to accompany you. For moral support."

"I'm afraid it would send the wrong message to Russo."

"Uh-huh."

"What's that supposed to mean?"

"You'll have been broken up with Jack for months by the time the wedding rolls around. You're still worried about what he'll think of you hanging out with Gem as a friend?" Jane shrugged and rose from the couch. "Interesting."

"I hate when you say *interesting* like that," I said. "It just means there's more you want to tell me, but you're not going to do it."

"I'm just saying to think about it. Why do you care so much about what Jack thinks? If you're having a nice time with Gem, don't you think you owe it to yourself to explore that as an option, even if you go about it just being friends?"

I gave her a stern look. "This isn't a fair conversation. I just woke up with a half-eaten fry in my hand. I'm disoriented."

"Then go and get some sleep," Jane said. "Sweet dreams. About Gem? Russo? Let me know what you decide."

Chapter 14

The rest of my night was blissfully fry-free as well as dream-less. I woke up the next morning feeling refreshed and focused on the case ahead of me. I grabbed another quick shower. My adrenaline was already pumping by the time I made it downstairs to grab coffee. That usually meant one thing—we were getting close to making significant headway on a case.

Jane had already made coffee and was enjoying her dose of caffeine in the kitchen. She'd wrapped a pink bathrobe over her signature yellow pajamas. I grabbed a cup of coffee and sat next to her.

"I see you needed another shower this morning." Jane winked. "Had to wash off all that grease from last night?"

"Ha ha."

"Hey, Kate, there's one thing I wanted to mention to you after we talked yesterday."

Jane looked a little uncomfortable. I gestured for her to go ahead with whatever she had to say.

"You know I asked you to be my maid of honor because you're my sister, right?"

I made a face at her. "I'm not sure how to feel about that. It seems like a little bit of a dig, you only choosing me be-cause we're blood relatives."

"Except it's not like that at all," Jane said hurriedly. "That's not how I wanted you to take what I'm about to say. You're my best friend, and you've been there for me my whole life. I'd never get married with anyone else standing next to me."

"Except Wes."

She grinned. "You know what I mean. My point is only that I understand if weddings are a little bit of a sensitive subject right now. You've been through a lot this year."

"Whatever I have or haven't been through has nothing to do with your wedding." I reached out a hand and gave my sister's wrist a squeeze. "You're my sister, Jane. I'd never dream of shirking my maid of honor duties because I had a breakup. A breakup that I'm completely over, by the way."

"You don't have to lie," Jane said with another glimmer of a smile. "It's okay for it to be hard on you. My only point in bringing this up was that I know mushy stuff probably isn't exactly what you want to be thinking about right now."

"I'm not thinking about anything mushy for myself. But I can do mushy for you." I grimaced. "That came out wrong, but you get the idea."

"I have other bridesmaids that I can ask for help if you ever want. That's all I'm saying. Not because you can't do it or wouldn't do it, but just to help you out. You've got a lot on your plate between your job and your personal life. I'm just trying to be sensitive to how you might be feeling. That's all."

I stood up and went to the sink, rinsing my cup out. I'd downed my coffee in about three seconds flat. Mostly to give me something to do while Jane stumbled through her offer.

"You just don't want me to plan anything," I said, my back to her. "You don't trust me to be sufficiently mushy for you."

"No," she said, horrified. "That's exactly the opposite of what I wanted you to get out of this. I want you involved, Kate. I just—"

I whirled around, a grin on my face. "I'm kidding."

"That was so rude!" Jane threw a grape from her plate at me. "Here I thought you were angry with me."

"Your offer's sweet. I'm willing to do as much or as little as you want me to do. I won't be offended if you don't want me to touch your bachelorette party—I know there are lots of other ladies in your bridal party who are a lot better at planning that stuff than me. But I'll still be there with bells and whistles. Nothing—and I mean nothing—is going to keep me from celebrating my sister's wedding."

Jane burst into tears, then rose from her chair and came to give me a hug. She clasped her arms around me. "That's the nicest thing you've ever said to me."

I patted her on the back. "I guess I need to say more nice things, then. That's pretty sad if that's the best I can do."

Jane laughed through her tears, then wiped her cheeks. "I just didn't want—"

"I know, I know. Trust me, it's not an issue. I'm happy to help however I can."

After a few more minutes of listening to Jane babble on about wedding ideas, I was beginning to rethink my offer to help. Eventually, I glanced at the clock and excused myself to get to the precinct. Jane sent me on my way with another teary hug. Apparently, the wedding hormones had hit her already. Fortunately, she seemed to be more weepy-Barbie bride than full-on Bridezilla.

I made my way to the precinct, relieved once again to have an excuse to push my personal life, and my sister's, out of my mind. There was a jitteriness in my bones that had nothing to do with the single cup of coffee I'd had this morning. Something about our interviews with Ricky Navarro and Henry Dunwoody had me thinking we were getting somewhere. That, plus Anthony Luzzi's insistence that this Mathematician figure was in town hankering for a big hit.

Garrett's four pseudo girlfriends lingered in the back of my mind. There was plenty of motive there, certainly, but my gut was pulling me toward this bigger theory. To have a hand in bringing down someone the FBI had been tracking for years was an exciting prospect. A criminal who might be hunting for a target right in my backyard.

I pulled into the precinct parking lot, debating the pros and cons of stopping into my mother's shop for a latte or pouring myself a second cup of black coffee from the squidgy grounds at the precinct. The fresh steamed latte won out.

"Oh, hi, sweetheart!"

The second I stepped through the doors of the Seventh Street Café, I knew something was wrong. I froze and looked up at my mother. She was using her super-high-pitched, everything-is-fine voice that meant the exact opposite. I stared at her for a moment, taking in her tense posture, the dramatic widening of her eyes, the white-knuckled grip on the counter before her.

I sensed the disruption in the normal atmosphere of the café before I actually saw the figure who had set my mother on edge. Two people stood in conversation off to one side of the room, obviously waiting for their drinks to be served. One of them was wearing a suit. An FBI sort of suit.

My throat went dry when I recognized the man inside the suit. I'd become very familiar with Jack Russo and his clothing choices over the past year, and I'd know his profile anywhere.

I had a good long second to watch him in conversation with someone I presumed was a business colleague—a very beautiful business colleague—before he noticed me. I understood my mother's high-pitched voice of alarm.

As much as I'd tried to hide it, my mother had seemed to sense that the breakup with Jack had hit me harder than I'd let on. She'd insinuated as much on our Hawaii trip. I'd shut down her line of questioning because I'd staunchly wanted the week to remain focused on my parents and the renewal of their vows, but I'd been touched by the sentiment nonetheless. I knew she worried about me even if she hadn't brought the subject up again. It was part of the reason I'd been dodging the café so much. I'd been trying to give her as few opportunities as possible to bring up the subject of "feelings."

Jack glanced over at me the second my mother spoke again. His eyes locked on mine, and we both froze for a long minute. I missed whatever my mother had said the first time. Maybe the second time. Eventually, she smacked her hand on the bar counter and said my name sharply, and the instinct to listen to my mother's voice kicked in.

I swiveled to face her. "What'd you say?"

"Venti pumpkin spice latte?" she said sweetly.

"Sure," I said. "Whatever."

My mother's eyes narrowed at me. "It was a test. You failed. You hate pumpkin spice lattes."

"Just a regular latte, then," I muttered. "Whatever. Please and thanks. I've got to get to work, Mom."

Elizabeth, the college-aged woman who helped my mother run the café, swooped in to save the day. She tapped some buttons on the register, gave me a big smile, and set to making my latte. I moved off to the side of the room, a little away from Jack, giving him the space to continue his conversation without acknowledging me, if that was what he wanted.

"Kate, hi," Jack said softly. "I didn't think I'd run into you here so soon."

I gave a confused smile and thumbed next door. "You know I work at the precinct, right? And my mother runs this shop? I'm here quite often. I'm actually surprised to see you here, considering you live a billion miles away."

Jack cleared his throat. "Right. Well, I should introduce you to my colleague, Agent Denise Price. She's been working the Mathematician's case for the last three years."

"You're one of the profilers," I said, thinking the name had sounded familiar the second it rolled off Jack's tongue. "I read your report."

Agent Denise Price extended a hand and gave me a brilliant smile. It didn't take my excellent deduction skills as a detective to reason that she used Crest whitening strips regularly. She probably also got Botox and hair extensions and had invested in fake boobs. It was impossible for someone to be that beautiful naturally.

I shook myself and took another look at her again. Unfortunately, her boobs didn't look fake. She had a nice smile with laugh lines. Her hair was pretty and looked au naturale. It seemed like she really was just a beautiful person. How annoying that she was my ex-boyfriend's new colleague.

I shook Agent Price's hand and returned my own, significantly less white and shiny, smile back at her. "Pleasure to meet you."

"Same to you," she said. "I've heard so much about you. I'm thrilled to meet you in person. I hope the report was helpful."

I was too busy staring at the woman's pretty little diamond necklace, wondering who'd given it to her, to put together what she'd said. I mumbled a nonsensical sort of, "Huh?"

"The report," she said. "I mean the profile on the Mathematician. I've been watching him for years. I'm a little bit obsessed, but not in the crazy way. I promise. I just can't figure how this guy has escaped any detection at all. It's one of those cases that really gets under your skin."

"I know the type," I said dryly. "I've had a few myself. Can I assume that's why the two of you came all the way to Minnesota in the worst part of winter?"

Agent Price nodded. "I was only too happy to get away from my desk. It doesn't happen all that often for me, but when Jack here asked about the case, I found myself digging into it. I made a few phone calls and talked to some nice women named Asha and Chloe. We're all in agreement that if this murder is linked in any way to the real Mathematician, this very well may be the closest we've ever gotten to him."

"We're not entirely convinced it is the Mathematician," I said. "Even if it is him, the chances are very good that we've already spooked him."

"That's the thing with this guy," Denise said. "Nobody ever knows for certain it's the Mathematician until he's in the wind. If there's even a slight chance that he's still planning to go ahead with his big hit in the Twin Cities, then I want to be here to help."

"Don't take this the wrong way, but the case is mine," I said, "and I hadn't heard anything about the two of you coming into town. Can I ask who gave you permission?"

Denise gave me an indulgent smile. "Of course. I should have explained. After my conversation with Asha and Chloe, I was so convinced that this case might be the real deal that I asked to be put in touch directly with your chief. He extended the offer late last night. I apologize. I thought he would've briefed you this morning."

"I'm just getting into the office," I said. "I'm sure he's waiting to share the good news right now. Well, welcome to the team. I hope you enjoy the coffee. I'll, uh, leave you to it."

Elizabeth had silently slid my latte onto the bar. I gratefully reached for it, then raised it in a salute to the two feds. I was headed for the door when I heard footsteps behind me, and a moment later, Jack's voice sounded beside me.

"We're actually headed to the precinct to meet the rest of the team," he said softly. "Maybe you wouldn't mind showing us around?"

"Sure." I gave him a big smile that felt fake even to me. "I'd be happy to show you around, Agent Russo."

***

I pulled open the door to the precinct and held it for Russo and his new partner *du jour*. Though it wasn't my intention, I found myself watching every movement that passed between Russo and Denise Price.

I wasn't sure if I was imagining her brushing against him as she passed through the door, or if it was really happening. When she smiled at Jack, I instantly wondered if there was more meaning behind it besides a simple thank-you. I gave a shake of my head as I followed them into the building and pushed all thoughts of the two of them into the recesses of my brain.

I reasoned that just because Jack was working with a new woman didn't mean he'd fallen in lust—or love—with her. Just because she was beautiful and probably very smart and competent and seemingly sweet didn't mean anything. Jack probably was like me, still reeling from our breakup.

As we passed through the lobby, I thought guiltily about how much I claimed to still be reeling from the breakup. Yet hadn't I just gotten off a jet two nights ago with a billionaire who'd just about kissed me?

"This is a nice space you guys have," Denise said eventually. "How long have you been here?"

"The TC Task Force has only been here a couple of years. We're a newer organization. As the name suggests, we're a group of detectives who work homicides that blur the St. Paul and Minneapolis borders to help with jurisdictional issues."

Russo rolled his eyes. "She's being modest. Kate's been here since the initiation of the task force. She's practically the backbone of it. And even if she tells you the reason this branch was formed was to help with jurisdictional issues, that's not true."

"It's not?" Denise raised her eyebrows at me.

"Sure it is," I said, shifting uncomfortably and shooting Jack a look. "That's exactly what it says in our mission statement."

"Right. Okay, but everyone knows that the detectives who work here were handpicked by some very important people to head up particularly grisly cases. Kate's team handles the highest profile murders, anything that might be a serial killer, and other especially complicated cases."

Denise winked. "The city cherry-picked the cream of the crop and put them all in one room. It's one of the smartest things I've ever heard of to come out of a bureaucratic decision."

"Tell me about it," Jack said. "It's brilliant. The close rates on their cases are some of the highest in the country."

"We're new," I said. "And we have good resources."

Jack and Denise exchanged a look that said they didn't believe me. It was my turn to roll my eyes.

"It looks like someone brought in some pastries this morning," I said, gesturing to one of the conference rooms we passed on the way to our smaller office space. "Why don't the two of you help yourselves, then meet me at my desk? You know where it is, Agent Russo."

"I haven't had breakfast," Denise chirped. "Thanks. This will go great with the latte. Your mother runs an amazing café, by the way."

"She'll be happy to hear it," I said with a little smile.

Denise Price was proving difficult to dislike even with her pretty hair and shiny teeth and sunny disposition. She seemed enthusiastic and pleasant to be around. It would've been annoying if it didn't seem so genuine.

I was especially grateful for whoever had brought the pastries in this morning. It had bought me a few extra minutes to gather my thoughts around this new wrinkle in my day. It was a step beyond shocking to have found Russo in my mother's shop this morning.

On the plus side, I didn't have the headspace to deal with it now. The most logical option was to shut off any feelings squirming in my stomach in favor of complete focus on the case. Compartmentalization was one of my strengths, and I planned to take full advantage of it.

I headed past Asha's station, which was currently empty, and into the office space for the TC Task Force. Jimmy was already at his desk. Frankie Dunkirk was slinking lower behind his computer, his eyes following me as I entered the room. An unexpected hush fell over the small group of detectives. I froze again, wondering what I was missing.

Then my eyes lifted, and my gaze traveled to my desk. It was like there was a magnetic draw to it, as if I could feel my attention being sucked toward the handsome man who'd made my desk his own.

I took a few more steps into the room, my heart racing. On a good day, I would've been caught off guard. Today, I was in full-on panic mode.

"Gem?" I asked, my voice coming out a few octaves too high. "What are you doing here?"

Gem sat back and grinned. "I thought I'd bring in some pastries for the team. A couple of coffees. Well, that's not entirely true."

I felt my throat start to close up as I heard footsteps behind me. As Gem started talking, I felt Jack and Denise arrive behind me.

"After the other night, I thought I owed you a coffee, so..." Gem trailed off as his eyes locked on mine, then slid quickly to the two people standing beside me.

There was a long, long, long moment of silence.

I could hear the crunch of Jimmy biting into his almond croissant, then the squeak as he sat back in his chair and folded his hands across his stomach, as if he were watching a spectator sport. A sport in which I was the main participant facing down my ex-boyfriend and the man who was trying to become my boyfriend. Sort of.

A trickle of sweat dripped down my back. Russo couldn't have walked in at a worse moment. There was no way he hadn't heard what Gem said, and really, it would be logical for Jack to entirely misconstrue what he'd meant.

"You're responsible for the pastries?" Denise raised her chocolate croissant in salute to Gem. "They are incredible. Seriously, the best I've ever had, and I lived in Italy for six months."

For having a badge that stated she was a federal agent, Denise had completely failed to pick up on any context clues that the situation was an uncomfortable one. I held my breath. I could feel Jack flexing his fingers next to me like it was a new nervous tic.

Gem, the most suave of the group, recovered first. A fleeting moment of uncertainty had crossed his eyes, then he'd turned on his charming smile that showed the world everything was all right. It was still odd to me, seeing him change like that. Then again, he hadn't earned millions by wearing his heart on his sleeve. He'd had years of practice to finesse the way he dealt with people. This could hardly be the most uncomfortable situation in which he'd found himself.

"We make our breakfasts and desserts in house at Gem Industries," he said with a smile. "I hired a pastry chef who has trained across Europe. In my opinion, he's the best in the world."

Denise's eyes widened. "I probably shouldn't have scarfed it down so fast. I feel like I should've savored the experience a little more."

"There are plenty where those came from. Please help yourself," Gem said. "It's a pleasure to meet you..."

"Oh, right. Sorry," I said, spluttering to attention. "Most of you know Agent Jack Russo. This is his new partner, Agent Denise Price."

"We're not partners," Jack clarified quickly. "Agent Price here has been running point on the Mathematician's case since it started. I'm just here as a liaison between the FBI and your team since we've worked together before."

"Worked together," Gem echoed quietly. "Of course. Makes sense."

Russo ignored him. Denise seemed oblivious to any discomfort once again.

"Agent Russo's just being modest," Denise gushed. "He's practically been a mentor to me these last few months. He helped me close this case I'd been working on for ages just by reviewing the case files. When I heard that Jack had worked with your team, plus the Mathematician might be connected to one of your cases, it was a no-brainer to get him to come along with me."

"Completely logical," Gem said smoothly. "Everyone here loves Agent Russo."

"And you are?" Denise glanced at me, then back to Gem. "Are you a detective here?"

If I wasn't mistaken, there was a hint of flirtation in Denise's voice. It was understandable. Not only had Gem brought in the most amazing croissants, according to the agent, but he was very easy on the eyes this morning. He'd dressed as he did to go into the office in nice slacks and a button-down, white shirt. His jacket sat on the arm of my chair. The curls in his hair dripped over his forehead.

I snuck a sideways glance at Russo, unable to keep from comparing the two once again. Jack Russo looked plenty sophisticated and suave in his own way, but his was a sort of rugged, tough-guy handsome as opposed to Gem's gorgeous features and polished attire. There was a hardness in Russo's eyes and a playfulness in Gem's. It was almost impossible for me to believe that I could be associated with both men as they were almost complete opposites in so many ways.

It did, however, throw a wrench in my assumptions that Denise and Russo were a thing. She wouldn't be flirting in front of Jack if she was interested in him, would she? Then again, I was pretty sure that Alastair Gem was a major exception. It seemed impossible for women not to flirt around him.

"No, I'm not a detective," Gem said when nobody else answered for him. "I guess you could say I'm a friend of the department. Well, I became a friend after they investigated me for murder."

Denise choked on the sip of her latte that she'd just taken. "Murder?"

If anything, Denise looked more intrigued. It annoyed me.

"He was cleared quickly," I said. "This is Alastair Gem, head of Gem Industries. His connections and assistance have been instrumental in a few of our recent cases."

"I see," Denise said. "Well, it's a pleasure to meet you."

"I feel the same way," Gem said. "But on that note, I should be letting the real detectives get down to business. It seems you are all very busy and have some catching up to do."

Jack cleared his throat as if that were the biggest understatement of the year.

"It was nice to see you again, Agent Russo," Gem said, standing and shrugging his jacket onto his shoulders. "Pleasure to meet you, Agent Price. Detective Rosetti, do you have a minute before you get to catching your killers?"

"I'll walk you out," I offered. "Agent Russo, please show Agent Price to the extra desk and the conference room. She can have her pick for where she'd like to set up shop for the time being."

Jack nodded, made another sound in his throat, and then gestured for Denise to follow him. I waved a hand at Jimmy asking him for help in getting the agents situated.

"This is for you. Was for you," Gem corrected, once we got into the hallway. "But I can see you've got the caffeine covered."

I looked down to find a latte in Gem's hand. It was half-heartedly extended in my direction, as if he wasn't quite sure what to do with it, seeing as I had a latte in my hand already.

"Actually, this is perfect." I reached out for Gem's latte. When we passed a trash can, I tossed my mother's perfectly good latte. "My mom made me a pumpkin spice latte. I hate them."

"Ah," Gem said, but in a way that told me he was only partially convinced that was true. "You're too kind."

I sighed. "I'm sorry. That was awkward. I didn't know he'd be here."

"You don't have to apologize. I should apologize. It wasn't my place to show up unannounced at your office. I don't know what I was thinking."

"Why did you come by?"

"Why?"

I waited a beat. When Gem didn't seem inclined to explain further, I prompted him. "Yes, why? I don't believe that you've started a second—or third, or fourth—career as a food delivery service."

"It's stupid."

"I'm not sure you can be feeling more stupid than me at the moment."

"I assure you that's not true." Gem rubbed at his forehead. "After the other night, I felt like you might've gotten the wrong impression."

"Can you clarify which impression you're talking about?"

Gem gave a chuckle. "I don't know if that's a good thing or worrisome that you came away with several."

I couldn't help but smile in return.

"I was referring to our discussion about dates and money and what is appropriate."

"I'm not following."

Gem glanced at me. "You made it clear that you disliked being taken to a vineyard in Canada on a private plane. It seemed too–what did you say?—contrived?"

"A little overkill," I admitted. "I'm not the glamorous type of girl."

"I wanted to show you that I could do"—Gem paused to add air quotes—"'normal' things too."

"Normal things?" I gave a little snort. "You mean, hiring a chef to personally make pastries for an entire police department?"

"I didn't hire the chef for you specifically." Gem sounded a little annoyed. "I just meant—"

"I know what you meant. I was just teasing."

Gem glanced at me, then relaxed. It was then that I realized the suaveness he'd shown in the face of an uncomfortable situation was a front and nothing more. He had been just as uncertain as the rest of us. He simply had a different way of showing it.

And a better way of hiding it. It struck me that while I assumed Gem had developed this shell of protection to deal with his business enterprises, that might not be true. It could have been developed much earlier, soon after his mother had been killed, leaving him an orphan.

He'd been on his own for so long, probably forced to keep his feelings to himself simply because he'd had no one else to share them with. The thought sobered me for a moment. The hint of vulnerability in Gem's voice was enough for me to latch on to and soften my own frustration at being caught unawares not once but twice in one morning.

"I just wanted to bring you a coffee and a pastry," Gem said. "It seemed like a very normal thing for a friend to do. But I was worried you'd misinterpret that as a romantic sort of gesture. I asked my assistant how to handle such a touchy situation, and she said I'd be covering my bases if I brought enough for the entire office."

I laughed. "You are overthinking things. I'm not upset about the other night."

"It seemed like you were at the time."

"Maybe I was. I think upset is the wrong word, but I can't deny that you have a point. I was just caught off guard, and I don't do well when my plans go off the rails. I'm a detective, a planner, and when someone surprises me like you did, it takes me a minute to pivot. It's not your fault. In fact, I ended up really enjoying the evening."

"Maybe it's good for you to be caught off guard once in a while, Detective."

Gem pushed the front doors of the precinct open and held them for me. He waited while I passed through. Then he fell into step beside me once again.

"I know you keep me on my toes," he admitted. "It's one of the things that intrigues me about you. One of the many things."

I took a sip of the latte. "This is really delicious. You didn't have to bring anything, but I appreciate the gesture."

"The other night—"

"We don't have to talk about it," I interrupted again. "I really did have a nice time once I got over my shock at being whisked away to another country. You have to understand that doesn't happen to me often."

"I get it."

"And I think I understand where you're coming from too," I admitted. "I can understand how these things are normal for you. How my reaction might've seemed like it came out of left field."

"Thank you."

"Thank *you*," I echoed. "It was the first time I'd gotten out of my head in a long while."

"Where are you now?"

"Now?" For a moment, I was confused. "Oh, do you mean Jack?"

Gem shoved his hands in his pockets and turned to face me. We were stopped outside of a shiny, black car I hadn't seen before. Judging by the lack of limousine and driver, I assumed he'd driven himself over here. Probably another attempt to be "normal". The thought made me hide a smile.

"I am still trying to wade my way through everything," I said. "I found him in my mother's coffee shop about five minutes before you saw him. I've had a lot of surprises this morning."

"For someone who hates to pivot, you must be feeling incredibly peeved."

I couldn't help another grin. "Well, you're making it hard to stay annoyed."

"That's not a bad thing."

"He's just here on business," I said. "It doesn't change anything either way. Jack and I broke up for a reason."

"I thought you might want to clarify for him what I meant earlier. What I was saying when he walked into the room."

"Ah, you caught that."

"Unfortunate timing."

I raised onto my toes, then lowered back down again, biding my time until I could come up with an appropriate response. I had no clue how to navigate the waters of a relatively uncomplicated relationship, let alone this mess I was trying to wade through.

"It doesn't make you a bad person to want to explain to Jack that nothing happened between us." Gem spoke quietly. His hands were in his pockets, and his eyes tracked my every movement. "I would understand."

"But I don't know if that's entirely true."

"Still."

"I don't want to lie."

"I'm not telling you to lie," Gem said. "But we didn't sleep together. You didn't kiss me. That's all the truth. I wouldn't blame you if you wanted to set the record straight with Russo."

I expelled a breath. "You're making it really hard to stay annoyed this morning. This is all very understanding of you."

"I will keep trying to prove to you that I'm not an arrogant rich guy for as long as it takes to convince you."

"I don't think you're arrogant." I gave him a little smile. "The rich thing, well, you can't argue with facts."

He laughed, his eyes sparkling. "I think it's time for me to leave you alone for a bit, Detective. Please consider this my notice that I'll be stepping back for a bit."

"Back from what?"

"You. The situation. Us. However you want to phrase it is fine with me. Whatever you tell Agent Russo is fine by me. Let me know what you tell him, and I'll corroborate whatever you say."

"I'm not going to tell him anything but the truth. And I might not say anything unless he asks. It's really not his business."

Gem reached out and touched my cheek. He brushed his thumb gently across my skin before dragging his hand away. "Just know that whatever happens, I understand."

"Gem—"

He gave me a smile and climbed into the car. "I'll wait for you to reach out to me. I meant it when I said that I don't want to complicate your life. If and when you decide you'd like me to be in your life—in any capacity—you let me know. In the meantime, I think the best thing I can offer you now is an uncomplicated space to figure things out."

I wanted to say something more, something that would make this easier. Something that would help everything make sense. But if there were words that could've been used, I didn't know them. Maybe there were no words. Maybe there was just a whole heap of uncertainty that needed to be navigated one step at a time.

As Gem drove away, the only thing I could do was raise a hand and give a wave. Gem waved back to me, then he left the parking lot without a backward glance. It felt strange seeing him go, knowing he wouldn't be contacting me unless I asked him to. Then I did what I did best and pushed it out of my mind. I turned on a heel and made my way back into the precinct.

Chapter 15

I found Jack and Denise set up in the conference room. Agent Price had gone ahead and brought in a few more pastries on a tray and set them in the center of the room. Jimmy wandered into the room as well and plopped in a chair across from the agents, probably drawn there by the scent of fresh food.

Agent Price had a second croissant on her plate, and for some reason, it annoyed me that on top of her perfect complexion and supermodel figure, she still ate like a normal person. It felt extra unfair. She was probably one of those people who ran marathons for fun on leisurely Sunday mornings to raise money for charity.

"You really need to try one, Jack," Denise said, dunking her croissant into her latte. "They're incredible."

"I'm not hungry," Jack said shortly.

I suspected his lack of appetite had something to do with the fact that the croissants had come from Alastair Gem's personal stash and nothing to do with his stomach. Russo had never passed up free food before, and especially not free food from Gem's parties. Obviously, something had shifted. It wasn't hard to guess what.

"Well, if this isn't a pleasant surprise." Melinda appeared in the door to the conference room. "How are you, Jack?"

"Just fine." Jack stood to give Melinda a hug. "How's my favorite ME?"

"Oh, now you're just sucking up to me in hopes I've got some good information to share." Melinda tossed her curls over her shoulder and grinned at Jack. "Fortunately, you're in luck."

"Really?" I asked, feigning off the annoyance that my best friend and my ex-boyfriend seemed to be on such great terms. "What sort of good news?"

Melinda took a seat at the table. "Where are these from? I haven't seen croissants this fresh since I was in Paris."

"That's what I said." Agent Price gave a small wave and introduced herself. "I traveled here with Agent Russo to assist in case the Mathematician is involved with your murder investigation."

"I'm Dr. Brooks," Melinda said. "Pleasure to meet you. So? Where's the secret stash of incredible croissants from?"

"Alastair Gem," Jack said. "Apparently, he brought them around this morning. I hadn't realized he was such a good friend to the department."

Melinda stilled, a croissant in her hand. She glanced at me as if checking to see whether I wanted her to put the croissant back or not. I nodded for her to go ahead and eat the thing.

"This is fun," Melinda said, "but I do actually have some exciting news for you all. I believe I've figured out the murder weapon."

"For the Garrett Landers case?" I asked, relieved to be back on track for business discussion.

A part of me wanted Melinda to wrap this case up for us right now and prove that the Mathematician had nothing to do with it, thereby rendering the two federal agents sitting before me useless in this investigation. They'd be forced to return back home to canoodle at Quantico.

"That would be the case I'm working," Melinda said, practically bubbling over with excitement. "However, I have a twist for you."

"A good twist?"

"I think so," she said. "It turns out, I think we might be dealing with a double homicide."

"How?" I asked. "We only have one body."

"Not true," she said. "You heard about the case Dunkirk picked up last week while you were gone?"

"Just a little bit," I said. "He said an old lady got bonked on the head. I didn't read the case files yet. I'm still catching up."

"I believe that old woman and Garrett Landers were killed by the same weapon. It seems like they were both struck by some sort of bat. Likely a baseball bat. We're still pulling fibers and swabbing for particulates to see if we can determine the specific type or brand."

I stared at Melinda. "What do Garrett Landers and an old woman have in common that would get them both killed?"

"That's for you to find out."

"This is where I come in." Asha stepped into the conference room, grinning around at the growing gang. "What's up, Jack? Hi, there. You must be Agent Price."

Denise gave a smile. "It's nice to meet you—"

"Guess who plays on a baseball league?" Asha, too, was brimming over with excitement so much so that she brushed Denise's greeting right off. She wasn't usually so short when meeting new people, but her eyes were locked on mine, and it was clear she sensed we were close to a break in the case. "Take one guess."

I blew out a breath. "Tell me it's one of my suspects."

"One Mr. Ricky Navarro," Asha said. "He used to be the captain of the team, but it seems like he got booted out of the spot. Probably because he kept forgetting to register the team for the league in time, and they kept having to bribe the judges for entry."

"How did you learn all this in five minutes?" Denise looked impressed. "You just got this information, right?"

"It's Asha," Jack and I said at the same time.

That seemed to render Denise silent.

"At least, that's the gist of what I gleaned from the online messages I was able to crack into between the team's current captains," Asha said, obviously in her element. "They're a gossipy bunch for a team of grown men."

"Then I guess we need to pay another visit to Ricky Navarro," I said. "Do you think this is enough for a warrant?"

"Already on it," Asha said. "The chief thinks Judge Klein will push it through for us. They should have it by the time you get to Ricky's place."

"You don't seem as happy about the news as I thought you'd be," Melinda said. "What's wrong?"

"No, this is great news. It's just..." I blew out a breath and glanced at Jimmy. I knew he was feeling the same way as me. "I would've bet good money that the killer wasn't Ricky Navarro."

"We're not convinced it *is* Ricky Navarro," Melinda pointed out. "We don't have anything concrete to tie Ricky to the bat that killed Garrett Landers. We don't even have anything that directly ties the two murders together yet. As unlikely as it may be, it could be that both murders were conducted with different bats. It could all be a coincidence."

The room was silent. Nobody truly believed in a coincidence of that magnitude, not when someone like the Mathematician was potentially involved.

"If we can link the two murders together, then it has to make us wonder about whether one of Garrett's girlfriends would actually be responsible for it. What would the motive be?" I asked. "The motives for all the girlfriend theories were based on jealousy or anger at a man double-or-triple-timing them. That would leave zero motive to kill a completely unrelated older woman a week before Garrett died."

"Agreed," Jimmy said. "Honestly, it seems far-fetched to believe there's a connection between the two victims at all."

"Trust me," Agent Price interrupted, "if this is the Mathematician, there will be a connection. We might not find it until it's too late, but eventually it will be clear as day."

"What's your take on this whole thing?" I asked Denise. "You've read the case files, and now you're up to date on the latest information we have. What do you think?"

"While there's plenty of motive for the ex-girlfriends to murder this guy, I don't think this is a case of jealousy. I do believe that this could be the Mathematician at work, but I'll know more after I get a chance to study the second victim. Or rather, the first. It's possible this woman could be a target of the Mathematician's. It's even possible the theft already happened, and as usual, we're a few steps behind."

"Well, I'm a few steps ahead on this one," Asha said, handing out folders around the table. "I've already got the files here for you all. Everything Dunkirk's found which, in his words, isn't much. He'll be here in a few minutes to brief you."

"My ears are ringing." Dunkirk appeared in the doorway. "Are those pastries up for grabs?"

"Only after you talk," Asha said. "These guys are chomping at the bit to hear more about your old-lady case."

Frankie Dunkirk waved a hand in greeting around the room, then sat without further ado. "The woman's name was Harriett Windsor. She was eighty-seven years old at the time of death and in perfect health, according to her doctors. There was no reason she should have dropped dead."

"Except for the fact that someone took a baseball bat to her head?" Jack asked skeptically. "That'll do it for most people, eighty-seven years old or not."

Frankie nodded. "My point is just that she was in great shape as reported by everyone who knew her. She lived over on Lake of the Isles in a pricey, old mansion on one of the lakes."

"Interesting," Denise interjected. "How pricey?"

"Out of this world pricey," Frankie said. "We checked out her house. She lived alone. She was married, but her husband died thirty years ago."

"How'd she get her money?" I asked.

"Family money. She was independently wealthy before she got married. Then she married a man who started several companies and sold them."

Denise sucked in a breath. "So she was ridiculously rich even though nobody knew her name."

"I think that's one way to put it," Frankie said. "I mean, you'd know it if you went to her house. But if you passed her in the grocery store, you'd have no clue who she was."

"She was invisible in public," Denise said. "That fits the profile for who the Mathematician would select as a target."

"What doesn't fit the profile is the fact that she's dead," I said, and then added, "Right?"

"Correct," Denise said. "The Mathematician is largely believed to be a nonviolent criminal. However, I believe the profile might need adjusting. You may have heard that we believe as much as fifty percent of the Mathematician's crimes have gone unreported. That leaves a lot of room for violence that we might simply be unaware of."

"I can see how that might happen," I said. "Take Harriett Windsor's case. If it weren't for some fortunate ties to Garrett Landers, a little help from the FBI, and a lucky break or two, we would never have connected Harriett Windsor's death to the Mathematician."

Denise nodded knowingly. "I believe something happened to throw the Mathematician off. If there's a chance he hasn't fled just yet, it might be our only hope to catch him before he disappears again."

"How would an eighty-seven-year-old woman pose enough of a physical threat to the Mathematician to the point where he needed to kill her?" I asked. "That just doesn't make sense. You said Harriett lived alone?"

Frankie nodded. "She has a housekeeper come by twice a week to help with cooking, cleaning, and groceries. The housekeeper has been there for thirty-six years and is seventy-four years old herself. I get the impression these two women are more friends than anything else, and that Harriett just keeps paying her because that's been the arrangement all along."

"Anyone else help out around the house?" I asked. "Anyone who might know how much she's worth?"

"There's a groundskeeper, but he's married to the housekeeper and has been there for forty-seven years," Frankie said. "He's got an alibi for the time of the murder. There are a few regular delivery guys and things like that, but nothing that's ever been reported as suspicious. That's the odd thing. There's been nothing suspicious about this whole case except the fact that she's dead."

"What did she collect?" Denise asked.

"Collect?" Frankie looked surprised. "How'd you know she had a collection?"

"This is the Mathematician," Denise said, sounding more and more confident the longer the meeting went on. "The Mathematician mostly targets private collectors. I'm going to guess some sort of art, just based on the woman's age and the lifestyle you're describing."

"That would be correct," Frankie said, looking more than a little impressed. "She had one of the largest private art collections in the state. She loaned it out several times to museums throughout the world during her lifetime."

"Let me guess," Denise continued. "None of the pieces are currently loaned out?"

"Correct," Frankie said, looking even more impressed.

"The Mathematician would've known all of this," Denise explained. "He would've waited for the best opportunity to make the biggest score."

"A time when none of the pieces were on loan," I filled in. "Frankie, did your guys come up with a list of all the pieces Harriett owned? Is anything missing?"

"We do have a log," Frankie said. "It was given to us by Harriett's niece."

"The niece," I said. "Do we suspect this niece of anything?"

"She has an alibi. Her boss confirmed that she was working at the time of the murder. Aside from that, she's been nothing but cooperative. Nothing's missing."

"No, no, that doesn't work," Denise said. "Something must be missing."

"Why?" Frankie asked. "Why would you think something's missing?"

"The Mathematician would never leave empty handed, especially if a murder occurred. A cost that high, and he would need to take something."

I shook my head. "I don't know about that. If what you wrote in your profile is correct, then I just don't see how that scenario fits. You wrote explicitly that you believe the Mathematician idolizes accuracy above all. That this is a criminal who is not ashamed nor afraid to abandon a situation that could be dangerous. You theorized that self-preservation is incredibly important to this individual."

"While that is true, I believe there are some things that might trump his desire for self-preservation," Denise countered. "After all, there are some conundrums within this individual. Self-preservation would dictate that this person does not steal anything at all. That would be the safest route.

Everyone weighs these sorts of decisions every day. Think about it."

Denise paused to look around the room.

"Driving under the speed limit is the safest way to get from point A to B. Not only for pure safety reasons, but because it doesn't attract attention from the law. Yet how many people speed?" Denise raised her hand as if to demonstrate that she herself was guilty of the offense. "People weigh the risks and benefits of speeding. We make these snap choices so quickly and frequently that it's often a subconscious thing. How urgent is it that we get to point B? Is it worth risking a ticket? Maybe even our safety?"

She shrugged.

"If a man was driving to the hospital and his wife was in labor, he might think it well worth the hundred-something-dollar ticket to press the speed limit. A week earlier, the same man might have been leisurely driving to visit his mother on a Sunday and might have made a different decision."

"How does this apply to the Mathematician?" I asked. "You think because there was bloodshed that he felt obligated in a way to make it worth his while?"

"That's exactly what I'm saying," Denise said. "I don't believe the Mathematician believes he's a bad person. I believe he picks his targets accordingly."

"A little Robin Hood action?" Jack asked. "The whole stealing from the rich thing, minus the giving to the poor?"

"Sure, that works," Denise said. "I think the Mathematician is willing to abandon a project if he senses he's in danger. But maybe he wasn't in danger. Maybe this poor woman ended up dead, and the way the Mathematician is reconciling her death is by making sure the score was worth it."

"It's still murder," I said. "And it doesn't match up with the fact that nothing is missing."

"That's why I feel like something isn't right here," Denise said. "It's not that I don't trust Detective Dunkirk's work—quite the contrary. I believe everything here to be true. I just don't think it adds up. Excuse the pun."

There was silence in the room.

"What would you guess, then?" I asked. "Do you think the Mathematician is still biding his time, waiting to hit Harriett Windsor's collection now that she's gone? Do you think something went horribly wrong with his plan? Or do you think this isn't him at all?"

Denise pursed her lips together. "I don't feel comfortable coming up with a theory on that just yet. I'll need a little more time to review the Windsor file. The only thing I'm comfortable saying is that I don't feel like things are as they seem here."

"That implies you believe the Mathematician is still involved," I concluded.

After a moment of consideration, she nodded. "I do believe so. I believe that, as usual, we're just missing key pieces of the puzzle. Or..." She raised a finger, her face drawn. "Or else something went horribly, horribly wrong."

Chapter 16

We spent another hour picking Detective Dunkirk's brain and going over Harriett's case file. Eventually, Melinda and Asha left the conference room to return to their work, leaving the rest of us behind. We were starting to go around in circles and rehash the same theories. Finally, I raised a hand and put a stop to our discussion.

"We just got the warrant to search Navarro's place," I said. "I'm going to head over there. Hopefully that'll give us something more concrete to work with."

I left my statement relatively open ended. We didn't need an entire train of people heading to Ricky Navarro's place to look around for a baseball bat. I wanted to offer Jimmy the right to come with me first as he was my partner on the case. But judging by the way he was avoiding eye contact with me, he would be more than a little bit happy to step back and let someone else go along for the ride.

"I'd love to go with you," Denise said. "I know I'm just the profiler, but I'm as invested in this case as anyone."

"I'd be happy to accompany Detective Rosetti as well," Jack said. "I'm up to speed on all the files. However, I understand if three's a crowd."

"It's fine," I said. "We can use the extra set of eyes. Not to mention, Navarro's a bit of a creep when it comes to women, and while I hate to say it, he might be a little more well behaved if there's a male present."

"I'm not afraid of a creep," Denise said. "I have a gun."

I smiled at her. It was the first time I genuinely found myself liking her without feeling twinges of jealousy. "Same here. But I don't want him getting handsy while I'm looking under his bed. It'll just be less paperwork if we don't have to shoot anyone because Russo was standing there."

Denise grinned back. "Fair point. He can deliver the warrant."

I nodded to Jack. "Sound good?"

"Happy to be of service," Jack said.

Jimmy grabbed a third croissant. "I'll hold down the fort here and go over the case files looking for more ways to link Harriett Windsor to Garrett Landers."

The four of us parted ways. Jack and Denise trailed me to my car, which I took to mean I was driving. It only made sense, seeing as I was the local and knew my way around the city. Not to mention, I had a habit of getting rental cars in trouble with bullets and whatnot, and I was willing to bet Jack hadn't forgotten how much paperwork it was to request a new vehicle from the bureau while traveling.

I climbed into the driver's seat. Denise walked around to the back without a word, leaving Jack to take the passenger's seat. As I started up the car, I couldn't stop the wave of nostalgia from crashing over my shoulders.

Sitting here in the car next to Jack and preparing to interview a suspect together brought back old memories that weren't as old as I liked to think. In fact, they were so fresh, I felt as if I could reach over and grab Jack's hand, and magically, everything would be as it was a few months earlier. Back when things were a little easier, a little more hopeful, a little less complicated.

The wave of nostalgia was broken when Denise piped up from the back seat, reminding me that Jack and I weren't alone. And also that we weren't still dating.

"How many cases have the two of you worked together?" Denise asked. "Jack told me he's been out here a couple of times."

I glanced sideways at Jack, and it dawned on me that Denise didn't know. He hadn't told her about our history. I wasn't quite sure how that made me feel. In a way, I understood. I wasn't exactly thrilled to be forthcoming with Jack about my current situation with Gem. At the same time, Gem knew of my history with Russo. He knew I was just getting out of a complicated relationship. I hadn't tried to hide the fact that I was hurting from Gem. If anything, I was trying to be brutally honest so that Gem knew exactly where I stood, moving forward.

Jack stared straight ahead, carefully avoiding any eye contact with me. It confirmed my theory that Denise was in the dark about the exact reason for all of Jack's trips to Minnesota.

"Plenty," I finally said. "I've lost count. At least three, and I think this might be four? I don't really remember. We'll just say enough."

Denise sat back in her seat and gave a tinkling laugh as if she thought it to be quaint. "It's really neat, you guys bringing two different agencies and departments together. Honestly, if it weren't for the two of you, I'm not sure we'd even be this close to the Mathematician. This sort of cooperation between agencies needs to happen more often."

I wasn't sure of a response to that, seeing as the reason we were so close was a little bit more romantic than she'd thought. "I guess that would be one way to do things," I finally agreed. "How long have you been with the FBI?"

"Six years," she said. "I graduated a year early. I've wanted to be an FBI agent my entire life. It's a dream come true, and it's even more of a dream come true to be working with Agent Russo. He's a bit of a legend. I guess you are too. I consider myself lucky to be working with two legends."

"I wouldn't go that far," I said. "Not to mention, if you've been given the Mathematician's case, that means the FBI thinks pretty highly of you too."

"I don't know that they gave it to me," she said. "I mostly elbowed my way on to it. I read everything I could. Put together profiles in my spare time. Finally, I was so well versed in the material and obnoxious about my interest that they had to let me help out. Three years later, here I am, still tracking the guy. It's just the case that I can't seem to let go."

"What made you so interested in it in the first place? Why this case and not a different one?"

"It's just so unique. There's almost a romance to it, the idea of this uber-intelligent criminal who thinks themself above the law. Until recently, we've largely believed him to be nonviolent, which also adds to the Robin Hood aspect of his personality, if you will. I'm convinced the Mathematician is already wealthy, independently or otherwise, and I think he steals for the thrill. I get the reverse thrill from tracking someone so passionate about their trade."

"It sounds like you respect him."

"I have to," she said. "Otherwise, I wouldn't be doing him justice. I don't agree with what he's doing, and I certainly don't condone murder. But I have to respect his intelligence or I'll never be able to catch him. I have to think on his level, or at least strive to."

"I can understand that."

"This guy's a genius. I mean, can you imagine? He's one person. I am also one person, but I've got the vast resources of the FBI behind me. There are multiple agents who've been on this case for years. We have computer algorithms that can track terrorist intelligence and surveillance that would blow your mind. Yet we haven't caught so much as a whiff of this guy. In our digital age, that's truly amazing. I think that can be recognized as a near fact."

I shrugged. "Plus, you don't have to look at dead bodies as much when dealing with a thief."

"It is a nice break from death," she admitted. "I've also gotten to peek at a lot of very extravagant collections. Art, cars, you name it. The guy has good taste."

Something about what she said struck me as interesting. "Do you know who has all of those things?"

"Who?" she asked, confused, as if I were changing the subject.

Jack Russo rubbed his forehead, understanding dawning. He cursed under his breath. I nodded.

"Alastair Gem," I said, glancing in the rearview mirror at Denise. "The man you met this morning."

"He's rich? I mean, I got that impression from the fact that he has his own chef, but still. What does he do?"

"He's a billionaire," I said. "He owns Gem Industries. You can do some Googling later, but suffice to say he has his hands in a little bit of everything: Fancy cars, art, coffee, food. You name it, he's got it. He would be a perfect target."

"Too high profile," Russo said. "Gem's graced the pages of half the magazines on stands as the 'World's Most Eligible Bachelor' or whatever."

"You sound jealous, Agent Russo," Denise teased.

Silence followed. Denise must have realized she'd touched a nerve because she cleared her throat.

"Sorry, I only meant it as a joke," she said. "I'll have to look into this Mr. Gem a little more thoroughly before I can draw a conclusion as to whether or not he fits into my profile. It is interesting though. In theory, it might work. He's not a celebrity in the traditional sense of the word; I haven't heard of him. He might be sort of a local legend, but it's not like he's Brad Pitt or someone whose face everyone knows."

Jack gave a grunt of disagreement, but he left it at that. I made a mental note to call Gem later and tell him to be careful. Maybe add a little extra security to his already large security arsenal. It couldn't hurt. Maybe I was just becoming paranoid, but I was beginning to think that the only way we'd catch this thief was by using paranoia to our advantage and pursuing every lead, every hunch, no matter how small.

"Here we are," I said as we pulled up in front of Ricky Navarro's motel. "I sort of doubt we're going to find the bat here. What sort of killer would leave the murder weapon in plain sight?"

"One who's either too cocky to think they'd be caught, or someone too..." Denise paused. "Well, someone who's too—"

"Too stupid to know better," Jack said. He still sounded a little stung from our conversation in the car.

I wasn't sure if it was the bit about Gem or if he was just sour over the fact that Denise had inadvertently revealed her lack of knowledge about my relationship with Jack, but he seemed to be in a particularly prickly mood as he approached the motel door and gave a firm knock. I suspected it wouldn't be a good idea for anyone to try and cross Russo today. He seemed a little twitchy, and I knew he had a gun at his waist.

A moment later, the door opened. I was standing closest to the entrance beside Jack, and his eyes landed on me first. He got a big smile on his face as he scratched at his bare chest. Then his smile got even bigger when he noticed the woman standing behind me.

"Hey, there, Hot Cop. I see you brought a friend," Ricky said. "I was just having a dream along these same lines. Come on in, and I'll show you what it was all about."

"Was I in your dreams too, pal?" Russo muscled the door open. "FBI. We've got a warrant to search your apartment."

"FBI?" Ricky looked at Russo as if he was more of a buzzkill for the party he'd been envisioning than anything alarming. He didn't seem particularly intimidated by the flashy acronym that made many criminals pause. "What does the FBI want with me? I didn't do anything wrong."

"Okay, then," Jack said, pushing past Ricky and into the motel room. "Then you won't mind if we take a peek around your space for the murder weapon."

"Murder weapon for what? Who do you guys think I killed?"

I followed Russo inside. I could feel Denise keeping close behind me. I could practically hear her thinking there was strength in numbers, especially when it came to warding off a half-naked Ricky Navarro.

Ricky left the door partially open behind him as he turned to face the three of us as we began scouring the room. He wore a pair of gray sweatpants and no shirt, but he hadn't taken off the gold chain around his neck. His feet were bare and very hairy.

The motel room smelled musty and closed in, as if it hadn't seen fresh air in a week. The mustard-yellow curtains were drawn. The television was on and showing a somewhat staticky image of an old movie rerun. The shag carpeting was bare in patches with several suspicious-looking stains.

Ricky's bed looked as if it'd been torn apart in a search already, with the covers twisted in every direction. I was suddenly grateful for the cracked-open door allowing a slight breeze of fresh air to brush through the stuffy space.

Russo and Denise had already started their preliminary search of the place. Judging by the way Denise was handling every item she touched with her gloved hands, by using two fingers, daintily, as if Navarro's things might be contagious, she was just as disenchanted with the state of the place as I was. I joined the search.

The next few minutes were spent sifting through Ricky's paltry belongings. The guy really hadn't had to move much when he'd moved in here. Even with a thorough search, we were done within fifty minutes.

Ricky had spent the first twenty minutes profusely protesting the invasion of privacy. He'd added a few jabs about Denise and her pretty looks along the way. Around the twenty-minute mark, Russo had uttered a few private words to Ricky that had shut him up very quickly. I wasn't sure what Jack had told him, but Ricky's face had gone pale. He'd then flopped on the bed and proceeded to watch his show silently for the next forty minutes.

"The warrant also covers your car," Jack said. "Do you want to come outside with me or just give me the keys?"

Ricky fished out the keys from his nightstand and tossed them to Jack. He looked hopefully at Denise, as if crossing his fingers she'd be left in the room alone with him.

"No luck, Bucko," Jack said. "They're coming with me."

Denise and I trooped out after Jack to the beat-up, old Camaro parked just outside his door. Jack did a quick check of the inside of the car and came up empty handed. I heard the exasperated sigh from Denise and had to admit I was feeling the same way.

I'd started to get my hopes up that Ricky Navarro might be the "too stupid to hide the murder weapon" sort of criminal, but it seemed he was proving me wrong. My biggest fear was that he had gone to Henry Dunwoody for help in getting rid of the evidence. I had no doubt that if Henry Dunwoody wanted to make a piece of evidence disappear, it would be gone forever.

"Bingo," Jack said, shaking me from my thoughts. "Here we go. Should've looked here first. He was dumber than I thought. It's in plain sight."

Jack seemed particularly harsh on his analysis of Ricky. I wasn't sure if it was because of Ricky's advances on Agent Price, or if Jack hadn't gotten out of the touchy mood from our car ride over here.

Jack reached a gloved hand inside the trunk and removed a baseball bat. There were no obvious signs of blood on the outside, but I knew Melinda and her team would be able to run their tests to tell us if this bat had been used to kill anyone. If it had, they'd find something. Damage to the bat, traces of blood, DNA, something. I felt a slither of satisfaction down my spine.

Jack looked up at the door to the motel. Ricky had appeared there, a satisfied smirk on his face. He scratched at his chest again, an annoying habit to watch.

Jack didn't seem thrilled with it either. He seemed to take extra satisfaction as he raised the bat and said, "Gotcha."

"Yeah, that's my bat," Ricky said. "So?"

"So thanks for admitting to owning the murder weapon." Jack gave an almost mystified shake of his head as he glanced to Denise and me. "Can you believe this guy? He's making this case a walk in a park. We didn't even need to fly out here for this."

"I didn't kill no one with that bat," Ricky said. He gave another sneer. He really wasn't getting how much trouble he was in, if his cavalier attitude was to be believed. "Unless you count the baseball I smacked out of the park at the game last week."

"Then you won't mind coming with us," Jack said. "We appreciate you making this easy on us. Though you could've spared us an hour by just pointing us to your trunk."

"I'm not going anywhere. I didn't do nothing."

"Anything," Jack corrected. "You didn't do anything."

"Exactly," Ricky said, now looking really confused. "I'm glad we understand one another. Can I go back to bed now? I'd really like to finish my dream."

"Where you're going, you're going to be having dreams of a whole different nature," Jack said. "Let's go, buddy."

"I thought you just said—" Ricky shook his head. "I told you, I didn't do nothing."

"Sorry, pal, you're coming with us," Jack said. "We're going to bring you down to the precinct to chat."

"I didn't kill anybody," Ricky said, then he revised. "I didn't kill him."

His slip-up would almost have been funny if not for the dark nature of it. I shook my head in disbelief.

Jack took a few steps toward Ricky. "You said this is your bat, right? And you've had it in your possession for the last couple of weeks?"

"All season," he said defensively. "I don't let anybody else touch my bat. It's my baby."

Jack's smile grew a little brighter and a little more dangerous at the same time. "That's what I thought you'd say."

"I'm not going anywhere." Ricky shook his head. "You're full of baloney."

When Jack took a single step toward Ricky, he bolted. It was a complete surprise, seeing as Ricky had no shirt, no shoes, and no socks on. He just took off running across the

parking lot. At some point he stubbed his toe and gave a gut-
tural yell of pain, but that didn't stop him.

"This is annoying," Jack said.

"Do you want me to chase after him?" I asked. "I'd really
prefer not to touch him."

Jack, Denise, and I all stood together watching as Ricky
made his way clumsily across the parking lot. He was headed
directly for a run-down playground in a field that was mostly
dirt. It wasn't that he was particularly fast or agile, but he was
determined.

"I'll go," Jack said with a sigh, then he took off at a jog
behind the fleeing criminal.

"I'll help him out," Denise said, pulling a gun from her
hip. "I've been wanting to do this for a while."

"No!" I said, horrified. "Don't shoot him. He might have
information on the Mathematician."

"I'm not going to shoot him." Denise raised her gun.
"I'm just going to spook him."

"No, Agent Price, that's a really bad idea."

My warning was cut short as Denise's finger squeezed the
trigger. A part of me had wanted to stop her from shooting him, but a larger part of me hadn't actually believed that
she'd do it. Even as the shot rang out, deafening me, I was in
shock. I was too busy staring at her to see where the bullet
had hit. I was afraid that she hadn't missed her target, and
that when I looked, Ricky Navarro would be bleeding out
under the monkey bars.

"Not too bad," she said, analyzing her own work with a
little frown. "It worked."

Her nonchalant attitude shook me. I knew some FBI agents and cops were good at compartmentalization—myself included—but I never took shooting at a target lightly. Ever.

Feeling a prickle of dismay, I snapped my head forward to survey the damage. I never thought I'd be so relieved to see Ricky Navarro alive and seemingly unharmed. He didn't have any bullets in his body, which was a good start, though he was laying on the ground and twisting in pain.

It took me a moment to figure out what Agent Price had been shooting at if not Ricky Navarro. Then I got it. He'd been running over some sort of contraption made of tires. Agent Price had put a bullet through the tire beneath Ricky's foot, sending him spiraling to the ground. It was a very impressive shot.

"Wow," I said. "I'm sorry to have doubted you."

"I've trained as a sharpshooter," she said with an easy shrug. "I told you I've wanted to be an FBI agent all my life, and I knew if they were going to let me carry a gun, I had to be good."

"Yeah, but not that good," I said. "They gave me a gun, and I couldn't have made that shot. I wouldn't even have attempted it, and I'm decent."

She gave a thin smile. "It's a passion of mine."

"Huh."

"It surprises a lot of people," she said, softly holstering her gun. She didn't take her eyes off Jack Russo. "A lot of people think profilers are useless, that our work doesn't really matter because it's not a hard science. I'm used to that. People don't think women can shoot as well as men. Again, I'm used to it. I always prefer people underestimate me anyway. Under promise, over-deliver, right?"

I glanced at Agent Price with a new respect. A new understanding, even. I'd been one of the people who'd misjudged her. Mostly because she'd been the beautiful woman standing next to my ex-boyfriend. I'd let my bias, and admittedly my jealousy, cloud my judgment of the agent.

"I'm sorry," I said. "Of all people, I shouldn't have—"

"It's fine," Denise said quickly. "I'm the new guy on the block. It's good to have a healthy dose of skepticism." She winked at me. "So long as you're open to changing your mind when I prove you wrong. No offense."

"Happy to be proven wrong."

She gave me a smile, and I returned it. Jack was making his way back with a grumbling Ricky Navarro cinched in handcuffs. As Denise smiled at Russo and complimented him on the arrest, I felt a pit in my stomach. A new sort of pit. Not the jealous sort of pit, not the petty, claws-out kind of pit.

It was a new feeling, one that was even worse than jealousy. As I followed Jack, Ricky, and Denise to my car, I knew it was the realization that Jack and I were truly over, and he had the right to move on. Whether or not he and Agent Price were an actual thing, the truth was that they could be, and there was nothing I could do about it.

Somehow, it made the situation both better and worse to imagine Jack getting together with Agent Price. There was nothing wrong with her. She'd proven herself to be a good agent, a thoughtful person, a very smart woman. She was beautiful, and I was willing to bet she didn't have the same commitment issues as me. She lived in the same city as Jack. In short, she was perfect for him, and even I couldn't argue with that.

The car ride back to the precinct was relatively quiet. We turned over Ricky Navarro for booking, to be questioned later, then made our way back to the main office. When Agent Price ducked into the restroom, Jack grabbed my hand and pulled me back into the hallway before I could make it to my desk.

"Jack?" I asked. "Is everything okay?"

"I was just going to ask you that," he said. "You were quiet on the way back. You did a good job. I know this doesn't wrap up the Mathematician's case with a pretty bow, but it's a big start. It's good work, Rosetti."

"Sure, good work by Agent Price," I said. "She's very impressive. You two make a great team."

Russo gave me a hard look. "She's very good at her job."

"I'm realizing that. The two of you are lucky to have one another as partners."

"Kate—"

"I'm going to touch base with Jimmy," I said. "I want to see if he's gotten any further with his research. Then I'd like to visit Harriett Windsor's niece. If you and Agent Price would like to come with, you're welcome to."

"Kate—"

I was already into the office as Jack called my name a second time. I kept myself walking forward. The conversation that was obviously on the tip of Jack's tongue was not one I wanted to have here, now, or maybe ever.

It was probably best for everyone involved to finish this case and get those agents back where they belonged—across the country from me.

Chapter 17

After a quick catch-up with Jimmy, it was decided that we'd part ways once again for the next phase of the investigation. Jimmy wanted to stay back with Dunkirk to combine forces when questioning Ricky Navarro. Now that we had the potential murder weapon, we were hoping he'd be more willing to talk.

Best-case scenario was that we'd find evidence on the bat linking Ricky to both murders. With any luck, then Ricky might consider cutting a deal with the DA in exchange for information that could get us closer to the Mathematician.

At the same time, I wasn't getting my hopes up. A criminal as meticulous as the Mathematician wouldn't leave loose ends. The fact that Navarro was still alive was a testament to his disposability. I was willing to bet that even if Ricky wanted to roll over on the people who'd told him to get rid of Garrett Landers, he wouldn't be able to provide us with any useful information. We might be able to pin Garrett's murder on Navarro, but if I had to guess, he'd be a dead end after that.

"Make sure you grill him about Henry Dunwoody," I said to Jimmy before we parted ways. "There's something funny about the two of them being connected. It might just be part of Dunwoody's cover, but if he really is the Mathematician, then he'll have selected Ricky Navarro for a reason. I want to know what that reason is."

"Because he's dumb enough to follow orders without questioning them?" Jimmy shrugged. "Let me know how things go at the Windsor house."

I left the precinct to meet Jack and Denise outside. They were waiting for me at the car, prepped and ready to visit Harriett Windsor's niece. Asha had gotten ahold of Nicole Harding, the niece, and had arranged for her to meet us at her late aunt's house. That way we could get a feel for the niece and Harriett Windsor's lifestyle at the same time.

The car ride was more subdued than the previous one. There was a slight overture of awkwardness between Jack and me after the way we'd left our broken conversation in the hallway. I wasn't sure if Denise's quiet was a sign that she'd picked up on the discomfort, or if she was just feeling the pressing importance of our progress in the case.

I parked in front of Harriett Windsor's house and took a moment to look up at the impressive place. I rarely made it to this part of Minneapolis. There was always traffic, the streets were narrow and full of one-ways, and the people who lived here were different. Not different bad or different good, just different.

While I was a St. Paulie girl through and through, even I could admit this neighborhood was a gem. Filled with arching old houses and tall, magnificent trees casting shade over the streets, the area had an almost European feel to it. People in these parts were willing to pay top dollar to feel as if they'd been transported to a different era.

The three of us headed up the front walk, currently covered with a light layer of snow. I could imagine pretty rosebushes leaning over the walkway in the summer, and a perky little herb garden in the window boxes out front. Pots of pansies bobbing on the front steps.

The door opened before we could knock. A woman probably in her mid-thirties stood before us in jeans and a crisp black blouse. Her brunette hair was pinned back, and she wore glasses with purple frames that made her look just eclectic enough to fit in with this part of Minneapolis.

"You must be the detectives," the woman said. "My name's Nicole. I'm Harriett's niece."

"Thank you so much for seeing us on short notice," I said. "I'm Detective Kate Rosetti, and these are my associates from the FBI, Agents Price and Russo."

Nicole shook our hands and invited us in. "I've got some tea set up in the solarium. It was my aunt's favorite room. It's sad to be in there because it reminds me of her so much, but at the same time, I feel like it would be what she wanted."

"We're very sorry for your loss," I said, following Nicole through a winding hallway covered in blue tile. "Your aunt's death is a tragedy."

"It sure is." Nicole gave a shake of her head as we reached the solarium, a room with curved, all-glass windows that let in a tinted, greenish-colored light. The space was covered in plants. "She was an incredible woman. You know, it's hard to hear people say she had a good, long life."

Nicole paused to sit at a bistro table. On it was a small aloe vera plant along with a tea set. The china was decorated with rhododendron blooms in a shade of purple that matched Nicole's glasses. It was dainty, pretty, and perfect for the room.

The four of us sat around the table and gave Nicole a moment of silence as she poured the warm beverage for us. The tea smelled minty, with a twist of floral notes, and tasted quite comforting on a chilly January day.

"Yes, she did lead a long life." Nicole resumed where she'd left off without missing a beat. "It was a good life. She had a good husband, good friends, wealth beyond most people's wildest dreams, but still—it was incomplete."

"Incomplete, how?" I asked.

"She was healthy and in good spirits. Her mind was as sharp as it'd ever been." Nicole gave a nostalgic smile as if remembering something witty her aunt had said. "She didn't deserve to die. She wasn't ready to die. It wasn't her time to die. Someone made that choice for her, and it's completely unfair."

"I agree wholeheartedly," I said. "The loss of your aunt, as I said before, is truly tragic. That's why we're here." I gestured toward Jack and Denise. "We are working with the best. Our team is very focused on finding the person who killed your aunt so we can bring him to justice."

"Him?" she asked, curiosity evident in her voice. "Do you have information about who killed her? Was it the groundskeeper?"

I blinked. "Why would you think it was the groundskeeper?"

"I thought that would be obvious in light of recent developments."

"Recent developments?" I asked, glancing at Jack and Denise. "I'm sorry. I'm not sure to what you're referring."

"I-I thought that's why you were here this morning," she said. "My aunt's will was read. She left her entire estate and art collection to her groundskeeper and her maid."

There was a moment of sharp silence broken only when Denise set her china teacup down a little too hard against her saucer.

"I'm sorry," I offered again. "I hadn't heard that."

"That's where I was when you called me, at the attorney's office," Nicole said. "I should've known you guys wouldn't have heard about that yet, but my brain has been a little foggy trying to help take care of things since my aunt passed. I'm still in a little bit of shock trying to digest the will."

"It must have been quite a shock."

"Tell me about it," Nicole said. "I didn't see that coming."

"From what I understand, you're her only living relative?"

Nicole nodded. "My Aunt Harriett and her husband never had children. My mom, Aunt Harriett's sister, passed away a few years ago."

"Were you close with your aunt?"

"You could say that," she said. "I wouldn't say we were like mother and daughter or anything. I was already an adult by the time my mother passed and well established on my own. But I'd call Aunt Harriett once a month or so. She'd send cards for special occasions. Once in a while we'd get together for a holiday or something, but it was rare."

"Do you live nearby?"

"Half an hour away," Nicole said. "But Aunt Harriett was quite content to spend most of her time alone or with her small circle of friends. She was a regular aunt. We were on good terms, but it wasn't like we knew every detail about one another."

"You mentioned she had a small circle of friends?" I asked. "Do any names in particular stand out to you?"

"I'm sorry, but no," she said. "Her best friend was her housekeeper, but I've already told you guys that. The housekeeper is married to the groundskeeper, and they've been close for years. Beyond that, my aunt had a small circle of ladies with whom she'd garden or play cards with, but I don't get the feeling she told them much of anything important. That particular circle of friends was made up of uppity older women—sorry to sound harsh—who mostly preferred to gossip and sip cocktails at noon."

I gave a small smile. "I see."

"My aunt wasn't really like that. Well, a little bit. She enjoyed the gossip, but she didn't get into it like all the other women did," Nicole said. "The way Aunt Harriett explained it to me, it was like she was watching a play. She listened to these women talk like it was pure entertainment. Something frivolous and fun, a light way to spend an afternoon."

"These women, they were all around the same age as your aunt? And the same social status?"

"Yes. If you're asking whether or not I think they killed her, I'd have to say no. I think the youngest member of the group was eighty-two years old. They're all plenty wealthy. I just don't see it."

"What about the groundskeeper?" I asked. "Or the housekeeper?"

Nicole cleared her throat. "My mind has been whirling since the will was read. I'm still trying to wrap my brain around it. A few weeks ago, I would've said there was no way they could have—or would have—killed her."

I glanced at Russo. "But?"

"But a person's got to wonder when something like this happens." Nicole's hands shook. "She left them a lot of money. The entire estate, all of her art, her savings."

"I hate to pry, but this is important," I said. "Were you left anything?"

"I was left a sizeable amount of cash. I'm grateful for it, of course. A few personal effects. In the scheme of things, it's still quite a lot of money. But in comparison to the size of her estate, it's a negligible percentage."

"That had to sting." I mixed up my face into the most sympathetic expression I could muster. "You're her only living relative. You had to think more would be left to you."

"Yes, of course. Don't get me wrong, I didn't expect to inherit everything. It wasn't like I was her daughter or something. But I was her sister's daughter."

"I'd be angry if that were the case," Denise piped up, obviously appealing to Nicole's shock at being mostly left out of the will. "It feels a little unfair to me."

Nicole, however, wasn't fooled by Denise's kind tone. "Maybe a little bit, but that's not what's bothering me. It's not the money that I'm upset about. Look, I'm a lawyer, and I make a very good living. My house is paid off; I have a boat; I'm very comfortable. I don't need any more money."

"What was it that bothered you?" I asked. "The house?"

"The house and the art," she said. "The home has been in the family for generations. I know my mom would be really upset to learn that her sister chose to pass the house down to a friend instead of a relative. It's just the principle of it. That, and the art. It's a priceless collection. It's not as if I would've turned around and sold it; I appreciated the art collection for what it was."

"What it was?"

"My aunt lovingly collected all of these pieces, not for the fame of it, but because she truly loved them all. That's why very few people understood the level of art collector that she was. She wasn't showy about her pieces. She rarely talked about them, never boasted about them. She was even stingy to loan them out to museums. She just really enjoyed them. I mean, I've never seen someone enjoy art like she did."

Nicole sat back in her seat and took a sip of tea.

"I've witnessed my aunt literally standing in a room for almost an hour just looking at a single painting. Each piece meant something different to her. Some reminded her of family members, others of friends. Sometimes she just admired the work of the artist or the particular skills it took to make a specific piece. Sometimes, she just bought a painting because it was pretty and spoke to her. Those were her words. She would say she could feel a piece of art calling to her, tugging at her, like it belonged in her collection. Then she'd just buy it."

"It sounds like a very special, very personally curated collection," I said. "I understand why you'd be upset that it was leaving the family."

"She could've left everything else, the rest of the money, everything, to her friends. It just hurts that she didn't trust me to take care of the things that meant the most to her. I wouldn't have turned around and sold them. That's the real kicker. Now the fate of her art collection and the house are in the hands of two people who aren't related to her at all."

"Let me play devil's advocate," Jack said. "Forgive me as I know this is a sensitive time, and I'm just coming on to the case. These two ladies here are the experts." Jack gestured to me and Denise before he continued. "But haven't the groundskeeper and his wife been a part of this estate for over three decades each? Isn't it possible they might know even more about your aunt's wishes than you?"

There was a moment of precarious silence that followed in which Jack, Denise, and I all watched Nicole for her reaction. This was the place where the interview could quickly turn ugly. To our collective relief, however, it seemed that Nicole had already considered this. She let out a quiet sigh, gave a nod of her head. A tear trickled down her cheek.

"I've thought about that," she said. "Maybe it's my fault for not making enough of an effort. I don't know. The thing that really gets me, though, is that her will was recently changed, and I can't help but think that wasn't a coincidence."

"What do you mean?" I asked. "Were you her lawyer?"

"No. I didn't want to work for family members, and she agreed that it would be a bad idea." Nicole waved her hands. "I keep a strict business-separate-from-personal policy. I didn't want anything to turn touchy."

"Smart," I said, deftly not looking at Jack, thinking my agreement was a little ironic seeing as I was sitting here working with my ex-boyfriend.

"But Aunt Harriett had asked for a lawyer recommendation, which I gave to her. She mentioned to me she was having her will amended. I didn't think too much about it. She needed to do that sometimes to accommodate changes to her art collection, if she bought and sold expensive pieces, things like that. Then, when the will was read, I realized she'd overhauled everything."

"You'd seen her will before?"

"Oh, sure. She was very open about how she'd be leaving me the house and her art collection. I think you can even see a previous version of the will somewhere. Maybe I have a copy, or maybe it's in her files somewhere."

"You didn't know she'd mostly cut you out of a the will?"

She shook her head. "No. Not that it mattered, really, but—"

"But it did," I interrupted. "It was a big change."

"Yes," she admitted. "And not only for me."

"You think she might have let something slip about the will amendments to her housekeeper?" I asked. "Or the groundskeeper, and that they suddenly got itchy fingers to get their hands on the money sooner?"

"I mean, they are of a certain age," she said. "They only have so much time left to enjoy the riches my aunt left them."

"My understanding was that the groundskeeper had an alibi for the time of the murder."

"There's two of them," she pointed out. "They could've been working together. Do you know what his alibi was? I mean, it doesn't mean that much if his wife gave him an alibi, does it?"

"Thank you so much for meeting us here and for being so forthcoming with your information," I said. "It's been very helpful. Do you think we could take a quick peek at your aunt's art collection before we head out?"

"Yes, of course. Right this way," she said. "I appreciate how seriously you're taking my aunt's death. I have to admit, I sort of thought that her case might slip through the cracks at the police department because of her age."

"She was murdered," I said. "Her murderer needs to be brought to justice. Age isn't a factor in our investigation."

"The truly ironic thing is that if the groundskeeper had simply asked for some money, my aunt would've given it to them. She was very generous with her finances, especially with her friends."

Nicole gathered up the tea set, then on second thought, left it on the table. She gestured for us to follow her down a hallway. There were several large, high-ceiling rooms adorned in furniture from a different time period.

"Here's her reading den. It's next to the library," Nicole said, gesturing toward the first two rooms we passed. "This one's sort of a trophy and awards room."

Nicole paused as I poked my head inside. I saw all sorts of awards and trophies mounted around the room. Medals from past wars, trophies from adolescent soccer and softball games, academic achievements pinned on the walls. Several diplomas hung behind the desk.

"The art room is this way."

"Do you have any trophies in there?" I asked.

Nicole showed us down a second, more private hallway. "I played a couple of sports and might have an old photo or softball mitt hanging in there. Nothing worth noting. I stopped when I got to college to focus on my law degree. Here's all of her art."

I stepped into the room first. Nicole let the two agents pass through before her, then she joined us a moment later. The room into which we'd stepped was different than the library, the trophy room, the reading den. There was an air of reverence to it. Like a museum or church. It had obviously been a place of great importance to the deceased.

The room itself was gorgeous with high, domed ceilings. The gildings around the room were a deep-copper shade and incredibly intricate. The whole space felt very Romanesque, almost otherworldly. I wasn't a particularly discerning connoisseur of art, but even I could appreciate Harriett's space.

For someone like her, someone who had loved art, it was easy to see how she could've spent hours in this room, wrapped in her own thoughts, musings, daydreams. Or simply appreciating the years of collecting she'd done.

I looked around the room for quite some time. The art was displayed in almost-matching frames. Each of the frames looked similar but weren't quite the same.

"She had a personal framer in France," Nicole said, noticing me inspecting the frames. "Each one hand carved and painted. They're all part of one collection, but they're each completely unique. The frames themselves are worth a ton of money."

"Half the time, the frames are more expensive than the paintings," I remarked. "That always annoyed me. Then again, I've only bought frames at Michael's."

"It didn't annoy Harriett in the slightest," Nicole said. "She loved the process of framing them herself. Then again, she had the funds to do it. The frame was almost as much of a piece of art to her as the actual image inside."

"Well, it certainly helps when money isn't an issue," I said. "That adds a little bit of freedom. Did she have a favorite?"

"Oh, sure," Nicole said. She wandered around the room for a moment as if lost in thought. Then abruptly, she pointed out a photograph on the wall that looked as if it had been painted. In it were various sprigs of flowers in ancient-looking chalices. "This one. For no reason. She didn't know the artist, didn't have any connection to it. She told me she just saw it and knew she had to have it. She could stare at this one for hours."

I studied the painting, trying to feel the same sort of attachment that the late Harriett Windsor had felt to it. I didn't get anything calling to me. The flowers were pretty and all, but apparently I wasn't educated enough to appreciate the nuances of this picture of flowers over the millions of other pictures of flowers that existed in the world.

"Nothing's missing from her collection?" I repeated. "Nothing at all?"

"Not a thing," she said. "I checked it against the roster. I gave the list of everything Aunt Harriett had to the other cops, so I'm sure they checked it too. Not to mention, it's pretty obvious. I mean, the room is set up around the art. Each frame is filled. No nail has a missing picture."

It certainly looked like a complete collection to me. "I'm sorry, I just have one last question for you."

Nicole gave a dismissive shake of her head. "It's fine. You can ask for my alibi, but I already gave it to the other cops.

My boss can confirm I was working late at the office the night my aunt died. My boss's name is Harvey Daniels."

"Thanks," I said. "Sorry to ask, but it's protocol."

"No problem," she said. "I appreciate you being thorough. Is there anything else I can help you with today? Otherwise, I should be getting back to work."

Nicole led us out of the house. Russo, Denise, and I made our way back to my car, none of us talking, each of us lost in thought. We didn't speak until we were on our way back to the precinct.

"What do you think?" I finally asked once we were on the road, giving a glance in the rearview mirror at Denise.

She'd been staring out the window when I spoke, her lips pursed. She seemed lost in thought and started at the sound of my voice.

"I'm not sure," she said, sounding somewhat uncertain. "I've got a few conflicting ideas rolling around in my head."

"You can shoot a few theories out to us," I said. "What's said in the car stays in the car, right, Russo?"

Jack nodded. "Sure thing."

Denise hesitated, then gave a nod. "This development has opened up a whole new can of worms. Or maybe I should say a whole new box of motives for people to want our victim dead."

"You mean the reading of the will this morning? It had to be a big shock to Nicole to find out she'd all but been left pennies compared to what she thought she'd be getting."

"Exactly. If she'd caught wind of the new will, then she would have had a motive to kill our victim. Out of revenge, or malice, or even just a passionate strike of anger," Denise said. "It's possible she even regrets it. Nicole seemed to be displaying real emotion. Which means she's either innocent, or she's struggling heavily with the guilt of what she's done, implying that it wasn't premeditated."

"Hit over the head with a bat doesn't exactly scream pre-meditation," I said. "But it's possible."

"I'm still having an issue with the bat thing," Jack said. "We think the murder weapon was the same for Harriett and Garrett. If that's true, and if the bat we found in Ricky Navarro's trunk is indeed the murder weapon, what's the connection between the two deaths?"

"I'm not sure yet," Denise said. "We can't forget there's new motive for the groundskeeper and his wife. If they'd recently learned that they were due to inherit a windfall when the mistress of the house died, they had financial motivation to make that happen faster."

"We're all thinking it," Jack said, "but I'm still not seeing a connection between any of this Harriett Windsor stuff with Ricky Navarro and team. Not to mention the Mathematician."

"Does this make you think we might not be dealing with the Mathematician?" I asked Denise. "It's almost looking like it could be two separate things. Ricky could've killed Garrett over an issue between them. We know Garrett promised Ricky a payday and never delivered, so there's financial motivation. Ricky was ticked he lost his job and his apartment, and he could've been getting back at his former buddy."

"Then we've got three good suspects for Harriett's murder," Jack said, "except two of them have alibis. But there's plenty of financial and emotional motivation here for a number of people to have killed her separate from the Garrett Landers case."

Denise was shaking her head by the time Russo finished speaking. "No, that's where you're wrong," she said, her gaze fixed on me. "On the contrary."

"On the contrary?" I asked.

"This makes me think more than ever before that we're dealing with the Mathematician."

"How?" I asked. "I'm not seeing the connection."

"Me neither," Denise said grimly. "And that's the problem. We won't see the connection until he wants us to see the connection. And by then, it'll be too late."

Chapter 18

"Hey, Asha," I said over the Bluetooth system as we cruised down the road. "Do you have news for me?"

"Hold on a second," she said. "I'll call you right back."

I glanced over at Denise and Jack in the mirror and raised my eyebrows. "That's a new one."

"I'm trying to figure out if that's a good or a bad sign," Jack said. "Asha doesn't often cut you off like that."

We didn't have to wait long to find out. A moment later, my phone rang, and I answered. I let Asha know we were all listening.

"Yeah. We're all here too," she said. "We've got news for you."

"Who's we?" I asked.

"It's Jimmy, Dr. Brooks, and me in the conference room," Asha said. "Y'all are on speaker. Melinda, you go first."

"It's looking like the bat could be a match as the murder weapon," she said. "We haven't confirmed anything with certainty yet, but we found blood and tissue on it—plenty for a DNA analysis. We're running it now. I can already tell you there's blood from more than one person on it. The killer tried to clean up but sloppily. An amateur job."

"The sort of job that would fit Ricky Navarro's style," I said grimly. "Jimmy, did you get him to crack on anything when you interrogated him?"

Jimmy sighed. "Not much. He told me to talk to the guys on his team, said they'd vouch for him. I don't know exactly what that means, but I'm going to do it anyway. I've

264

called in a couple of guys. They're headed to the station. I don't think I'll get anything from his baseball buddies, but it can't hurt to poke around some."

There was a moment of silence on both ends of the phone.

"I thought you'd be happy about that," Melinda said. "We've got a murder weapon. We've got a guy who has already admitted to owning the murder weapon. You found it in his trunk. There's literally blood on it. That's should be enough to arrest him with everything else you've got, and a conviction is looking pretty good."

"But it's not right." Denise spoke before I could. She caught my eye in the rearview mirror and shrank back a little bit. "Sorry to interrupt, Detective Rosetti. But it's not right."

"I've never known you guys to turn down evidence before," Melinda said. "Do you think I made a mistake?"

"Of course we don't think you made a mistake," I said hurriedly. "But I do agree with Denise. We're missing something. Why would Ricky Navarro have killed Harriett Windsor? What was his motive?"

"Maybe it was some sort of a low-paying hitman job," Melinda suggested. "If you suspect the Mathematician is involved, then maybe he just hired this guy to off a few people as some part of a greater master plan."

"It's possible," Denise said. "It just doesn't fit with his MO. It's messy and sloppy."

"Yes, but he's essentially framing someone else to go down for murder. If we assume that to be true," Melinda said, "he gets off scot-free."

"Right, but that's not his MO," Denise repeated. "He doesn't get a thrill from making a splash. He doesn't murder for fun, for convenience, for anything, really."

"That we know of," Asha corrected. "It's possible he's been linked to other murders that simply haven't been solved."

"It's just not his style," Denise insisted. "Not to mention, nothing is missing, and there've been two deaths. What's the point?"

"Let's move on," I said. "What else do we know?"

"We know that there's a little more incentive than even Nicole knew for the groundskeeper and his wife to need the money they were left in the Windsor will," Asha said. "A very expensive reason they might've wanted Harriett dead."

"I thought he had an alibi."

"He does, but it's not a solid alibi. He was home with his wife," Asha said. "Which doesn't help because she has the same reason to have wanted Harriett Windsor dead."

"A reason besides a ton of money?"

"The housekeeper, Anna Gertens, has cancer," Asha said. "She got the diagnosis a few months ago. I won't bore you with the details, but I'll tell you it's a rare type of cancer with a low survival rate."

"Yikes."

"There are a few experimental drugs that have been shown to help slow the progression. The one she needs has just been approved and isn't yet covered by most insurances. Don't ask how I found out, just know that I did."

"Let me guess," I said, "they wouldn't be able to afford the medical bills on their current salaries?"

"Bingo."

"But if they found out they were listed in the will," I said, "and they helped Harriett to an earlier grave, they'd be able to pay for it."

"Get this," Asha said. "Anna Gertens went in to receive her first treatment the day before Harriett died."

"That sounds like premeditation to me," Russo said. "The only thing I'm struggling to figure out is how this all matches with the baseball bat linked to Ricky Navarro. Could the Gertens have hired him to do the dirty work?"

"That's where my mind went," Asha said. "They could've done some Googling on the darker internet sites and found Ricky Navarro. It's definitely possible."

"That would link them together," Melinda said. "Ricky could've hit Harriett Windsor first, gotten a taste of killing, then decided he was mad enough at Garrett to finish him off too."

"Or maybe it was just another job," Jimmy said. "Maybe he'd gotten a taste of contract killing and thought it was easy money. Someone—even the Mathematician—could've hired him to get rid of Garrett."

"I think we need to pay a visit to the Gertens and hear what they have to say," I said. "Though you'd think if you'd hired a contract killer, you'd make sure you had a better alibi than a flimsy one saying you were home with your wife."

"I've got some baseball guys and a few of Garrett's ex-girlfriends on their way here," Jimmy said. "I'll let you know if I turn up anything new."

"Any movement on Henry Dunwoody?" I asked.

"Nothing yet," Jimmy said. "I've been checking in with surveillance regularly, and he hasn't moved from his house."

"Either he's really confident we're not going to catch him," I said, "or he's not the Mathematician."

"We'll find out soon enough," Asha promised. "We're getting there. I can feel it."

***

Steven and Anna Gertens lived on a property not far from Harriett Windsor's, though the neighborhood had a completely different feel to it. The houses on the Gertens' street were tiny and over a century old. Some were immaculately kept up, others not so much. The homes were close together, squished into a neat little line under a canopy of mature trees.

Even so, the houses weren't cheap due to their proximity to the nicer parts of the Minneapolis neighborhoods. I suspected that the Gertens had bought their property quite a long time ago. A good investment, considering how much it had likely appreciated over the duration of their ownership.

We slid out of the car, and I made my way up the front walk. The lawn had gotten a recent haircut, and the landscaping, though sparse, was immaculately maintained. I knocked, and the door opened almost at once.

An older woman with gray hair tied back in a ponytail stood there smiling at us. The house smelled like fresh-baked bread. Mrs. Gertens wore a red gingham dress and waved us in as if we were old friends.

"I'm just pulling some sourdough rolls out of the oven," she said. "Would you like to come in for a bite?"

"We haven't introduced ourselves," I said, unable to help myself.

"There's plenty of time for that over warm bread," she said. "I just put the coffee pot on. Decaf, of course, at this hour. Bread never tastes as good as it does fresh out of the oven, so I'd hate to miss our window."

As Mrs. Gertens led us into a kitchen decorated like a fifties' diner, I introduced myself and the two FBI agents. If the woman was shocked to have us in her house, she didn't give any sign of it. She merely continued to slice bread and pour coffee into cups and serve us each a roll with a cup of coffee and a splash of cream.

"This is delicious," Russo said. "Thank you."

"It's my grandmother's recipe," she said with a smile. "I've been making it for years. I have to give so much of it away because my husband and I can't eat it all. It's a pleasure to have company to share it with."

"Mrs. Gertens," I said, feeling a little guilty steering the conversation almost immediately to business, "we have a few questions to ask you in regard to the death of your former employer."

"Ms. Windsor," she said. "We already answered questions for the police."

"We're following up with some new information." I took a sip of coffee from the dainty little mug. "As you know, Ms. Windsor was murdered. We're doing everything we can to find her killer."

Mrs. Gertens nodded. "I've been told as much. That's very good. She was a good woman. She didn't deserve to die."

"Nobody deserves to die from cancer either," I said, watching for her reaction. "But that doesn't change anything."

Mrs. Gertens set her cup down. The slightest clink of china on china sounded. "You heard about the will."

"Yes," I said. "We also found out that you signed up for a new treatment for your condition the day before Harriett Windsor died. Pretty risky move, considering you didn't have enough money to cover the bills that were sure to head your way."

"I suppose it looks that way."

"Is it supposed to look a different way?"

"I suppose it doesn't exactly matter what it looks like," she said. "What matters is the truth, and the truth is that I didn't have anything to do with Ms. Windsor's death."

Anna's eyes teared up at the mention of her former employer. She raised a hand and gently wiped at the corner of her eye, not trying to hide it. She didn't seem to care that we'd witnessed her moment of sadness. Either it was genuine, or she was a great actress.

"Do you have an alibi for the time of your former employer's death?"

"You keep doing that." She stared at me with light-blue eyes, still a bit misty from the tears that had pooled there a moment before. "You keep referring to Ms. Windsor as if she were simply my former employer. But that's not how it was at all. She was a friend, a very dear friend. Family, one might say."

"Yet you call her Ms. Windsor," Denise noted. "That's an interesting choice of words."

"She was still my employer. I suppose that's technically correct, but the way you say it, it's as if that's all she was to me. That's just not true. Ms. Windsor was my friend and confidant, and I didn't kill her. I don't need an alibi to prove that."

Jack cleared his throat. "No, but it'd help an awful lot. If you could just give us an alibi, ma'am, we would be able to ease up on the questioning."

"My husband already told you that he was with me at the time of the murder. That would mean he's also my alibi." She gave a dainty one-shouldered shrug. "But I suppose that doesn't mean all that much to you since you probably think we were in on it together."

"Why did you sign up for this new treatment?" I asked. "Especially considering the timing? We know you didn't have the funds to cover it."

"No, but Ms. Windsor did."

"You mean in the will?"

Mrs. Gertens shook her head. "I mean she gave me a check to cover it. I had no clue she would include us in her will at all, let alone to the magnitude that she did. We weren't counting on any of that money. We don't need it. Frankly, I don't know what to do with it."

"You had no clue about the will?" I watched her carefully. "Who did you think she'd leave it all to?"

"I didn't think much about it. Why would I? It wasn't my problem. Look at me; I'm practically ancient." Anna gave a small smile. "I'm happy here. I have my husband. We have enough money to retire. I love—loved—working for Ms. Windsor. These days, the things that make me happy are puttering around in the garden and baking fresh bread. We get brunch every Sunday after church at my favorite little deli. I go to a book club once a month. I am fulfilled."

I could hear the earnest tone in Mrs. Gertens' voice. She struck me as a very unlikely culprit to have caused Ms. Windsor's death—either by swinging the bat herself or by hiring someone like Ricky Navarro. Of course, that didn't count the husband out, nor did it prove her innocence entirely. But my gut feeling was that this was all wrong.

"Not only am I fulfilled in my life, and not only am I ancient, but I'm dying." She gave me a warm smile. A smile that was almost jarring, considering the nature of her statement. "I didn't want to get the treatment."

"You didn't?"

"I didn't tell Ms. Windsor about my diagnosis. I didn't want her to worry or cut my hours or treat me differently. My husband, however, is desperate to keep me around just a little longer, that sweet man." She gave a fond, nostalgic glimmer of a smile. "Steven told Ms. Windsor, without my knowledge, about my diagnosis. He signed me up for the treatment. He has the check that was to be cashed to pay for it."

"A check you don't need anymore," Jack pointed out, "seeing as you have more money than you'll ever know what to do with."

She nodded again. "I wouldn't have cashed the check anyway, and I wouldn't have let my husband do it either. My dear Steven, I love him to the ends of the earth and back, and he'd give his life for me. But I'm not a medical science experiment. I have lived a long, happy, healthy, fulfilled life. What's left is for me to enjoy it and make memories. If I had one wish, it was simply that Ms. Windsor hadn't left this earth before me."

Mrs. Gertens paused to give a tiny throat clear. Her voice came out a little hoarse.

"She was a very kind, generous, lovely woman. She was the picture of health and had many happy years ahead of her. It's a shame that was stolen from her."

"It is a shame," I found myself saying, "which is why we're hunting for her killer. Ms. Windsor deserves to have closure, justice, and we're going to give that to her."

"I know, dear." Mrs. Gertens nodded. "You're just doing your job. I respect that. And while you might think that my husband had incentive for murder, possibly even more than me, I can tell you he'd never harm so much as a fly. We spent the night together here. That's the truth."

"We're looking into the possibility that the person who killed Ms. Windsor was hired," Jack said. "Is it possible—"

"I wouldn't know where or how to find a professional killer." Mrs. Gertens gave a little laugh. "And it's even more preposterous that my husband would. I imagine one would need the internet or a cell phone of some sort to do that, and my husband rarely uses either. He doesn't have a cell, and I check his email for him. You can verify that, I'm sure."

"Then would you have any idea who might have wanted Ms. Windsor dead?" I asked. "Initially, we suspected that a very high-caliber thief was after her art collection, but from what we can tell, nothing was stolen."

"How would you know what was stolen?"

I was a little taken aback by the question. "We went to the house today. Ms. Windsor's niece, Nicole, showed us the room where the artwork was housed. Nothing was missing from the frames or from the walls, and it matched the roster she gave us that listed all of Ms. Windsor's pieces."

"I'm sure it did."

"Do you have a reason to believe that's not true?" I asked, exchanging a quick glance with Jack and Denise. "Do you have any reason to believe Nicole might have killed her aunt?"

"I suppose she had an alibi," Mrs. Gertens said. "Not that it makes much difference if the person who killed Ms. Windsor was hired. That makes it almost worse, don't you think? A hired gun is so impersonal. I feel if one person decides they can play the role of God, they should have the guts to do the dirty work themselves, no?"

"So you do think it's a possibility Nicole killed her aunt?" I asked.

"I think if Nicole had caught wind of the fact that the will had been updated, she might have been very angry."

"I would imagine so," I said. "Do you think it's possible she found out about the will?"

"Of course. Nicole is very smart. It's also possible she caught wind of the check Ms. Windsor had given my husband and simply suspected all was not right."

"What did you mean about the art?" I asked. "You said something about how of course it would match up with Nicole's list?"

"Do you have Nicole's list handy?" Mrs. Gertens deftly peeled off a tiny piece of bread and took a bite. "I can tell you from a glance if it is comprehensive or not. The police never thought to ask me about it before, and I never thought to say anything. I was grieving my friend."

I nodded to Russo. He removed a photocopy of the paper Nicole had given to us and set it on the table. Mrs. Gertens finished chewing, swallowed, then pulled the paper closer and scanned it over top to bottom. Her expression was unreadable.

"That's a comprehensive list of the main room," she said with a nod. "It's very good that nothing's missing from there."

"You say that as if there should be another list," I said. "Was this Ms. Windsor's entire collection?"

Mrs. Gertens shook her head. "She had a different room tucked away from the rest of the house. By that, I mean it was a small fortress. Fake bookshelf doors, locked entry, the whole thing. It was where she kept her most precious pieces. She called it the family room. Often, she bought these pieces anonymously or through a third party to keep her identity hidden."

"She didn't want people to know she owned these pieces?" Jack asked. "Why?"

"She loved them because of the art," Mrs. Gertens said, a brief whisper of joy flitting across her face. "She genuinely loved these pieces. She cherished them, gave them a good home. It wasn't about show and wasn't about status. Nobody knew who she was. But she knew, and that was enough. I always respected that about her."

"How did you find out about it?"

"I found out about six months ago," Mrs. Gertens said. "About the same time she hired her lawyer to redo her will."

"I thought you said you didn't know the details of the will."

"I didn't," she said. "But I was the housekeeper and friend of Ms. Windsor. I overheard conversations, saw lawyers come and go. I even heard an argument between Ms.

Windsor and her niece. Nicole wanted to act as Ms. Windsor's lawyer, but she refused."

"Ms. Windsor refused?" I clarified, thinking that wasn't the story Nicole had given me at all. "Are you sure?"

"Positive. She was quite appalled at her niece's behavior and told me so. That's all I know. The next week a new person came to the house several times, and I assumed it was the lawyer. The day after he left was the day Ms. Windsor showed me into the family room."

"She showed you her private collection?"

"She gave me the code, showed me where she kept the paperwork that verified each piece was authentic."

"You didn't think that was suspicious?"

"Ms. Windsor could be whimsical, a bit spontaneous. She did things like this on occasion. I had no idea it could be linked to the fact that she was getting her affairs in order, which is what, in retrospect, I believe she was doing."

"You're saying you know where this room is located, and you could show us into it?" I glanced at Jack. "Are you free to come with us right now? This could be very important."

"Sure. Just let me prepare a little sandwich for Steven and leave a note. He'll worry when he gets back from the grocery store if I'm not here."

We waited for several minutes while Mrs. Gertens tottered around the kitchen. Then she followed us outside and insisted on driving herself to Ms. Windsor's place. Ironically, now it would be her place, but I got the feeling Mrs. Gertens wouldn't be ready to refer to it in that regard soon, if ever.

"She didn't do it," Denise said as soon as we'd pulled away from the curb. "I haven't met the husband, so I can't say for certain about him, but I highly doubt either of the Gertens is the murderer."

"We don't have any evidence of that," I said. "The husband had quite a bit of motive."

"A guy who barely uses the internet?" Denise raised her eyebrows. "How do you think he ran into Ricky Navarro if not on some dark website pimping out rookie contract killers? It wasn't him. Just saying."

"My focus now is figuring out which crimes were actually committed," I said. "Let's see what this family room situation is all about. If Nicole has been lying as much as it sounds like, she's probably hiding something."

I parked back outside of Ms. Windsor's house. Nicole's car was gone. Mrs. Gertens pulled into the driveway, into a space I highly suspected she'd parked in for the last several decades. The way she got out of her car and slung her keys into her purse with such ease gave me the feeling she'd done this many times before.

"This way," she said, letting us into the house.

Mrs. Gertens wove her way through a few hallways, past the trophy room, past the library, to the room where the majority of Ms. Windsor's art was stored. Then she led us through a small door on the opposite side of the wall into a reading room of sorts.

I remembered the whole secret bookshelf thing and was mildly impressed as I watched Ms. Windsor maneuver a fully loaded bookshelf away from the wall. A large lock was behind the bookshelf, and Mrs. Gertens twisted the dial until it clicked open. Then she put her hand against an invisible pressure button and waited a moment. Eventually, the door swung away from her. She gestured for us to follow her inside.

"This is the family room." Her face went pale. "No. No, it can't be."

"What is it?" I asked, an arm extended in case Mrs. Gertens collapsed. "Is everything okay?"

I didn't need an answer. As I glanced around the room, I understood the reason the blood had drained from Anna Gertens's face. The small, intimate room was completely devoid of artwork. There were, however, clear impressions where art had been, the nails hanging lonely on the walls. It was clear that the room had housed several items that I presumed would be worth quite a lot judging by the secrecy behind which they were stored.

"Can I assume this isn't the way Ms. Windsor left things?" I asked. "This is where she'd kept her most precious art?"

"It's gone," she murmured. "All gone. Stolen. Everything including the paperwork."

"Do you have any idea how much her art was worth?"

"It was priceless to her," she said sharply. "It wasn't about the money."

"No, but it would be about the money to a thief."

Mrs. Gertens nodded and gave a slow exhale. "Millions of dollars. Two, three, four million? All of it... just gone."

Chapter 19

I drove us back to the precinct. It was getting to be late afternoon, and I was starving. Jack must have had the same thought because he offered to duck out and grab sandwiches for us. Denise volunteered to go with him.

"Thanks, I'll take my usual," I told Jack, feeling Denise's eyes land on me as I spoke. "I mean, whatever you think. I'm not picky."

"Got it," Jack said quickly, too quickly.

I should've known a profiler would have picked up on my word choice. That was what she did, listened to words and watched actions and pieced together stories about other people's lives. It was helpful when it came to cases, but I was starting to feel like it was very invasive when her attentions were focused on me. I quickly turned away from them and muttered something about making a phone call.

In all honesty, I did have a phone call to make. As Denise and Jack made their way in the opposite direction to grab some food, I headed for the lobby of the precinct. I made my phone call in the hallway before heading into the inner offices.

"Detective, to what do I owe the pleasure?" Gem's smooth voice slid over the phone. "I didn't expect an invitation to dinner so soon."

I knew Gem couldn't see the small smile that I hid, but I trusted he could hear it over the phone. I hoped he could. "It's not that, unfortunately."

"I'll take it. At least you see it as unfortunate."

"I wanted to call and warn you to be careful."

"Can I assume this is related to your investigation?"

"We have a savvy thief on our hands who robs very wealthy individuals. We think they hit a target near us. I guess I thought of you and wanted to give you a heads-up."

"Thank you, Detective. Though I can assure you that me—and all my possessions—are well secured. Not to mention, things are just things. They can be replaced."

"Usually," I said, thinking of Harriett Windsor and her priceless collection that couldn't be easily replaced. "Not always."

"Things are things," Gem repeated. "But I appreciate your concern."

"I think you should be careful," I reiterated. "Just keep an eye out for the next few days until we catch this guy or until he leaves town."

"You'll catch him. I've no doubt."

"The FBI haven't gotten close to catching him yet, and they've spent three years tracking this guy."

"The FBI doesn't have Kate Rosetti."

"Another one of your lines," I said with an eye roll. "Just watch out, Gem. I'll talk to you once this is over."

"I understand. And if I find myself afraid for my life, shall I give you a ring?"

I gave a laugh. "I'm pretty sure your security guards will be able to help a lot faster than me." I hesitated. "But sure. If you want to call me sometime—whether your life is in danger or not—that'd be fine."

I hung up the phone and made my way to our offices. As I did, I had the thought that my call to Gem hadn't really been necessary. Sure, for a moment it had crossed my mind that Gem could be a potential target. That was before the thief had hit Harriett Windsor's place.

According to the profiles on the Mathematician, this guy didn't hit twice in the same location. Which meant that if the Mathematician was behind the art theft, then he'd be long gone. Gem would be safe. So why did I still feel the need to call him? Because I was worried? Or would Agent Price have said I was simply looking for an excuse to talk to him?

"What's on your mind?"

"Huh?" I looked up and found myself standing before Jimmy's desk. I barely remembered making my way there. "Oh, sorry. Just preoccupied."

"Case stuff?"

"Yeah." I made my way to my own desk. Jimmy didn't seem convinced, but he didn't press. "Did you learn anything?"

"Sure did, but I'm going to let Melinda inform you. She was just about to call you. I'll let her know you're here."

By the time Melinda came up from the lab downstairs, Jack and Denise had returned with sandwiches from next door. We gathered in the conference room and those who were hungry grabbed food. I noted Russo had gotten my exact favorite sandwich down to the spicy mustard and kalamata olives that had to be ordered special as extras. I didn't say anything, but I saw Denise watch as I deftly reached for my particular sandwich. When I met her gaze, she hurriedly looked away.

"Okay, now that you're all fed, let me tell you about the bat," Melinda said. "It's not the murder weapon that was used on Harriett Windsor."

"Sorry?" I asked, choking down a bite of the spicy mustard. "I thought you said—"

"We did find blood on Navarro's bat from more than one person," Melinda continued. "We weren't wrong. We've got Garrett Landers' blood on the bat, but the second person's DNA doesn't belong to Harriett Windsor. It's Ricky Navarro's blood."

"When I asked him about it," Jimmy said, "he told me that he'd gotten his nose bashed in after a game the previous week and had bled on the bat some. He said he just wiped it off real quick."

"That's about right," Melinda said. "The blood was smeared, but it hadn't been bleached or anything. It was a pretty weak effort to conceal evidence if that was what he was trying to do. I'm sorry, Kate, but it seems like we're back to square one when it comes to Harriett Windsor's murder weapon."

"I wouldn't say we're at square one," I said. "The weapon that killed her is still something resembling a bat, right?"

"Correct."

I blinked, a long-shot idea dawning on me. "Jack. Did you see inside the trophy room at Harriett's place?"

Jack's face pinched in concentration for a moment, and I could tell he was trying to figure out the connection I'd drawn. Then, as I'd known he would, he gave a nod and his eyes brightened. "Nicole mentioned she played softball."

"She had a couple trophies. One of them was a softball trophy. There was an empty space in the case next to it," I said. "It could've fit a bat."

Jack cursed under her breath. "She's no Ricky Navarro. She's smart enough to have gotten rid of the bat as soon as it was safe."

"Maybe," I said, "but if we could prove it was there, with photos or testimony from Anna Gertens, it might give us something to work with. It should be enough to at least get us a warrant to search for Nicole's car and house."

"I'll make the call," Jimmy said. "But before I do, there's something else y'all need to know. It's about the bat."

I looked at Jimmy. "Ricky's bat?"

Jimmy nodded. "I spoke to a couple of guys on Ricky's team. Turns out they had a guest player the week of Garrett Landers' death. A real ringer. This guy hit three home runs without breaking a sweat. Turns out, Ricky was the one who invited this guy to play with them. Better yet, this guy was using Ricky's bat all night."

"Don't tell me Henry Dunwoody subbed for Navarro's team."

"He sure did." Jimmy pointed in my direction. "Henry had full access to the bat the week Landers ended up dead. We know Dunwoody was at the game, and we know he had the bat. He could've taken it. Could've probably even replaced it in the back of Navarro's car, framing him for the deed. Ricky said he didn't go in his trunk between games, so he wouldn't have known if it was missing."

I pursed my lips. "It's not enough to hold up in court, but it's something. It warrants another visit to Henry Dunwoody. Between that and the missing art collection, we've got enough to pressure Dunwoody again. I'm honestly just shocked that he's still hanging around his house. What do you make of that, Agent Price?"

Denise looked surprised at me personally addressing her. "I'd say he's either extremely confident in his ability to dispose of evidence, or it's not him."

"I could've told you that," I said. "Which scenario do you think it is?"

Denise bit her lip. "I don't think it's him. I don't think he's our mastermind."

"Why?"

"There are too many discrepancies between him and the profile of the Mathematician. The sheer fact that we're getting close to him tells me this isn't right. Something's not right here. Of course, I might say differently if I had the opportunity to meet him in person."

"Then let's make that happen," I said. "Jimmy, are you coming with Agent Price and me to the Dunwoody house?"

"I'll let the feds accompany you," Jimmy said. "I've got two more girlfriends to interview."

"Why'd you call the girlfriends down to the precinct?" I asked. "Did you learn something new?"

"I didn't call them," he said. "All four of them showed up earlier today insisting their innocence and asking about the case."

"That's odd."

"Tell me about it," Jimmy said. "I don't know what that was all about, but I didn't tell them anything. I mostly sent them home. I've talked to Dominique and Marissa already.

They're both gone now. The other two are still waiting for me."

"Have fun with that," I said. "Russo, Agent Price, let's get to Henry Dunwoody's place and see if he's interested in talking now that we've got some new information. Jimmy, let me know when that warrant comes through for Nicole's place. We can swing by on our way back from Dunwoody's place to look for her bat."

"I should have it within the hour."

The group dispersed, leaving Jimmy and Melinda to stay behind at the precinct while I headed out with Russo and Denise behind me. When we got to the car out front, I was surprised to find a slip of paper under my windshield wiper. Frowning, I untucked the piece of paper and flipped it over to read the words written on it.

Except there were no words written on it. There were only numbers.

$1+1=3$

By the time I looked up, Denise and Russo had sensed something was wrong. They stood, their bodies tense, outside of the car. Jack's gaze was already swiveling around the parking lot in search of the person who'd left the note. His hand had slid close to his waistband, inches from his gun.

I handed the paper over to Denise without a word. She took a look at it, and her face went pale.

"He was here," she whispered. "This is from him."

"Who?" Jack asked sharply. "Dunwoody?"

Denise shook her head. "The Mathematician."

Chapter 20

"Do you have any notes like this that you've associated with the Mathematician before?" I asked. "Has he ever confronted a law enforcement officer working his case prior to this?"

Denise shook her head from the back seat as we headed to Henry Dunwoody's place. "Not once."

"What does it mean?" Jack's voice had taken on a heightened, tense quality. He spoke sharply, his eyes focused on some point outside of the car. "Why would he target Kate?"

"We don't know it was for me," I said. "Both you and Agent Price have been driving around with me all morning. It's possible that they were targeting Agent Price. She's the expert on this case."

"Nope," Denise and Jack said at the same time.

"I'm sorry, but you just can't know that." I glanced at both of them. "We've been operating as a unit. What makes you think it was me specifically?"

"You're the thing that's changed," Denise said. "I've been tracking him for years. If he was worried about me, he would've confronted me a long time ago. He's concerned about you. Very concerned. He's breaking his patterns. This is about you, Detective Rosetti. Not to mention, it was your car. Even the Mathematician couldn't have known that Jack and I would be joining you at the exact same moment you returned to your car. You were meant to find it."

"Then what do you think it means?" I asked. "There are no words on it."

"It's more telling than that. He's taunting you."

287

"Taunting me, how?"

"He's telling us that he knows. He knows we call him the Mathematician."

"One plus one is three," I said. "He's telling us that we're missing something. That things aren't adding up right, and he knows it."

"Exactly," Denise said grimly.

"You sound worried about this," Jack said, sounding more than a little worried himself. "Why does this seem to worry you more than anything else you've seen so far in the case?"

"Because this is the first time he's completely breaking his trend." Denise sounded slightly breathless. "He's escalating. He's threatened."

"That's good," I said. "It means he could make a mistake."

"Or it means he could come after you," Russo said, sounding annoyed. "I don't think that sounds very good at all."

"I have to agree with Agent Russo," Denise said. "I think it's a sign he's getting more reckless. A combination of reckless and confident. He's testing his boundaries. He feels like he's met some sort of match against you, and I believe if he feels cornered, he might try to take it out on you."

"I can handle myself."

"You need a security detail put on you until he's behind bars," Jack said. "I'm going to call this in to the chief."

"No," I said. "I'm not doing that. It'll just give him the satisfaction of thinking he's rattled us."

"He has rattled us," Denise said quietly. "At least me."

"Then I'm staying at your place tonight," Russo said. "And if you say no to that, I'll sit outside. The note, however, does need to be reported. It's evidence."

"I'm not hiding the note," I said. "I'll call Jimmy and let him know once we get to Dunwoody's place. He'll let the rest of the team know including the chief, if necessary. That doesn't mean I'm accepting a security detail parked out front of my home."

"Then I'm—"

"We'll discuss it later," I said. "I want to focus on Henry right now."

"How could it be Henry?" Jack asked. "If there's a squad car watching him at all times, how could he have slipped out to deliver the note?"

"If Henry really is the Mathematician, he could've gotten around a cop car," I said. "Or he could've had someone else deliver it."

"It's not him," Denise said. "He's not the Mathematician."

"You keep saying that, but I'm not hearing a lot of alternative theories."

"It's a woman."

I parked outside of Henry Dunwoody's house. "Excuse me?" I swiveled in my seat. "Every profile I've read states that this guy is a male. You've been saying *he* this whole time—we all have. What makes you suddenly think it's a woman?"

"We were wrong," she whispered. "We were all wrong. It's always been a woman."

"I don't understand," I said. "What caused the sudden change?"

"The signs were always there. I just missed them. We all did. We focused too much on the exacting and calculating and cold nature of this person's process, and our brains all automatically assumed it was a male."

"But?" I prompted.

"But that wasn't right. This thief, this person, is a woman. It's the crimes that spell it out for us. The sorts of crimes, the type of violence, the way everything has been set up. I don't know who it is, but I know that we're wrong. It's not Henry."

"Well, we're here," I said. "So I'm going to go in there and have a chat with Dunwoody regardless. I still find it weird he was playing softball with Ricky Navarro the same week that Garrett Landers ended up dead."

Jack was already getting out of the car. He went to talk to the guys in the black SUV across the street. They weren't exactly doing a great job at disguising their presence, but then again, maybe they weren't aiming for discretion. He returned a moment later.

"Agent Price, you'll wait out here for now," Jack said. "Detective Rosetti, I'd like you to wait outside as well while I knock on Henry's door."

"Fat chance of that," I said. "Not happening."

"Can I say fat chance also?" Denise asked. "I'd really like to meet this guy."

"You can meet him," Jack said. "But I want the first crack at him."

"You're ridiculous," I said. "I'm coming with you. This is my case. You're not even on this case."

"No," Jack said, "but I came here to help, and I rank above Agent Price. I'm sorry to pull rank, but I'm doing it anyway."

"What did the guys in the SUV say?" I asked. "Hasn't Henry just been hanging out inside?"

"So they say. They haven't seen any movement through the windows for the past two hours."

"Which means he could've slipped out," Denise said. "You think he might not be there? Or he might have booby-trapped the place?"

"Look, I know you changed your profile and don't think it's this guy," Jack said sternly to Denise, "but I'm not about to take the risk that you're wrong. Sorry."

"I'm not offended. I wouldn't expect you to do anything else," Denise said. "I wish you'd let me come in with you, but I'm happy to wait outside if you think that would be best."

"Wait outside," Jack said. "We'll let you know once the house is clear. Come on, Kate."

Denise's gaze flicked between us again, and I had the feeling she'd noted his use of my first name, along with the interesting timing of it. Namely, the fact that in a high-pressure situation, he'd reverted to using my first name instead of my appropriate title as he'd done for Agent Price. I shivered, thinking that working side by side with a profiler was starting to seriously mess with my head. I was turning everything into a psychology lesson, which was exhausting.

Denise stood outside of my car. She gave a wave to the guys in the SUV while Jack and I made our way to the front door.

"Why'd you make her stay back?" I asked. "Really?"

"You and I work well together. We know each other inside and out. Our work processes," he added quickly. "Agent Price is a profiler. Her experience in the field is extremely limited. While I trust her opinions, I've been in the field. I've seen people injured because they missed a step. I'm not taking that risk."

"You think she'd be a liability if Henry's up to something?"

"I think it's a valid possibility. One I'd be foolish to ignore."

I knocked on the front door. When there was no answer, I knocked again, harder. By the time I knocked a third time, I was starting to get a creeping sensation down my spine.

"Something's up," I said. "I don't like it."

Jack took out his phone and dialed. From the street, Denise answered, and Jack didn't waste any time speaking. "Call for backup. I'm going in. We're not getting an answer, and I heard someone call for help."

Jack hung up. I stared at him.

"What?" he said, avoiding eye contact. "Just because you weren't listening carefully doesn't mean I made it up."

"Right," I said, tensing as I prepared to enter the house behind Jack.

Once he got the front door open, he barreled through, announcing his presence. I followed shortly behind doing the same thing. We both had our weapons drawn. There was still no answer, which was very peculiar, considering the man we were supposedly visiting hadn't left his house in days.

I was beginning to think Agent Price had been wrong this whole time, and we would find evidence that Henry

Dunwoody had flown the coop. Proving once again that we didn't have what it took to capture the Mathematician.

Jack cleared the front room, then moved quickly toward the kitchen through the hallway. I checked the other hallway, then found myself moving toward the dining room. I saw the pool of blood before I saw the body.

"Jack, in here!"

Russo whirled around from the opposite entryway with his gun drawn. I faced him from the opposite side of the room. Together, we looked down to find Henry Dunwoody on the floor. Dead.

I rushed to the body while Jack covered the rest of the room, looking for the person who might have shot him. I found the bullet wound in his chest still bleeding, and I pressed my hands to it. Then I heard a hoarse breath, and Henry's eyes fluttered open.

"She's still here," he murmured.

I thought for a moment I'd heard him wrong, but then I quickly called to Jack to let him know Dunwoody's warning.

"Stay with me, Henry," I prompted. "You'll be okay. Just stay awake. Backup is already on the way, and once they get here, they'll fix you up in no time."

Henry Dunwoody's lips parted once more, but the only thing that came out was a small gasp. Then he was gone. I knew it, though I continued trying to save him as best I could until Russo laid a hand on my shoulder.

"He's gone, Kate," he murmured. "Leave him. Backup will be here in minutes. We need to sweep the house to see if the shooter's still here."

"She is," I said. "Agent Price was right. Russo, I think this was a trap. I think we need to get out of here before—"

"Neither of you will be moving, or I shoot her."

The voice came from behind us. When I turned, I found a woman I'd seen before, several times, in fact. A woman I'd suspected in the murder of Garrett Landers for entirely different reasons.

"It was you this whole time," I said. "This whole thing was a setup."

"You just about ruined everything. You should know better." Marissa, the wannabe PI, stood holding a gun pointed at me. "Nobody ruins the Mathematician. I'm smarter than you all. I don't know why you don't just accept that as fact."

"Because we're here with you," I said. "We found you. It's too late."

"It's not too late," she said. "I rerouted backup to a different location where there's a bigger threat present. Agent Price is gone and so are the chumps in the SUV. They're all headed in the opposite direction. It's just us."

"Good, then you have a few minutes to explain how you pulled this off before you kill us."

Marissa cocked her head to one side, her messy bun bobbing with her movements. She didn't look like a killer. She wore stretchy black pants and a form-fitting zip-up black sweatshirt. She looked like a young mom finishing her shopping trip at Lululemon. Except for the gun pointed steadily at me. There was no way Russo or I would be able to get a shot off without her hitting me first.

"I thought you'd have it all put together." She winked at me. "After all, you're the famous Kate Rosetti, catcher of killers, aren't you? Did you know there was an article about you in the papers? There's never been an article about me."

"Is that what this is about? Fame? If so, why target people like Harriett Windsor?"

"She's rich. Thieves like to steal. It's more fun to steal a million-dollar painting than a big screen TV. Trust me."

"You framed Ricky Navarro," I said. "How'd you do it?"

"How'd I do it?" She looked unimpressed. "I used his bat and put it in his trunk? The guy's a bumbling idiot."

"Why? Why'd you have to kill Garrett Landers?"

"He was supposed to help me get inside the Windsor estate. It turned out I didn't need him, and he was pestering me. He wouldn't give it up. He tried to set a bomb on my car, as if I wouldn't notice. I don't take kindly to death threats."

"So the whole friendship with him, the failed romance, the PI shop, all of that was just bogus?"

"It was for a purpose. I don't do anything without a reason. The PI firm was mostly for fun, though it did help me to get into Harriett Windsor's house. She was hiring a couple of new security guards. She was getting paranoid in her old age that someone would come for her fortunes."

"She was right. Maybe she suspected."

"She couldn't have known," Marissa said. "Nobody knows what my plans are ahead of time."

"We made it here."

"Mostly luck, mostly a setup," she said. "I figured poor Henry Dunwoody would fit that stupid profile your girl had come up with. He was neat, single, smart. That was really all it took. Profiling is such a joke. I know they all thought the Mathematician was a male. You, of all people, should appreciate the leaps and bounds I've made for women everywhere. We're always underestimated, aren't we, Kate?"

I just shook my head at her. "We don't need strides where you've made them. How'd you get inside the Windsor estate?"

"That's my little secret. I can't tell you everything. See, your life might be coming to a close, but I've got big plans for my future."

"So you killed Garrett because you didn't need him once you'd gotten inside the Windsor estate. You framed Ricky Navarro—hence the sloppy murder. You knew we would've suspected someone else if the job had been a clean hit."

"I guess you've earned a little bit of the reputation they've given you. I still don't know that I'd call you the smartest cop to grace the streets of St. Paul, but we can agree to disagree."

"Why kill Henry Dunwoody?"

"To get you here. I wanted you alone. I needed Henry out of the way, but he hasn't been leaving his house lately. So here we are."

"Why'd you go through the trouble of getting all three men linked to you? Why'd you show them the treasures you'd hidden away?"

"I told you, I had a front I needed to keep up for Harriett. As far as she knew, I was a private security company that supplied highly trained, highly discreet guards. We're called Diamond Security. Check it out. We've got a fancy website and everything."

"That's how you got in," I said. "She trusted you and showed you her home. She either told you about the secret room or you knew about it." I paused, shook my head. "No, you'd have already heard about the secret room before you picked her as a target, otherwise she never would've been a target in the first place."

"I am starting to think you might've earned about half the praise that article gave you," Marissa said. "Of course I knew about it. I'd heard through my channels about this old woman who collected art privately. Didn't tell anyone about it. You know, I was the one who suggested she might look into a private security firm. I met her at one of her garden clubs. I might have even suggested Diamond Security as my husband's preferred choice to guard our own precious art collection."

"All lies."

"I prefer to consider it a carefully constructed story. It's nothing more than a form of entertainment, a fictional tale. Like a book or a movie."

"Except your twisted tales have cost three people their lives and counting."

"If Garrett had just left me alone, if Harriett had just been out of the house like she told me she'd be, none of this would've happened."

"And Henry?" I asked, looking at his motionless body on the floor.

"That's all their fault. Harriett's fault. Garrett's fault. They all caused his death. If they'd just behaved, the case wouldn't have spiraled and gone off the rails. It's not my fault. I had it planned carefully."

"Then Kate came along," Jack said, "and ruined every-thing. Which is why you left her the note."

"That was just a little joke between us girls," Marissa said. "I was at the precinct anyway, flooding your partner with a series of interviews to keep him busy. An entire baseball team plus four women who all have a grudge were enough to keep him busy for the day."

"What about the second murder weapon?" I asked. "The bat that killed Harriett?"

"You'll find it wiped clean in Nicole's safe. The code is 1890."

"You made this crime a little neater, a little tidier, just enough to fit with Nicole's style. Otherwise, we wouldn't have believed it. What about her alibi?"

"An anonymous tip from a concerned coworker will hit your partner's desk in a day or two that suggests Nicole was actually sleeping with her boss. That part is not a lie which is why my plan works so well. That'll make her alibi a little shakier since it's only the word of her lover. There are no emails sent, no timecards punched, nothing else. It's certain-ly enough to cause some reasonable doubt."

"Who do you plan to frame for our deaths?"

"Do you remember your little friend Denise Price out there?" She grinned at the two of us. "Don't you think it's weird, a little stalkerish even, how obsessed she is with me? What if *she* was the Mathematician? She follows me around; she thinks she understands what makes me tick... She can even fake a profile with the wrong gender to keep people from looking in the right direction."

"The feds would never believe that."

"Not even when the murder weapon turns up with her prints on it?" Marissa flicked her gaze at the gun in her hand. "I don't know. That's pretty damning evidence, if I do say so myself, though I'm no fed."

"They'd never believe it," I said. "It just wouldn't happen."

"Don't underestimate me."

The way she said it was quietly confident. It invoked far more fear in me than if she'd simply snapped a response. Her delivery was like a threat in and of itself, and I had no doubt in that moment that if Marissa—or whatever her real name was—wanted to frame Denise Price, she'd get away with it.

After all, didn't we already have Ricky Navarro in prison? Weren't we here because we'd suspected Henry Dunwoody as the Mathematician? And wouldn't we inevitably find the bat in Nicole's safe and assume she'd murdered her aunt as well? We'd followed in the exact footsteps that Marissa had laid out for us, and there was no reason to believe that would change now."

"I see you working through the situation, but trust me, I've already worked through it," she said. "I'm more than a couple of steps ahead of you. You're thinking that you've followed my plan exactly so far which means there's no way out of here."

I didn't respond.

"That's correct, and it's why I haven't been caught. It's why nobody's come close. It's why most of the world still believes I'm a male thief. You'll never catch me. Once the two of you are gone, I'll disappear for a long, long time. I don't need the money."

"This has never been about money," I said. "There are other ways to get rich. This is about the thrill for you. You won't be able to stop, and you'll get caught. Not to mention, Russo is FBI, so you'll get a whole team of people looking for you with a massive grudge."

"They can look." Marissa raised the gun. "They won't find me."

I raised my hands. "You don't have to shoot us. You can disappear and let us live. I guarantee you'll have an easier time getting away if you let us live. You've already got three murders on your hands. Add the deaths of two law enforcement officers, and you won't make it across state lines."

"I don't need to." She smiled, her finger tense on the trigger. "I'll hide right here for a while. Let things die down. Not that it'll matter to you when you're dead."

I saw Russo move, out of the corner my eye, a split second before the gunshot rang out. There were two gunshots in rapid succession. The shattering of glass. The deafening silence in the wake of the shots. Then came the groan of pain and the blood.

I found myself on the floor, an arm over me. My ears rang as I struggled to sit up and piece together the events that had transpired in the blink of an eye. A quick inventory of my own limbs told me that I wasn't bleeding anywhere. I didn't feel injured, but there was blood on me. That's when I realized it belonged to Russo.

"Jack!" I leaned over him, simultaneously reaching for my gun to point it in the direction of Marissa. But as I flung myself over Jack, I caught a glimpse of Marissa. She, too, was sprawled on the floor in a pool of what could only be her own blood. She wasn't moving.

"Jack," I said again, "where are you hit? What'd you do that for? That bullet was meant for me."

He blinked, his eyelids fluttering with the effort. "That was the problem."

"You shouldn't have done this," I said, rapidly searching for his wound. I found it on his shoulder and pressed my hands against it. "You're going to be fine. You hit her."

"I didn't fire my gun."

"What?" I shook my head. "But my weapon didn't discharge either."

"Are you okay?" The front door burst open and in came Agent Price, her eyes wild as she glanced around the room. "I saw her getting ready to pull the trigger. I just did the first thing I could think of, and—"

"You fired the shot?" I asked. "Marissa said you were gone. That she'd rerouted backup."

"She did," Denise said. "The guys in the SUV are gone, and backup went to a different location. I stayed behind. I just knew something wasn't right."

That's when I pieced it together. Denise had made an almost impossible shot firing through the window. Marissa had still managed a shot that had hit Russo, but it hadn't killed him. For that, we had Denise to thank.

A low moan sounded from the direction of Marissa. Denise hurried over and slapped handcuffs onto her, then moved Marissa's weapon well out of reach. Denise was on the phone calling for more backup by the time she joined me at Jack's side.

"Jack," Denise whispered, "hang in there."

"He jumped in front of a bullet for me," I said. "That's why he was hurt. The bullet was meant for me."

"I know." Denise's eyes were shiny as she looked at me. "I understand, Detective."

A few minutes later, the sirens arrived. The paramedics quickly took over. It was far too late to do anything for Henry Dunwoody, but they began work on Marissa and Russo immediately. I didn't let go of Jack's hand, my heart pounding as his face paled and his grip loosened.

"You have to let him go," the paramedics said. "We're taking him to the hospital."

"I'm going with," I said.

"We're going to need you to stick around to take your statement," a cop said. "I'm sorry."

"He'll be fine," the paramedic promised. "Come see him when you're finished here."

"I won't leave him," I said.

"Stay," Jack said. "Come visit me later."

"Jack, you took a bullet for me. I'm not letting you out of my sight."

"Do your job, Kate," Jack said, taking a breath that sounded painful. "Marissa's going to survive. Make sure you get a conviction. Follow the rules. I'll be waiting for you when you're done."

Chapter 21

I knocked on the door to Jack's hospital room. When I heard his voice grant me entry, I slipped inside and found him sitting up in bed. I gave a low whistle as I took a look around the room.

"Wow," I said. "They've got you set up here like a king."

"Tell me about it." Russo glanced my way with a smile. "Do you know anything about that?"

I raised both of my hands. "I had nothing to do with this. I came straight from the crime scene. How are you doing?"

"I'm fine. The bullet didn't hit anything important. A couple of weeks in this stupid sling, and I'll be good as new."

As I stepped farther into the room, I glanced around, taking stock of the fancy, private space. It definitely wasn't an average postage stamp-sized hospital room. This space felt like a penthouse complete with a fancy little coffee machine and an oversized TV that was broadcasting some sporting event.

Jack reached for the remote and clicked the television off. "Thanks for stopping by. You didn't have to rush over here. You could've gone home first. Showered, maybe."

"Is it that obvious I haven't showered?" I grimaced. "The best I could do was throw on the sweatshirt that's been sitting in the back of my car for months."

I made my way over to the side of the bed and took a seat. Jack leaned back in bed. Without thinking, I reached up and took his hand in mine. It felt nice, right. Not romantic, just comfortable. Jack looked over at me, his brown eyes holding a complex emotion I couldn't quite decipher. I was pretty sure the expression on my own face matched it right back.

"I don't know what to say, Jack," I finally whispered. "You jumped in front of a bullet for me."

Jack gave me another smile, but this one was a little hollower. "Just my instincts, Kate. Don't read too much into it. I saw her finger tensing to pull the trigger, and I just acted."

I swallowed. "No, yeah, of course. I didn't mean you did it for me because it was, well, *me*."

"I admit knowing that you were on the receiving end of her shot influenced my decision a little bit."

"That's sweet, but we both know you'd do the same thing for anyone."

"Don't read into this situation too much, Kate," Jack repeated. "You and I were both just doing our jobs."

"Right, right," I said quickly. "No, of course. I guess what I mean is thank you."

"You're welcome."

I gave Jack's hand a squeeze, then released it. "How have you been, Jack?"

"I've been okay." He looked at me, gave a slow nod. "The bullet wound's not exactly what I was hoping to get out of this visit, but I'll take it if it means we caught the Mathematician before she could hurt anyone else."

"What *were* you hoping to get out of this trip?"

"The Mathematician." Jack cleared his throat. "I came here to work."

"Well, it's a good thing you did. A good thing and a bad thing," I muttered, nodding toward his arm. "Without you and Denise, we wouldn't have caught her. But you also wouldn't have been injured."

"Oh, you would have caught her, Rosetti. You always do. Now you just have to share credit with the feds."

I gave him a little smile. "You can have all the credit. You deserve it."

There was a moment of easy silence as Jack glanced out the window, and I looked down at my hands. I wasn't sure where to go from here. We hadn't had a chance to talk about our private lives since Jack had arrived in Minnesota. But this didn't seem like the time or the place to get into the nitty-gritty details of our failed romance.

"I didn't tell Denise about us because it was too raw for me to talk about," Jack murmured finally. "I wasn't trying to hide anything. I wasn't trying to hide you from her."

"I didn't think that."

"You did."

"Okay, I did," I admitted. "But I understand, I really do. And Denise is a great person. She's smart, capable, pretty—heck, she saved our lives. She's a great shot. If she was my type, I'd date her too."

"Kate, it's not like—"

"Oh, there you are. I was starting to get worried they'd sent me to the wrong room." Denise entered without knocking. She paused at once and looked horrified when she saw me sitting at Jack's side. "I'm so sorry. The nurse told me to go right in. I didn't realize you were here, Detective Rosetti."

"I was just leaving." I stood and looked down at Jack. "I can't thank you enough for saving my life today." Turning, I looked at Denise. "The same goes to you, Agent Price. Your shot probably saved both of our lives."

"It was nothing," she said. "I was just doing my job. I should have been in there with the two of you."

"It's a good thing you weren't." I smiled gently at her. "You were right where you needed to be."

Denise gave a nod. "Can I speak to you for a minute outside, Detective Rosetti? Whenever you're done in here. No rush."

"Sure. I'll be out in just a minute."

We waited until Denise left the room, then I faced Jack again. "Can I get you anything? I should probably get home and take a shower now that Denise's here to see you."

"I want to explain, Kate."

"You have nothing to explain," I said. "Whatever is—or isn't—going on between you and Agent Price is none of my business."

"But—"

"I promise I understand," I said, reaching for his hand again. I gave it a squeeze. "I care about you, Jack, and I want to see you happy."

"I want to see you happy too. I just don't know what that looks like."

"I'll let you know when I figure it out."

"It was really great to see you again, Kate."

"I know," I murmured. "I agree. I hope we can still be friends. If you want."

"Of course I want that. I don't jump in front of bullets for just anyone."

"I thought you were just doing your job."

Jack winked. "That's what I'll put on my reports."

"Take care, Jack."

"Same to you."

I turned away from Jack and made my way out of the room. I found Denise waiting a few paces down the hallway. I headed toward her, and she looked up, almost surprised to see me.

"I'm sorry I interrupted you," she said. "I didn't know you were in there. I mean, I should've figured it out after you dropped me back at the precinct, but anyway, I'm sorry."

"No apologies needed," I said. "I just came by to see how Jack was doing and see if he needed anything. And to thank him for saving my life."

"So nothing big." Denise grinned.

"Right. Nothing big at all."

"I wanted to apologize for not realizing what the two of you meant to each other sooner." Denise bit her lip. "I should have known, should've guessed it."

"It's not a big deal. Jack and I, whatever we had, it's over. We're just coworkers now."

"Uh-huh."

"And friends," I added. "We're friendly, but that's it. I'm sure Jack didn't tell you about me because it's not important anymore."

"I beg to differ."

"Sorry?"

"I think he hasn't mentioned you because you meant so much to him. But that's just my unprofessional opinion as an FBI profiler."

"It's only been a month since we broke up," I said. "It's still fresh."

"There's nothing happening between Jack and me."

"It would be fine if there was. Like I said, we're over. We tried, it didn't work, end of story."

"I don't think all stories end that easily," Denise said. "Not that it's any of my business."

"Look, I appreciate this little talk, but if you were looking for permission to, I don't know, pursue Jack or something, you don't need it from me." I raised my hands and faced Denise. "Jack and I aren't a couple. As much as it pains me to admit it, you'd be great for him. Probably even better than me."

"You can't say that," Denise said. "Even a professional profiler can't predict love. The heart wants what it wants."

"It's more complicated than that." I took a deep breath. "Anyway, I need to get home and shower, and I know you came to see Agent Russo. Thanks again for your help on the case."

"Thank you, Detective Rosetti. We never would've closed this case if not for you and the team."

I nodded, then turned to leave. Denise called after me down the hall.

"And thanks for the other stuff you said." She looked a little sheepish. "I appreciate it."

"Anytime," I said. "Just treat him well."

As I left the hospital, Jack, and Denise behind, my heart felt heavy. It was hard to see Jack moving on in front of my eyes. If what he and Denise had both said was true, nothing had happened between them, but that didn't change the potential I'd seen either.

Jack might still be hurting from our breakup, but Agent Price was clearly interested in pursuing Jack, and there was nothing I could do to stop it. Not that I'd want to. Jack deserved to be happy, and if I couldn't make him happy, then he deserved someone who could. Agent Price might just be that woman, and it was hard to hold a grudge against the person who'd saved my life with her expert shot.

As I reached the front doors, I glanced down at a message blinking on my phone from Melinda. She'd asked if I wanted to meet her and the other girls out tonight or if I wanted to be left alone. As much as I appreciated the offer to get together with my friends, I did not feel like discussing Jack over margaritas just yet.

I was in the middle of politely declining her invitation in favor of going home for a shower and some Lean Cuisine when a voice startled me out of my thoughts.

"There you are, Detective."

I found a man leaning against my car when I got outside. I was already smiling by the time I glanced up. "How'd you know to find me here?"

Gem grinned back. Then he grabbed a pizza box he'd set on the roof of his car. "I heard you got into a firefight today."

"Who calls it that?" I asked. "We're not in some old western movie."

"Bullets were exchanged. People died. I thought you might want dinner."

"That's an interesting train of thought," I said, but as my stomach rumbled at the smell of pepperoni, I added, "though it's not entirely wrong."

"You've got two choices, and I want you to know that I won't be offended by whichever one you choose. You can take this pizza home with you and enjoy a quiet night alone, and I certainly wouldn't blame you."

"Option two?"

"I can accompany you home and share the pizza. Or you can join me at my place. Or we can picnic at a neutral rendezvous spot somewhere in between."

"I need to shower."

"I can wait in the car if that'd make you more comfortable."

I swallowed, glanced at the pizza, and considered. Gem seemed to sense my silence as hesitation.

"I understand things are complicated with the agent," Gem said. "I understand you're not ready. This offering is purely to feed a friend who almost died today."

"Did you have the pizza flown in from Sicily?"

"I picked it up myself from the local shop down the street," Gem said with a smile. "How very normal of me, right?"

"I'm proud of you. Now, fess up, did you have anything to do with the fact that Agent Russo's hospital room is nicer than my house?"

Gem shrugged. "I'm a friend of the department. It's what friends do."

"That was kind of you."

"He saved your life, from what I hear. I owe him for that."

I turned my attention back to the pizza. Then I looked up at Gem. I had a fleeting thought of Denise and Jack in the hospital room. I thought of my sister probably canoodling with Wes, and my parents, happily encased in their honeymoon glow. I thought of Chloe with her Agent Brody cocooned in their DC apartment.

"You know, I think I'd like company tonight," I said. "Alastair Gem, would you join me for a slice of pizza?"

THE END

Author's Note

Thank you for reading! I hope you enjoyed another adventure with Detective Kate Rosetti and team.

I'm excited to say there will be more books in the series to follow—please sign up for my newsletter at ginalamanna.com to be notified when they are available. And, if you enjoyed the book, please consider taking the time to leave a review at your retailer of choice. It is much appreciated and helps other readers find books they love!

Thank you for reading!

Gina

List of Gina's Books![1]

** **

Gina LaManna is the USA TODAY bestselling author of the Magic & Mixology series, the Lacey Luzzi Mafia Mysteries, The Little Things romantic suspense series, and the Misty Newman books.

List of Gina LaManna's other books:

Women's Fiction:
Pretty Guilty Women
Three Single Wives
Detective Kate Rosetti Mysteries:
Shoot the Breeze
Riddle Me This
Follow the Money
Riddle Me This
Nail on the Head
Sleigh All Day
Time is Money

Murder in Style:
Secrets and Stilettos
Lipstick and Lies
Mascara and Murder
The Hex Files:
Wicked Never Sleeps
Wicked Long Nights
Wicked State of Mind
Wicked Moon Rising
Wicked All The Way

---

1. http://www.amazon.com/Gina-LaManna/e/

B00RPQDNPG/?tag=ginlamaut-20

Wicked Twist of Fate
Wicked Ever After
Lola Pink Mystery Series:
Shades of Pink
Shades of Stars
Shades of Sunshine
Magic & Mixology Mysteries:
Hex on the Beach
Witchy Sour
Jinx & Tonic
Long Isle Iced Tea
Amuletto Kiss
Spelldriver
Mint Julep
Mermaid Mimosa
MAGIC, Inc. Mysteries:
The Undercover Witch
Spellbooks & Spies (short story)
Reading Order for Lacey Luzzi:
- Lacey Luzzi: Scooped
- Lacey Luzzi: Sprinkled
Lacey Luzzi: Sparkled
- Lacey Luzzi: Salted
- Lacey Luzzi: Sauced
Lacey Luzzi: S'mored
Lacey Luzzi: Spooked
Lacey Luzzi: Seasoned
Lacey Luzzi: Spiced
Lacey Luzzi: Suckered
Lacey Luzzi: Sprouted
Lacey Luzzi: Shaved
The Little Things Mystery Series:
One Little Wish
Two Little Lies
Misty Newman:
Teased to Death

Short Story in Killer Beach Reads
Chick Lit:
Girl Tripping
Gina also writes books for kids under the Pen Name Libby LaManna:
Mini Pie the Spy!